OTHER BOOKS BY CHARIS COTTER

The Ghost Road
The Painting
The Swallow: A Ghost Story
Screech! Ghost Stories from Old Newfoundland
Footsteps in Bay de Verde: A Mysterious Tale
The Ferryland Visitor: A Mysterious Tale
A World Full of Ghosts

Born to Write: The Remarkable Lives of Six Famous Authors
Wonder Kids: The Remarkable Lives of Nine Child Prodigies
Kids Who Rule: The Remarkable Lives of Five Child Monarchs
Toronto Between the Wars: Life in the City 1919–1929

THE DOLLHOUSE

CHARIS COTTER

tundra

for Sarah Legakis and Ruth Redelmeier,
two bright lights

Text copyright © 2021 by Charis Cotter
Jacket art copyright © 2021 by Chloe Bristol

Tundra Books, an imprint of Penguin Random House Canada Young Readers, a division of Penguin Random House of Canada Limited

Library and Archives Canada Cataloguing in Publication

Title: The dollhouse : a ghost story / Charis Cotter.
Names: Cotter, Charis, author.
Identifiers: Canadiana (print) 2021009124X |
Canadiana (ebook) 20210091274 | ISBN 9780735269064
(hardcover) | ISBN 9780735269071 (EPUB)
Classification: LCC PS8605.O8846 D65 2021 | DDC jC813/.6—dc23

Published simultaneously in the United States of America by Tundra Books of Northern New York, an imprint of Penguin Random House Canada Young Readers, a division of Penguin Random House of Canada Limited

Library of Congress Control Number: 2020951912

Edited by Samantha Swenson
Designed by Emma Dolan
The text was set in Harriet

Printed in Canada

www.penguinrandomhouse.ca

1 2 3 4 5   25 24 23 22 21

Penguin
Random House
tundra   TUNDRA BOOKS

To sleep, perchance to dream—ay, there's the rub;
For in that sleep of death what dreams may come

—William Shakespeare, *Hamlet*

Part One

THE HAUNTED HOUSE

PRELUDE

Fizz

I slept for a long, long time.

Now and then sounds filtered through heavy layers of sleep. The murmur of voices. Faint, faraway music. Summer rain pattering on the roof. Birds chattering high in the branches of trees. Wind whistling around the corners of the house. Thunder. People calling to each other. Children laughing. Someone walking in the garden, singing.

And every so often the train whistle, blowing sharp and lonely through the night, rising and falling as the train approached, passed and then faded away into the distance.

I turned over with a sigh in my soft, high bed and fell deeper into sleep.

I slept for a long, long time.

Chapter One

THE TRAIN

The train rumbled through the gathering dusk. Every so often it gave a long, mournful hoot that echoed through the countryside. I shivered. Our house was near the railway tracks in the city, and I had always loved hearing that lonely, haunting sound when I lay safe and warm in bed at night. But it was very different to be inside the whistling train, in the very heart of that desolate cry, hurtling into an unknown future with my mother sitting rigid beside me, tears falling in a steady stream down her face.

We had been on the train for five hours. I first noticed that she was crying somewhere in the middle of hour one, and her tears had been ebbing and flowing ever since. Every now and then I reached out and gave her hand a squeeze, and she'd come out of it for a moment, shaking away the tears impatiently and wiping at her face with the handkerchief she kept gripped in her fist. "I'm all right," she would say. "I'm fine."

But a little while later, when I turned back to her from the hypnotic view of houses, trees and roads, the tears were slipping down her face again, and her eyes looked far away at something that was not visible to me.

It was all wrong. Tonight we were supposed to be in a rental cottage with Dad by a small lake far to the north of the city. We'd arranged for me to get out of school a week early because these two weeks were the only time he could get off work. He traveled a lot, and lately it seemed like we hardly ever saw him. We hadn't had a summer holiday together for years, and we were all looking forward to it. At least, I thought we were. Yesterday when I came home from school, charging happily into the kitchen, bubbling over with that fizzy school's-over feeling, I ran smack into a big fight.

Mom was yelling, "It's the last straw, Stephen, I won't take it anymore," and he was shrugging his shoulders and saying calmly, "What can I do, it's my job," and then Mom started yelling again. "If you loved us, you would make this holiday happen, the way you promised. You never keep your promises to me or to Alice, and I told you, if you let us down this time, I was leaving. That's it." Then she turned and saw me, standing at the door with my heavy knapsack full of everything I'd cleaned out of my desk from the year at school: notebooks and books and markers and colored pencils.

"Alice," she said, her face crumbling, "I'm sorry, honey, we're not going to the cottage. Your dad can't make it—so none of us are going."

I looked from one to the other.

"Dad? . . . Mom?"

"I'm sorry, Ally. I'm really sorry, but I absolutely have to be in LA tomorrow. It came up at the last minute—"

"It always comes up at the last minute," yelled my mom. "I warned you, and as always, you didn't listen. We're done."

"Done?" I said in a squeaky voice.

"I'm leaving you, Stephen," said my mom. "And I'm taking Alice with me."

My knapsack fell to the floor with a thud.

"For goodness' sake, Ellie, don't be so dramatic," said my dad.

She shook her head, tears falling, and picked up the telephone.

"Who are you calling?" he demanded.

"The Wilsons. I'm canceling the cottage."

"What are you talking about? We'll lose our deposit! You and Alice can still go."

My mother spoke remarkably calmly into the telephone.

"This is Ellie Greene. I'm calling to cancel our booking at the cottage. There's been a family emergency. Please call me back when you get this message." She hung up the phone just as my father lurched toward her to try and grab it.

"It's done, Stephen," she said. "Go to LA. Alice and I will not be here when you get back."

I stood, gaping at her, feeling the floor tilting beneath my feet as my family slipped sideways and fell in pieces.

* * *

That was yesterday. Dad left an hour later to catch a flight to Los Angeles, where a building project urgently needed his attention for the next few weeks. He hugged me before he left, the familiar, peppery smell of his expensive aftershave filling my nose as he held me longer than usual. When he pulled away, he automatically smoothed down his snappy designer jacket in case I'd wrinkled it, like he always did, but his eyes were full of tears and his mouth tight.

"I'm sorry, Ally," he said, his voice cracking. "We'll fix this, I promise."

Behind us, my mother snorted. She was really mad. And we all knew how many times he'd promised things would be different, and they never were.

This afternoon Mom and I boarded the train to Lakeport, a small town a six-hour ride from the city. Mom made a few phone calls last night and accepted a job there looking after an old lady who had broken her leg.

My mother's a nurse and works on contract. The agency had called her earlier in the week to see if she would take this job, and now they were happy to hear she was available after all. It started right away, a live-in position, and a twelve-year-old daughter was no problem. Lots of room, they said. A big house.

I didn't see why we couldn't go to the cottage and leave Dad *after* our holiday, if we had to leave him at all, but Mom was determined. Maybe she thought if she postponed it she would lose her nerve.

So now here we were on the train, speeding into the future, with lush green countryside flashing by and tears trickling down my mother's face.

I watched as city gave way to suburbs, then green fields framed with rows of trees, then a few farmhouses, some small towns and, finally, the lake.

The lake was enormous. The train ran close to the shore for a while, and all I could see was water going on and on to the horizon. Then the train veered inland again and rattled along past farms and villages, rivers and woods.

When we went through small towns, the train slowed down, and I stared into backyards at swing sets, flower gardens and kids playing. As the light began to fade, some of the windows lit up, and I had brief glimpses inside kitchens and living rooms. I wondered about all those people's lives, and I was filled with a sense of longing—if only we could stop, walk into one of those kitchens and find Dad waiting for us, then go on with our lives in another place where everything was okay and there was no fighting.

It could happen. We could get off the train and drive away from the station, up a hill and into a house where we were a happy family. I could see my mother smiling at my dad and him taking off his glasses to give her a hug.

Wait a minute. My dad didn't wear glasses. This was a different dad, a chubby, comfortable kind of dad who wore old flannel shirts and baggy pants, with a bald spot and a job that didn't involve getting into airplanes and flying away from us.

I glanced at my mother. The tears had stopped, but she was still gripping the handkerchief tightly in one hand, and she still had that sad, faraway look in her eyes.

I sighed and looked out the window again. I didn't really want a new dad. I love my dad. But I had a bad habit of getting lost in my imagination. Sometimes it got me into trouble. Not just trouble from my teachers and Mom, who were constantly telling me to stop daydreaming and pay attention to real life. That was nothing. I mean serious trouble, when I would scare myself so much that I would forget what was real and what was just in my head. One time when my mom was half an hour late coming home, I thought maybe she'd had a car accident. Then I saw the accident happening and then I saw me and Dad at her funeral, then we were packing up her clothes and bringing them to the local thrift store, then Dad got a girlfriend, and they got married, and I had a wicked stepmother, and it went on from there.

I'd got so lost in the story that when my mother came in the door complaining about the traffic that had held her up, I was so happy to see her there instead of lying dead in a graveyard that I threw myself into her arms, sobbing.

That took a little explaining.

The problem is that this kind of thing happens to me all the time. Every day. I always have stories running in my mind, some good, some bad. I try to stop myself when I get started on a bad one, but it's hard to put on the brakes. I get caught up in it before I realize what's happening.

And ever since Mom and Dad have been fighting so much, my fantasies have veered way out of control: Mom and I shivering in a horrible apartment with no heat and people being murdered down the hall in drug deals gone wrong while Dad moves to Singapore and forgets all about us. A horrible custody battle where I have to choose between them. Mom getting a boyfriend who I hate. Dad getting a girlfriend who hates me. These worst-case divorce scenarios made me feel even more sick about them fighting, but I just couldn't stop.

Now that it had finally happened, it was a relief in a way. At least I wasn't an orphan in foster care with both of them dead or in prison. I tried to look on the bright side. Maybe Dad would finish early in LA, come looking for us and talk Mom into going home. Maybe we could rent the cottage after all, later in the summer. Maybe.

Or maybe not.

I gazed out at the landscape. It had changed. We were running through woods now, thick stands of trees. The train seemed to have picked up speed, swaying from side to side. It gave a sudden lurch, then kept barreling forward.

I looked over at Mom. "Umm . . ." I began. "Isn't it going kind of fast?"

She turned and I watched her eyes slowly focus on me as she pulled her attention back from that sad place she'd been in ever since we boarded the train.

"What did you say, honey?"

The train lurched again.

"The train. Isn't it going a bit too fast?"

She looked out the window. Trees were flashing by.

"Oh, I'm sure it's fine. They speed up between towns."

I wasn't so sure. I'd heard about train accidents. Trains just kept gathering speed and then they'd run off the tracks, leaving upside-down rail cars smoking, bloody bodies, people stumbling through the wreckage—No. I stopped myself. I didn't want to get lost in a gory train-wreck fantasy. I'd think about Dad again, and how maybe he would come next week, and this would all be over and we could be a happy family.

That's when it happened. With a tremendous screech, the train came to a sudden grinding halt, and I slammed forward into the seat in front of me. Everything went black.

Chapter Two

THE MOON

My head hurt. I could feel people moving around me, voices raised in alarm. Someone was crying.

"Alice," came my mother's insistent voice. "Alice, are you okay?"

I opened my eyes. My mom was leaning over me, her face full of concern. A conductor appeared behind her.

"Does she need first aid?" asked the conductor briskly.

"Alice?" said my mother again.

"Am I dead?" I asked in a shaky voice.

"I'll take that as a yes," said the conductor, leaning past my mother and taking my wrist. She held it for a moment, counting, then put it down.

"Her pulse is fine." She reached over and gently raised each of my eyelids.

"Possible concussion," the conductor said to my mother. "You might want to get that checked out. The train will be starting in a few moments, and we'll be in Lakeport in fifteen minutes."

"Is it okay if we move across the aisle away from these broken seats?" asked my mother.

For the first time, I noticed that the seats in front of us were leaning crookedly toward ours.

"Of course," said the conductor. "Now, I must go and see to the other passengers."

"I'm a nurse," said my mother. "I'll come and help as soon as I get Alice settled."

Mom gave me a hand getting around the broken seats and into the window seat across the aisle. There was something wet on my forehead. I put up my hand to feel and it came away covered with blood.

"Am I dead?" I whispered.

My mother clicked her tongue. "For goodness' sake, Alice, you're not dead. You just had a bump on the head."

"But the train crash!" I said. "It went off the tracks. There was blood everywhere. Dead bodies."

"There was no train crash!" said my mother. "We just had a very sudden stop and you hit your head. The lights went out and you were unconscious for a few seconds, but you've come back." She took my wrist, the way the conductor had. It was comforting to feel her cool fingers on my skin.

She peered into my eyes for a moment. "No dilation," she muttered. "I think you're okay."

"But I remember the crash," I said in confusion. It was clear in my mind, like a snapshot. I could taste blood in my mouth, and I could still hear the echoes of people screaming. I looked out the window. We had stopped at the foot of a hill. It was getting dark, but I could just make out an old house at the top of the hill—a large, grand old house with a row of tall windows along the first and second floors, a fancy entrance with pillars, and twin wrought-iron staircases curving down to a stone terrace. Vines snaked up the house to the roof.

"A haunted house," I murmured.

"Alice!" said my mother sharply. "Can you stop your imagination for just one minute and pay attention. I asked you what day it is."

I turned back to her. Weird. I hadn't heard her talking to me. I had an odd, floaty feeling, like I was seeing everything through a haze.

"Saturday?" I said. "June 21, 1997."

"And what's your name?"

That was just silly.

"Alice Felicity Greene," I said. "Duh."

My mother's lips twitched with annoyance.

"Alice, I'm serious. You could have a concussion. That was a nasty crack you got. Do you feel dizzy?"

"Sort of."

She reached out her hand and touched my forehead lightly.

"You're going to have a big bump."

I put my hand up and traced the swelling. She was right. Maybe that was why I felt so weird.

An announcement came over the sound system.

"We apologize for that sudden stop. There was an obstacle on the tracks and we had to brake suddenly. We've called ahead to Lakeport and there will be medical personnel at the station waiting for us. Anyone who has been hurt will be attended to. We are clearing the tracks, and we should be on our way shortly."

"I'll be back soon," said my mother. "I'll just see if anyone needs my help." And she was gone.

I peered outside. The house was almost invisible now, fading into the gloom. But then a glowing light appeared behind it, and the house stood out in silhouette for a moment. As I watched, the light grew brighter. Then I realized what it was: the moon, slowly rising above the house—a glowing silver circle.

An almost full moon, shining above a haunted house. On June 21, the summer solstice. The longest day of the year.

I shivered.

There was something strange about this whole trip, hurtling through the darkness to some unknown place where we were going to spend the summer without Dad. It didn't feel quite real. As if I'd fallen inside one of my fantasies and couldn't get out.

The train began to buzz, the lights flickered, and with a lurch, it started moving down the tracks. As I turned to watch the house disappear into the darkness behind us, I saw a small tree that had fallen down and had been pulled away to one side. I wondered if that was the obstacle that had brought the train to such an abrupt stop.

The train trundled through the woods, slowly picking up speed. It was dark enough now that I could see my reflection in the glass. My face looked pinched, my eyes a bit wild, and my forehead had blood smeared across it.

I've never been too happy with my looks. I think I look kind of insignificant. I have straight, light-brown hair I'm trying to grow longer and pale brown eyes. I'm small for my age, and Mom always says I look a bit like a waif. That's an old word for a poor little abandoned creature. That's exactly what I looked like tonight, a little skinny thing with haunted eyes and my head kind of floating along outside the train window.

The Lakeport train station was a small, old-fashioned building with a peaked roof and the name Lakeport painted on the brick wall. An ambulance stood outside, with a growing line of people waiting to see the paramedics.

Mom turned toward the taxi stand. "Let's not bother with that," she said. "I know as much about concussion as they do. You can take some painkillers when we get to Blackwood House, and I'll keep an eye on you for the next few days."

She said it in her brisk, no-nonsense nurse's voice, the one that brooked no argument. We gathered our suitcases, got into a taxi, and soon we were rolling through the dark streets. I couldn't see much. The road we were on left the town behind, and a deeper darkness settled in around us.

"So you're going to Blackwood House," said the taxi driver. "Rather you than me."

"What?" said my mother, irritated. I pricked up my ears.

"That house stood empty for nearly seventy years. Something happened to the family and the house was locked up. All the furniture, all the dishes—everything left just as it was. Spooky, I call it. Not a person went in it all that time—except a cleaner who was paid to look after it and keep her mouth shut. You wouldn't catch me setting foot in that house. It's a legend around here."

"Is it haunted?" I asked breathlessly.

"Haunted! I would say so. By all accounts that house has seen more sorrow than most, ever since it was built way back in the 1830s. It's the oldest house in the neighborhood, and there's been more sudden deaths and accidents there—"

"Nonsense," said my mother. "Any old house has seen its share of deaths and accidents. That doesn't mean it's haunted."

"No good ever comes to people who live in that house," intoned the taxi driver, ignoring my mother. "Old lady Bishop, who lives there now? They say she came here all the way from England. She bought the house last summer, restored it to its former glory, so they say, but two weeks ago she fell down the main staircase, and they never found her till the next morning. If she'd been there much longer, she would have been dead, sure as shooting."

"Shooting?" I said. My head was spinning.

"That often happens with old people who live alone," said my mother. "If they fall, they have no way of calling for help. Nothing to do with the house being unlucky."

"So you say," said the taxi driver. "But you mark my words:

Blackwood House is an unhappy, lonely place, and if I was you, I would go back to where I came from and—"

"That's enough," said my mother. "We don't need to hear any more of your scaremongering, thank you very much. I'm a nurse, and I'll be looking after Mrs. Bishop and living in the house with my daughter, and there's no need to fill her head with this foolishness."

The driver grunted. "Just don't say I didn't warn you," he said.

The car turned off the road and up a steep, curving driveway through a stand of trees. When we pulled out on top of the hill, he stopped the car.

"Here you go," he said.

Standing before us, illuminated by the silver shining moon, was the haunted house I'd seen from the train.

Chapter Three

THE DARK ANGEL

Mom paid the driver and he drove away, muttering. We stood and stared up at the house. It was large, with a row of tall windows on each floor. Thick vines crawled up the stone facade, which looked slightly blue in the gentle light of the moon. It was definitely the same grand house I'd seen from the train, but something was different.

I frowned. The porch roof was supported by pillars, but it wasn't the fancy entrance with the curving iron staircases I'd noticed before. A few stone steps led up to the front door. Then I realized this must be the back of the house, and what I'd seen was the front. Or this was the front, and that was the back.

My head was still a little fuzzy.

"Mom," I whispered. "We're going to live in a haunted house? Really?"

Beside me Mom stiffened. "No," she snapped. "We are not. This house is not haunted, it's just old. There is no such thing as ghosts, and I don't want you starting off your summer letting your imagination get the best of you!"

Just at that moment the front door swung open with a creak. Mom jumped. I squeaked.

Light flooded out and a dark figure appeared in the doorway, its face in shadow and its head lit from behind, like a halo. It was draped in some dark material that fell from its shoulders to the ground.

A dark angel welcoming us to the haunted house? Yikes. I grabbed Mom's arm.

The figure stood there, motionless. Then slowly it began to move toward us, and as it stepped under the porch light, it shrank into a girl about sixteen with long dark hair and a blanket draped around her shoulders. Underneath she wore shorts and a T-shirt.

"Hi!" she said. She was gazing at us in rapture, as if we were her long-lost best friends.

"Hello," said my mother. "I'm Ellie Greene, and this is my daughter, Alice. I think we're expected."

The girl walked right by my mother to me. She reached out a hand and lightly touched my hair.

"Alice," she said, smiling even more widely. "Are you going to be my friend? I think so."

I glanced at my mother. She was trying to convey something to me by nodding her head and blinking her eyes, but I wasn't sure what. I looked back at the girl, and I couldn't help but smile back at her.

"Yes, I think I am," I replied, and the girl responded by throwing her arms around me and giving me a big hug. After a small hesitation, I hugged her back.

"Lily?" called a voice from within the house. "Lily, are they here?"

The girl broke away from me and yelled, "Yes, they are, and Alice is going to be my friend!"

A woman bustled out of the house and then stopped, looking at us. She was short and rather plump, with curly brown hair, wearing jeans and a red sweater.

"Welcome to Blackwood House," she said, reaching out to shake hands with Mom. "I'm so glad to see you safe. We heard the train stop suddenly, and Mrs. Bishop was ever so fussed about it, worried that it was some terrible accident, but I called my friend Marsha, whose husband works at the station, and she told me no one was badly hurt, and we were so relieved! And now here you are! Come on in and let us help you with those bags."

She and Lily started hauling our suitcases in the door. The woman kept up a running commentary as we entered the house.

"I'm Mary Barnett, call me Mary, and I help out Mrs. Bishop with the cleaning here, and you've met Lily, my daughter, and . . ."

I didn't hear whatever it was she said next. We had walked into a wide hallway with big doors opening off each side. An alarmingly steep, curving staircase climbed to the second floor. I gulped. If that was the staircase Mrs. Bishop had fallen down, the one the taxi driver was telling us about, I'm not surprised she broke her leg. A fall down those stairs could easily have killed her.

The ceiling was twice as high as any ceiling I'd ever seen, with a glittering chandelier floating in the middle, hung by a metal rod that disappeared into the murky shadows above. Dark woodwork on the walls and doors reflected the light from the chandelier. Huge, gloomy paintings in gilded frames lined the walls. A tall grandfather clock stood just to the left of the door.

It reminded me of a historic house my dad and I visited last summer. As usual, he didn't have time for a proper holiday, but my mother had booked us some rooms at a bed-and-breakfast in a small town for a long weekend. On the Saturday, Mom felt like sitting on the porch reading a murder mystery, and Dad and I went exploring. We found a historic house in a nearby town that had been restored and turned into a museum, and we spent about two hours wandering through the rooms, with Dad filling in details about everything we saw. Dad and I loved doing stuff like that: he's an architect and he also knows all about antiques, and he used to take me to antique markets every once in a while. Before he got so busy. The house we saw that day was Georgian, Dad said, built in the early 1800s, but it wasn't as big or as grand as this one.

Mary led us up the staircase, talking all the time. The stairs were so steep on the curve that Mom and I held tight to the banister, but Mary and Lily just charged up without any hesitation. Mom was staring at everything as much as I was. The stairs had a thick, dark-blue carpet, and my feet sank into it a little with each step. When we got to the second floor, that hall was just as big as the one downstairs, furnished with a small desk and a couple of armchairs. A soft light emanated from a lamp on the desk, but it did not penetrate the dark shadows that gathered near the high ceiling.

Mary lowered her voice and leaned in close to my mother. "Why don't we get your daughter settled, and then I'll take you in to meet Mrs. Bishop. She's had a bad day, and she really doesn't like children very much—"

She opened the first door on the right and we went in.

I stopped inside the threshold and just stared. It was the most luxurious bedroom I had ever seen.

Chapter Four

THE GREEN BEDROOM

I couldn't believe that this was going to be my room. Nothing could be more different than my little boxy bedroom at home that looked out over the railway tracks.

To start with, it was enormous. You could fit at least four of my bedrooms in here. It was hard to see exactly how big it was because it was too dim to make out where the shadows ended and the ceiling began. A softly glowing lamp on the bedside table was the only illumination. There was just enough light to see the light-green wallpaper printed with little vines and tiny yellow and blue flowers.

Long, silky green curtains that reached from ceiling to floor were drawn partway across two tall windows with window seats upholstered in the same material. On the far wall was an old-fashioned fireplace with a mirror that reflected the lovely room back at us, making it seem twice as big, as if there was another room just like this one beyond the fireplace. Two slim silver candlesticks stood on the mantelpiece, and an armchair covered in dark-green velvet stood to one side of the fireplace.

But the most impressive thing by far was the bed. It stood against the far wall, a four-poster enclosed in flowing green curtains hanging from a carved wooden canopy.

Lily dropped my suitcase and ran forward, pulling me with her, the dark blanket still hanging round her shoulders like a cloak.

"I helped Mama make the bed for you," she chirped. "Look what I left you!"

She held back one of the curtains so I could see what lay inside. Propped against a heap of pillows was an antique baby doll with a china head and auburn curls peeking out from under her white lacy cap.

"She's Mrs. Bishop's, but Mama said I could touch her if I was really careful. She said you could too. But you have to be careful! And not play with her in the dirt. I think so."

Her mother came over. "I thought Alice would be old enough to take care of the doll. Lily is a little careless, so she's not allowed to play with it on her own."

I was too old to play with dolls, but I didn't say anything. Lily was grinning at me, and her mother was looking on fondly. I couldn't quite figure Lily out. She was so pretty, with her dark hair and eyes, and she had the body of a teenager, but she acted and moved more like a six-year-old.

"It's a lovely room," said my mother. "Why don't you unpack

your night things and get ready for bed, Alice? She had a bit of a bump on her head on the train," she said to Mary, "and it's been a long day."

"The poor child," said Mary. "I'm sure you both need an early night. I've made a little lunch for you both downstairs, and Lily and I must be on our way soon."

Mom and Mary left, and I took another look around the marvelous room. There was a row of built-in mahogany closets along one wall. Two of the doors opened up into a large clothes closet, and another into a cupboard fitted with shelves where there were a few more dolls and some children's books.

"Shall I help you unpack? I think so," said Lily, hovering over my suitcase.

I noticed she kept repeating that one phrase, "I think so," and nodding her head as she said it, as if to affirm that everything was okay.

"I'm going to wait till tomorrow to unpack, Lily. I don't feel so good."

Lily came over and examined my face. She reached out a finger to lightly touch the bump on my forehead.

"Does it hurt? Is that where you bumped your head?"

I nodded. "I have a headache. I'll feel better in the morning."

Her eyes were glued to me as I opened my suitcase and pulled out my summer nightie. I hesitated, reluctant to get changed in front of her.

"Where's the bathroom?" I asked.

"Oh, I can show you," she said quickly, jumping to her feet and grabbing my hand. "Come on."

She pulled me out into the hall and started toward the far end. We passed two doors on our left. The second one was slightly open, and I could hear someone speaking in a low voice that crackled with age. Lily grabbed my arm and put her finger to her lips, shushing me.

"As long as your daughter keeps out of my way and doesn't make a racket, I can put up with her being here, but she must respect my property. I have a lot of valuable possessions, and the last thing I need is a thoughtless child causing an uproar. Lily's bad enough!" She had an English accent and she sounded very cross.

Lily looked at me with big eyes and clapped her hand over her mouth to stifle a giggle.

"Now, Mrs. Bishop," chimed in Mary, "you know Lily's a quiet, good girl and has never caused any trouble. And I'm sure Alice will be the same. Nothing to worry about."

"Alice and I are very happy to be here," said my mother in her soothing, everything-will-be-all-right nurse's voice. This was in sharp contrast to her no-nonsense, do-as-I say-right-now nurse's voice. "And Alice is very mature and I'm sure she won't be any bother. Now, Mary says you've had your evening pills?"

I frowned. Mom had never called me "mature" before. Usually the opposite. She clearly wanted this job to work.

Lily pulled me along and through a door at the end of the hall into a luxurious bathroom with a large claw-foot tub and a pedestal sink.

"Mrs. Bishop is a witch!" whispered Lily, making a face and giggling as she shut the door behind her. "She has a long nose! If you make her cross, she gets really mad and yells." She waved her arms around the room. "This is the bathroom. It's way nicer than our bathroom at home. I think so."

She stood there, looking at me expectantly, a big smile on her face.

"Lily, can you go now? So I can . . . um . . ."

"Oh!" she said and giggled again. "Okay," and she left.

Once I was changed into my nightie, I tiptoed out of the bathroom. Now the door to Mrs. Bishop's room was shut tight.

Lily was sitting on the bed waiting for me, tracing her fingers gently along the doll's rosy cheek. "Her name is Lucy," she said. "You need somebody sleeping with you in this scary room. I think so. I asked Mama if you could have Lucy and she said yes."

"Thanks," I said.

Lily turned to me, her eyes wide and her expression serious. "I won't sleep in this room ever again, not even with Lucy. Never."

"Why not?"

"It's the ghost room."

A little shiver crawled down the back of my neck. I had known this house was haunted from the minute I first saw it from the train, and I was about to get proof.

"What do you mean 'ghost room'?" I whispered.

If possible, her dark brown eyes got even wider. "I saw a ghost here once," she whispered back to me. "Sleeping in this bed. I think so."

29

Chapter Five

THE LUNCH

Our mothers came in before Lily could say anything else, and Mom had a glass of water in her hand and stood over me while I swallowed a painkiller she'd dug out of her suitcase. Then Mary bustled us all down to the basement. There was a big modern kitchen down there with French doors leading out to the terrace.

Mary's "lunch" was laid out on the kitchen table: lemonade, cheese, pickles, bread and butter, potato salad, oatmeal cookies and a green jellied salad with weird little bits of something orange floating in it. Either orange mini-marshmallows or diced carrots, but I wasn't going to investigate. Mom and I sat down and started loading up our plates. We'd had sandwiches on the train, but no real dinner.

"Why do you call it a 'lunch'?" I asked Mary as I sat down and prepared to dig in. "It's nighttime, not lunchtime."

Mary laughed. "That's just what we call a snack, whenever it happens. We have dinner at noon, supper at night—"

"It's a country thing, Alice," said Mom. "My grandmother on the farm used to serve up what she called a 'lunch' to company any time of day. Let's just say it's a substantial snack."

It certainly was. Lily wanted to stay and eat with us, but her mother told her to have a cookie and come away, because we needed our rest. Then Mary stood and talked for another ten minutes, with Lily beside her slipping one cookie after another off the plate and into her mouth as her mother rambled on.

"I don't usually work on a Sunday," said Mary, "but I'll drop in tomorrow afternoon to see how you're getting on and do a few things. Everything's been at sixes and sevens since Mrs. Bishop got out of the hospital last week, and what with the other nurse not working out and the temporary nurse leaving yesterday, and me waiting on Mrs. Bishop all day, I'm a little behind on the cleaning."

"Why didn't the first nurse work out?" asked Mom, pausing with a forkful of potato salad halfway to her mouth.

Mary rolled her eyes. "Mrs. Bishop is very particular," she said, lowering her voice as if the old lady could hear her two floors away. "Everything has to be just so. I'm used to it, although she's enough to try the patience of a saint. Even though she can't walk around and inspect my work the way she used to, she's been grilling me every day about keeping up with the dusting and the polishing and the sweeping and everything else. There are so many priceless antiques in this house, you've no idea! And they all need to be cared for to her specifications, not that I haven't been cleaning profession- ally for twenty-five years! And my mother before me. And hers before that. Our family has been cleaning houses in and around Lakeport for the last hundred years! But I don't take it personally," she added, laughing. "She's eighty years old and I suppose she has a right to fuss in her own house."

"But why did the first nurse leave?" asked my mother, trying to get Mary back on track.

"Well, poor Mrs. Bishop, she's been through so much these last few weeks, with the fall, and her broken leg, and the head injury, and she's more difficult than usual. She's just not her- self sometimes, and she can get quite nasty. The doctor says that's the head injury, that it can change a person's behavior. But the truth is, it's kind of funny because Shirley Bassett is a very cheerful kind of person, really a bit too cheerful you might say, and she treated Mrs. Bishop like she was a child, and Mrs. Bishop couldn't stand her smiling all the time and saying things like, 'We need to get our sleep,' when she meant Mrs. Bishop needed to get her sleep, and well, Mrs. Bishop lost her temper and told her—well, she said terrible things, her language! I'm glad Lily wasn't there because it was quite shocking, but you know, Mrs. Bishop was a journalist in England, and I suppose she's seen it all and heard it all, but before the accident she would never use that kind of language." Mary laughed again, a loud, happy laugh. "Anyway, Shirley had to go. Mrs. Bishop fired her on Monday, and then Lily and I held the fort that night, and then Mr. Brock got in touch with the agency again and a temporary nurse came for a few days, and she wasn't too bad, but when I heard that you were coming, I was so relieved."

"She might not like me either," said Mom, taking a sip of lemonade.

"Oh don't you worry about that. I could see she likes you already. You're straight with her, and kind, but not too cheerful, and you don't treat her like she's stupid. She hates that, and Shirley really does have a problem in that department. She speaks to everyone the same way. I suppose she can't help herself. Anyway, it's late and I know you're tired, and Lily and I must get going—Lily! How many cookies have you had?"

The plate was nearly empty, and Lily was reaching for another.

"Just a couple," said Lily, trying to paste an innocent look on her face.

"A likely story," said her mother. "Well, there's more in the tin. I'll take my greedy girl home, and we'll be back tomorrow afternoon. About two, after we've been to church and had our dinner."

And finally, they left, Mary's voice fading away as she admonished Lily all the way up the basement stairs.

Mom and I exchanged a look, then we both started to giggle.

"She's a talker," said Mom, and opened the tin of cookies.

When we went upstairs to bed, Mom checked my eyeballs one more time.

"How's your head?" she asked.

"Better," I said.

"The food probably helped. If you wake up in the night and it's worse, come and get me. I'm in here." She pointed to the door opposite mine.

When I was alone in my room, I stood for a moment, looking at the bed with its flowing curtains and the pretty doll propped against the pillows, wondering about Lily's ghost. This room didn't feel haunted: not like the hall downstairs or the shadowy dining room we had walked through to get to the basement stairs. This room was pretty and quiet. Restful.

I yawned. I was exhausted. I knew I should just jump into bed and go to sleep and not give myself time to start thinking about ghosts and haunted houses. But I wasn't quite ready to bid goodbye to the day.

I walked over to the window closest to my bed and looked out on the moonlit landscape. The window was open, and the sweet country smell of grass and trees and flowers floated in. I curled up against the soft cushions of the window seat and pulled the velvety green afghan over my knees, drinking in the peaceful summer night. I had a feeling that this was going to be my favorite perch.

In the light of the moon, I could see that the stone terrace was built along the entire side of the house, with steps down to a lawn that stretched off to the edge of the hill that led down to the railway tracks. Beyond that were shadows.

I sighed. So much had happened since the day before when I walked in the kitchen door and found Mom and Dad fighting.

My whole world had been turned upside down, shaken and then set right-side up again, leaving me and Mom in a haunted house in the country and Dad on the other side of the continent. It was hard to believe that any of it was real. Instead of the familiar city noises of traffic and sirens, I heard the high hum of crickets.

I had been looking forward to this summer so much. It was going to be the best summer ever. First, and most special, was being at the cottage with Dad and Mom, but I had plans for the rest of the summer too. Me and my best friends Aleisha, Laura and Jenny were going to hang out together—we were already signed up for the reading club at the library and swimming lessons at the local high-school pool. We were going to spend our afternoons in our various backyards—lying on blankets in the shade, drinking lemonade and eating cookies. It was the first summer I was old enough to be left by myself and not packed off to day camps while Mom worked, and the four of us had worked it all out with our parents. Now they would all be having fun without me. I missed them already.

And Dad. Suddenly I missed him so much that I could hardly bear it. If he and Mom couldn't work it out, when would I see him? It was hard enough for him to find time to spend with me when they were together, but if our family split up—I sighed again. It was too much to think about. I had to push it all away and let time work it out for me.

Then I yawned again. I was so tired now that I just had to sleep, ghosts or no ghosts, so I turned away from the beauty of the moonlit lawn, climbed into the bed and closed my eyes.

My last thought before I fell asleep was of the silvery moonlight falling gently all around me like some kind of starry snow and the crickets gently singing me to sleep.

Chapter Six

THE GHOST ROOM

I don't know what woke me up. I opened my eyes, and for a moment, I wasn't sure where I was. I seemed to be floating in some kind of pale-green bubble, faintly lit from outside by a white light.

My first thought was that I had somehow fallen into the jellied salad, but then I woke up a little more and realized that the green was the bed curtains that hung all around the bed, and the white light was from the moon.

Someone sighed beside me in the semi-darkness.

I froze.

"Mom?" I squeaked.

The person sighed again, and there was a movement beside me, as if they had turned over.

There was somebody with me in the bed!

Was it the ghost Lily had told me about?

I felt icy cold and burning hot all at the same time. I couldn't breathe. I tried to turn and look, but I couldn't move. It was as if I was suddenly paralyzed. I swiveled my eyes to the right.

Something was there. A lump under the covers, a head on the pillow.

"Mom?" I whispered, and then I managed to turn my head, ever so slightly.

A girl lay beside me, sleeping. She was about my age, with dark red hair and a few freckles across her nose. She was breathing softly.

I stared at her. Was this the ghost Lily had seen? Who else could it be? But she didn't look like a ghost. Her chest was rising and falling gently as she slept.

I have never been so scared in all my life. I wanted to scream but I still couldn't move. All my limbs felt heavy, like I could never lift them. A pressure was building up in my chest, and I felt like I would burst. I needed to breathe but I couldn't—

She opened her eyes and looked at me. They were green, like the bed curtains. She blinked a couple of times.

"Hello," she whispered, smiling. "Is it time to wake up?"

The scream ripped out of me and just kept on going, getting louder and louder. I shut my eyes tight so I wouldn't see her anymore. Everything grew very dark.

After what seemed like a very long time and a lot of screaming, there was a fumbling at the door and my mother was at my side.

"Alice, Alice, are you okay? What's wrong?"

I opened my eyes. The girl was gone. The doll lay where she had been, with her head on the pillow and her auburn hair peeking out from beneath her lacy cap.

For the second time in twenty-four hours, I saw my mother looking into my face with a worried frown. Her hair was every which way from sleeping.

I started babbling about a ghost and a girl and Lily and the moon and finally my mother gave me a little shake.

"You've had a bad dream, that's all. I'm not surprised, with everything that's happened in the last two days. Take a deep breath. And another."

Obediently I did my best to breathe slowly, but I could see the doll out of the corner of my eye, her red lips curved in a little smile. I pushed my mother away and picked up the doll. As I tilted her upright, her eyes opened.

They were green.

I started screaming again.

My mother took the doll and crossed over to the toy cupboard.

"No!" I yelled. "Not in here, not in here! Take it away!"

"Honestly, Alice, you're much too old to be carrying on this way about a doll and a dream," complained my mother, but she left the room, taking the doll with her.

I tried to calm my breathing again. I could see the moon through the window, a silver ball, almost completely round. Scrambling out of bed, I went over and crouched on the window seat. I wrapped the green afghan around my shoulders and looked out at the moon. It had crossed the sky while I slept. The terrace and the lawn were just as peaceful as they had been earlier, but the shadows were leaning in the opposite direction.

Gradually I stopped trembling. My mother seemed to be taking a very long time hiding the doll. Then I heard muffled voices from the other side of the house.

Great. I'd woken up the old lady.

I got up and tiptoed across the hall and through the open door into my mother's bedroom. A door on the right led into a bathroom, which was connected to Mrs. Bishop's room by another door. I crept in and stood, half-hidden by the bathroom door, watching my mother bending over another four-poster bed, larger than mine, talking to someone lying there under a blue bedspread.

"I'm so sorry, Mrs. Bishop. She hurt her head in the train earlier tonight, and it was very upsetting. It was just a nightmare, and she's okay now."

"Nightmare?" squawked the old woman. "Nightmare! I thought at least she was being torn apart by wild animals. I never heard such a fuss."

"Let me make us all some warm milk," said my mother. "Then we can all go back to sleep. No harm done."

"No harm done?" snapped Mrs. Bishop. "A ruined night's sleep? I'll pay for this tomorrow and so will you."

"I'll be right back," said my mother, and came toward me. I stepped back and retraced my steps through her bedroom and into the hall. She caught up with me and put her finger to her lips. We went down the steep staircase in silence. I clung to the banister around the curve.

As we descended into the shadowed hallway below, I kept looking over my shoulder. It felt as if there was something lurking behind me, watching.

"Where did you put the doll, Mom?" I asked, clutching at her arm.

"I tucked it away in my room, so you don't need to think about it again," she replied.

We went through the dining room past the elegant table and chairs to the doorway in the corner that led to the basement stairs.

Once we were in the kitchen, Mom turned on the light. The room felt modern and ordinary. I took in a shaky breath and sat at the table while Mom made the hot milk. I persuaded her that mine should be cocoa.

"It was just so real, Mom, not like a dream. I was awake. I'm sure I was awake, and Lily told me she'd seen a ghost in that bed before, and she was so real, a girl with red hair—"

"So it was Lily who put the idea into your head. Honestly, Alice, you have to get control of your imagination. And I wouldn't pay too much attention to what Lily says."

"Why not? What's going on with her, anyway?"

"Her mother was telling me. She's always been a bit slow to develop, ever since she was a baby, and they can't say exactly what it is, but they think she'll never really grow up. She's like

41

a small child, and she'll probably remain that way. So you see, even though she looks older than you, she's still at the stage where kids believe in ghosts and fairies and magic—"

"Mom! I'm still at that stage! I believe in ghosts! Maybe not fairies, but definitely ghosts. If you could have seen this girl tonight, you would have screamed too, honest. It was terrifying; she was right in my bed, just like Lily said!"

Mom prepared a tray with three mugs and some of the homemade oatmeal cookies that were left from Mary's lunch.

"Turn out the light, Alice," she said, heading for the stairs. "You had a nightmare, that's all, and you imagined the doll was a girl sleeping in your bed. You need to get some rest, and tomorrow you'll be laughing about this."

"No I won't," I muttered, and followed her up the stairs.

Chapter Seven

BREAKFAST

When I woke up, the room was filled with the bright light of day. I was alone in my bed. Last night Mom had said she'd stay with me till I fell asleep, but I didn't remember anything after she said that, so I guess I fell asleep pretty fast.

I sat up. I still couldn't believe that this lovely room was mine for the summer. The curtains stirred in the soft breeze that was drifting in through the open window. The flowery wallpaper and the green bed curtains made me feel like I was in some kind of fairy garden. Maybe the girl in my bed was a fairy and she came because it was Midsummer's Night. But who ever heard of a fairy with freckles?

I don't believe in fairies anyway. Not really. I like to imagine they're possible, but there is a part of me that knows they aren't. And that girl had looked like a real, live person, not a fairy or a ghost. Now that I wasn't scared anymore, I realized that she had looked like the kind of girl I'd like to get to know. Something about her smile. She looked like she'd be fun to be around.

But maybe Mom was right and it was a dream. Dreams could seem as real as waking, I knew that. Like that train crash last night.

I got out of bed and went to settle in my little nest in the window seat. I couldn't see the train tracks, but I knew they were there somewhere, past the garden, at the bottom of the hill. I tried to remember what had happened. I'd been thinking about train crashes—and then the train stopped suddenly, I hit my head, and everything went black. But I had these very clear pictures in my mind of twisted train tracks, a train car on its side and dead bodies. It was so clear, just like it had really happened. Sometimes my imagination played tricks on me, and it took awhile for me to sort out what was real and what was in my head. I must have imagined all that about the train crash.

My door opened and my mom poked her head in.

"So you're finally awake," she said. "You've been sleeping for hours. Come downstairs and get your breakfast. How's the head?"

The head was fine, no trace of headache, and I told her so and went down for bagels and peanut butter at the kitchen table by the open French doors, with the warmth of the summer and all kinds of sweet country smells wafting in.

Mom made herself a cup of tea and sat down opposite me with a pad of paper and a pen.

"I need to make a shopping list," she said, "so let me know if there's anything special you want me to pick up."

I looked at her. "How about Dad? I could use one of those."

She raised her eyebrows. "I'm not going to discuss that with you right now, Alice. Let's just give ourselves some space for a few days and settle in here. That's the whole point of us coming here: to get some space."

"But what am I supposed to *do* all summer? Aleisha and Laura and Jenny and I had it all worked out. You know we did! The reading club, the swimming lessons. Baking cookies. Being on our own. We've been planning it for months. Now they'll go on and have our perfect summer without me. And I'll be stuck here in this haunted house with nothing to do."

"I'm sorry! I know you're missing a lot. But I just didn't have any choice, Alice. I had to do this, and you had to come with me. That's all there is to it." She got up and started opening random cupboard doors and slamming them shut and scribbling things on her shopping list. She was upset.

I felt bad for her. And I felt bad for me. And I felt bad for Dad.

"Mom?" I said. She turned to me, and her expression made my heart turn over. She looked cross and sad at the same time. Poor Mom.

"What?" she snapped.

"Um . . ." I wanted to say I was sorry and I knew it was hard for her, but I didn't know how to start. "Umm . . . How's the old lady today?"

Her face relaxed and she rolled her eyes. "She's going to be a challenge, let me put it that way. She's got an electric buzzer beside her bed that she's going to ring every time she needs me. When I brought her breakfast, she gave me a ten-minute lecture on how to bring you up that started out, 'Although I never had children of my own, I've learned through careful observation that it does no good to indulge them . . .'"

I laughed. "She sounds a bit like a dragon lady, Mom. But do you think Mary's right? That she's a bit wonky because of the fall?"

Mom poured herself another cup of tea and sat down opposite me.

"I don't think so. She has had a head injury, and I understand it's affected her moods, but according to the case notes the other nurses left me, it wasn't severe. She does tend to get a bit confused at times, and rambles on about her life in England, but a lot of old people talk about the past and get mixed up about times and places. She called me Betsy a couple of times, and she seemed to think the train accident was a lot more serious than it was, but I set her straight.

"She's actually very interesting: she was a journalist for years and she told me she'd written stories about the evacuation of children from London during the war. I think you'll enjoy her stories. And that reminds me, I do have something in mind for you this summer. Just a little summer job helping me."

"Mom—" I began. "You know I don't like all that nursing stuff."

I was no good when people around me were sick or hurt: whatever their symptoms were, I'd start feeling them. Once a girl at school cut her finger with scissors, and there was a lot of blood. I had to sit down and put my head between my knees or I would have fainted.

"Nothing like that. I just want you to help with the housework and sit with Mrs. Bishop sometimes when I have to be out."

"I thought Mary was here to do the housework."

"She comes three times a week, but she's got other houses. Part of my job is as a housekeeper: grocery shopping, cooking the meals, making the beds, laundry, a bit of dusting, that sort of thing. There's a lot you can help me with. I'll give you five dollars an hour. You can put it in your travel fund."

I was saving up for a school choir trip to New York next spring. Aleisha and Laura and Jenny were saving up too. We are all in the choir. That's another thing we were going to do this summer: work on a couple of musical numbers with dancing, just for fun.

"Okay," I said. "I can do that. How much do you want me to work?"

"A couple hours a day would be about right," said my mother. "But for today, just get your suitcase unpacked and settle in. When Mary comes, you and Lily can spend some time together."

"Can I explore the house first? I haven't had a chance to see it yet."

"You can take a look around the first floor on your way upstairs, but don't touch anything! You heard what Mary said about how Mrs. Bishop feels about her antiques. You didn't make a very good impression on her last night with all that screaming, and we're both going to have to work hard to persuade her you're mature enough to be trusted with her treasures."

"Well, I'm not going to start screaming again if that's what you're worried about," I protested. "Unless there are more ghosts in this house . . ."

"That's enough, Alice. No more haunted house nonsense. For goodness' sake, just keep a low profile for a couple of days and I'm sure you can win Mrs. Bishop over."

Chapter Eight
THE PHOTOGRAPH

T he dining room was spooky even in the daylight, crowded with deeply polished mahogany furniture. Two ornate gold candlesticks stood majestically in the center of the dining table. The walls were painted the exact same shade of dark red as the long velvet drapes that blocked out most of the light from the windows. A fireplace stood against the far wall, with a gold-framed mirror hanging above it. In the far corner, opposite the door to the basement stairs, was a closed door.

I had to investigate.

The door led into a small passageway lined with built-in china cabinets with glass fronts. Stacked behind the glass were plates, bowls, cups, and various serving dishes in at least five different patterns.

At the end of the passage, another door led me into a study. Two tall windows faced the driveway, and the walls were lined with bookshelves. There was a big old-fashioned desk at one end, a dark brown leather couch, and a fireplace. Did every room in this house have a fireplace? I guess that's all they had to heat it in the old days. Two glowing brass candlesticks stood on the mantelpiece.

There were all kinds of old books with leather backings, and I wanted to take some down off the shelf and look at them, but Mom had said not to touch anything, and I had to try my best to be mature. Even if it had been wishful thinking on her part last night when she sang my praises to Mrs. Bishop. Most of the time she was not very impressed with my maturity. She was always saying things like, "Take responsibility for yourself," "Stop daydreaming!" "Pick up your clothes!" or "Alice, get a grip!"

So today, after disgracing myself with the nightmare and the screaming, the least I could do was not touch anything. At least, not on my very first morning.

I went out the far door and crossed the hallway into the living room. I stopped just inside the door and just stared. I had never been in a room as grand and beautiful as this one. It was twice as big and twice as luxurious as the living room in the historic house I toured last year with Dad. The room stretched from the front of the house to the back, with an archway across the middle.

My feet sank into a thick cream-colored carpet. The pale-green walls were lined with paintings, like an art gallery. Each section of the room had its own seating area. Silky sofas and elegant wing chairs, fancy lamps and embroidered footstools. Green-and-white marble mantels crowned the two matching fireplaces, and the tall windows were draped in floor-to-ceiling curtains in ivory silk. Dad always told me to pay attention to fabrics in a restored house: he said that was the key to whether it had been done properly or if they cut corners on cheaper materials. No one had cut any corners in this house.

I felt I needed to hold my breath, it was so quiet and still. And somehow sad, as if no one had come in here for a long time. Even though it was full of lovely furniture, it seemed empty.

I tiptoed in, half-afraid that my feet would leave footprints in the thick carpet. There were all kinds of things in here I wanted to touch: the blue silky material on the nearest chair, a collection of glass animals on a side table, a gleaming silver candlestick. I stuck my hands in my pockets to keep them out of the way of temptation.

There was a hush over the room, as if it were held in some timeless kind of bubble. I felt a bit like I was in a dream. The rest of the house was sunk deep in silence, as if I was the only person in it.

Something drew me toward the far corner, where a pretty little desk with curvy legs stood half hidden by one of the green wing chairs. A delicate china shepherdess stood on top, a china lamb curled at her feet.

As I came closer, I could see she was wearing a deep-red skirt and a ruffled white blouse, and she had bright blue eyes peeking out from her red bonnet and an enticing smile on her painted lips. I sat down on the small desk chair and looked at her. Her expression suggested she might break out in a little tinkling laugh any minute. My right hand came out of my pocket and snaked toward her.

No. Mom said not to touch and I wasn't going to touch. I pulled back my hand. I examined the desk instead. Several little compartments were lined up under the little shelf where the shepherdess stood, with a small drawer in the center. My hand snaked out again, but this time I didn't stop it. What was the harm in opening a drawer?

It pulled out easily. It was empty. I pushed it back in but it didn't close all the way. I pulled it out, tried again. It wouldn't close. I pulled it again, harder, and the whole drawer slipped out in my hand.

I peered in. It was too dark to see anything. I tried putting my hand in and feeling around. My fingers touched a crinkly piece of paper. I gave it a pull, and it wouldn't come at first, then all of a sudden there was a little ripping sound and it came.

It was a photograph, torn at the edge. It must have got wedged in behind the drawer when I opened it the first time, and that's why it stuck.

The photograph was black-and-white, faded and old. A woman with dark hair cut in a swinging bob and a shining, smiling face was hanging on to the arm of a big man wearing a hat. A young woman, barely more than a teenager, stood squinting into the camera, holding hands with a girl of about my age. Their matching dresses were cut straight to their hips, then flared out in small pleats to just below their knees.

They were standing in front of a tall doorway with white pillars to each side. It looked like the front of this house.

I looked closer at their faces. The teenager was remarkably pretty, with the same dark hair and eyes as the older woman— her mother? The man had a big, easy smile and he looked like he was just tickled pink to be standing with the three of them. The father? And the young girl—

I felt a chill start at the back of my neck and I stopped breathing.

The young girl had lighter hair than the others, red or dark blonde I guessed, and a smattering of freckles across her nose. She was grinning and her eyes flickered with mischief.

It was her. The girl in my bed last night. The ghost.

Chapter Nine
THE LOCKED DOOR

The quick, high notes of a buzzing bell broke the stillness of the house. Almost immediately came the tip-tapping sound of someone coming up the stairs from the basement, then a door creaked open, and I could hear my mother's swift footsteps in the dining room.

I fumbled the photograph back into the drawer, shut it tight, then got up and moved quickly away from the desk, breathing hard. Now I could hear my mother going up the hall staircase. I stood beside the door and listened. A slight creaking overhead, and then it was silent again. The house seemed to muffle sounds.

With one glance back at the quiet elegance of the double living room, I went out and ran upstairs to my room, my heart still hammering in my chest.

I stood just inside my room, the door closed behind me, staring at my bed.

The ghost bed. The ghost girl. Now I was sure. It wasn't a nightmare. How could I have dreamed of a girl in a photograph that I'd never seen before? She had to be a ghost. It was an old photograph, black-and-white, taken before they had color film. And the clothes were old-fashioned too—those short haircuts and drop waists reminded me of a movie I had seen on TV that was set in the 1920s—*Thoroughly Modern Millie*. The 1920s were—I counted on my fingers—seventy years ago. If the girl I saw in my bed was the girl in the photo . . . that would make her a ghost for sure. Lily was right. Mom was wrong. This room was haunted.

But it didn't feel haunted. It felt peaceful, like it had all along. I knelt on the window seat and looked out past the lawn to the trees that grew down the hillside and climbed up a slope opposite.

The long, wailing cry of a train whistle pierced the air. I leaned out to look. Through a gap in the trees far to the right of the garden I caught sight of a train and soon it was clattering past the house, invisible in the dip. I listened until it had rumbled into the distance and the countryside was quiet once more.

I turned back into the room and took a deep breath. This room was where I was going to live for the next few weeks, so I had to somehow make my peace with it. I walked over to the bed and started smoothing the sheets and pulling up the covers.

Once the bed was made, I dragged my suitcase over to the built-in closet and opened the doors. Then I opened my suitcase. I would unpack, like Mom said, proving once again how mature I was and how I did what I was told.

The closet was huge, with a rail to hang things on across the middle and a set of built-in mahogany drawers on the right. I quickly filled up two of the drawers with my shorts and tops, underwear and socks, and then hung my three sundresses on the railing. A couple of big clothing bags hung over to the left, but it seemed like the closet went back beyond that, so I slid the bags out of the way to see what was there.

I felt around on the inside wall, and sure enough, there was a light switch. I flipped it on. The closet flooded with light.

To my surprise, there was another door at the far end of the closet. I tried the handle, and it opened to reveal a set of steep, winding stairs.

Wow. A secret passage! All the stories I had ever read about secret passages in spooky old houses crowded into my head. Sometimes they led to a tower where a beautiful woman was held prisoner by a cruel husband. Sometimes they led to a secret room full of treasure. Sometimes they led to a hidden door so you could get out of the house unseen.

I went back into my room, opened the door, poked my head out and listened. The house was quiet. Hopefully Mom would be busy with the old lady for a while. I pulled my head back into the room and shut the door. Then I went back into the closet, and with a sense of setting out on an adventure, I started up the stairs.

Each stair was nearly twice as high as a regular stair, and I had to lift my knees way up to get from one step to the next. My feet left clear footprints in the thin layer of dust that covered the stairs, and there was a staleness to the air, as if no one had been in there for a long time.

When I got to the top, there was another closed door. I tried the handle. It opened with a squeak.

I stepped into a large room with sloping ceilings on either side and very wide, unfinished wooden planks on the floor. At the far end was a large half-circle window about as tall as I was. Light filtered in from outside, illuminating the dusty floorboards.

The attic was completely empty. I took a few careful steps, wondering if the floor was safe, but it seemed sturdy enough. The planks must have come from very big trees, because they were more than two feet wide. Mom had told me the house was built in the 1830s, so I guess there were forests with huge trees here then.

I crossed to the window and looked out. It was very high up, and I could see through a canopy of treetops to the country-side beyond the house. The lake was off to the left, powdery blue, and the train tracks curved into the distance.

I turned back into the attic. Now I could see that there was a solid wall built across the far end of the space, with the door I had come through in the center. Another door stood off to the left, just under the eaves. I crossed the open space again, taking care not to make too much noise. I was walking above where I thought the old lady's bedroom was, and I didn't want her to hear me.

I tried the handle, fully expecting it to open for me the way the other doors had. But this door was locked. It was made of the same heavy, dark wood that ran through the house, and it wouldn't budge. The wall it was set into was a dingy, faded color that might have been white when it was first painted, years ago.

Years ago. How long had this door been locked? And who had locked it?

I thought back to what I knew about the house. The taxi driver had told us that it had a tragic history, plagued by sudden deaths and accidents.

I shivered. This whole house could be full of ghosts from all the bad things that had happened here. I looked nervously back over my shoulder, but the attic was still empty. There were shadows under the eaves, but it didn't feel as scary as the downstairs hall or the dining room. It felt more like my bedroom: peaceful, with gentle light sifting through the dirty window and the smell of dusty old wood tickling my nose.

This attic had stood empty for a long, long time.

I turned back to the door and tried the handle again. Why lock a door in a place that no one ever goes anyway? And what could possibly be in there that had to be locked away? It couldn't be a person . . . could it?

No. A person had to be fed, and no one had walked up those dusty stairs for a week or two.

A precious treasure? But the house was filled with valuable objects; why lock anything away?

A book full of magic spells that was too dangerous for anyone to read?

I had to laugh at that one. Magic spells. Not likely.

But how likely was it that I'd seen a ghost last night? And that Mom and I were here in the first place, instead of sitting on a dock at a cottage in the north woods, Mom sipping a gin and tonic and me dangling my feet in the cool lake water? That was supposed to be what was happening this summer, not a headlong flight from the city to a haunted house in the middle of nowhere with an old dragon lady who had a buzzer beside her bed.

I tried the handle again. Okay, so if the door was locked, there must be a key somewhere.

I had to find it.

Chapter Ten

THE OLD LADY

I hurried down the stairs, intent on beginning a search for the key. I was moving too fast for those steep, winding stairs, and suddenly I lost my balance. I had that sickening feeling when you know you're falling but you haven't hit the ground yet. Luckily, as I lurched forward, I fell sideways into the wall and crumpled to a stop, one knee bent under me.

My heart was pounding and adrenaline coursed through my body. My knee began to hurt, a lot, and I carefully untangled myself. Ouch. The arm I had fallen against was hurting too.

I sat on the step for a moment, catching my breath. These stairs were dangerous. They were a lot higher than normal steps, so you really had to be careful. If I had kept tumbling, I would have hurt myself badly. And how long would it have taken for somebody to think of looking for me here, at the end of my closet, behind the secret door? I could be lying mangled at the foot of these steps for hours, or even days. I thought of the old lady, hurtling down the main staircase and breaking her leg, then lying helpless until Mary found her the next morning.

I stood up and picked my way carefully down the remaining stairs, shaking off my brief vision of staircase disasters.

Then I began to search. That key had to be somewhere.

First, I felt along the top of the doorframe of the door to the attic, then I got down on my knees and looked in all the corners of the closet, then I went through each of the built-in drawers at the far end.

I spent a few minutes looking in all the drawers in the bedside table and the shelves in the toy cupboard.

Nothing.

Where would someone keep a key? In a desk drawer? On a hook in the kitchen?

There was a sharp tap on my door and then it opened. Mom stuck her head around the corner.

"Have you finished unpacking?" she asked, looking around the room.

"Yes," I replied, zipping up the empty suitcase and standing it upright.

Mom looked me up and down and frowned.

"What have you been doing? You look a little . . . disheveled."

I turned to look in the full-length mirror inside the closet door. My hair was a dusty mess, my knees and elbows smudged with dirt from the stairs, and a trickle of blood ran down my leg.

"Quick," said Mom. "Go into the bathroom and get cleaned up. Mrs. Bishop wants to meet you. And brush your hair!"

I obeyed, and after a few swipes with a washcloth and my hairbrush, I looked a little more presentable. Mom was waiting for me outside the bathroom, and she seemed a bit jumpy.

"Try to make a good impression!" she whispered, then opened the door and gave me a little push.

I still felt a little breathless from rushing. I'd only had a glimpse in here last night, and the room had been dark and full of shadows. This morning it was filled with light streaming in the tall windows: so bright I had to squint. I was looking at a pretty blue and white room with a fireplace on the far wall and a majestic four poster with dark-blue velvet curtains on my right.

But I took all this in at a glance, because the figure in the bed was beckoning me with a crooked finger to come closer. She was wearing pale-blue pajamas with a pattern of tiny white flowers. Her thick white hair was neatly brushed, falling in a straight chin-length cut, with bangs and a blue hairband. She didn't look anything like my idea of a fussy old lady. Or a witch. Although she did have a long, sharp nose. And her chin was pointed.

She took me in with a head-to-toe examination that made me acutely aware of my dusty clothes and scruffy flip-flops.

"So you're the screaming one," she said in a dry tone, her eyes boring into mine. I couldn't quite tell what color they were because they were half-hidden under her jutting eyebrows. She spoke with an English accent.

"Uh, sorry about that," I said, shifting from one foot to the other.

"Your mother said it was a nightmare," she said. "Are you prone to nightmares? I need to know, because if you are, either I'm going to need earplugs, or you are going to have to move into the basement."

Was she making a joke? Hard to tell, because her eyes were still boring holes through to the back of my head.

"I don't usually have nightmares," I said. "I'll try to be quiet."

Her eyes narrowed. "Your mother tells me you're going to help her with some of the housekeeping. You understand, this house is full of valuable antiques. I hope you can be trusted not to break anything. I would be extremely put out if any of my things were damaged because of your carelessness."

I blushed. I was feeling a little guilty about opening the drawer and looking at the photograph. It shouldn't be a big deal, but somehow I felt it was.

"Have you been through the house yet?" she asked. It was almost as if she could read my mind.

"I took a look downstairs," I said. "But I never touched any of the china or books or glass animals because Mom told me not to." It all came out in a bit of a rush.

"Well, she has vouched for you and tells me you're trustworthy, so if you take your time and exercise caution, I will allow you to touch some of my things, under your mother's supervision at first, of course, and then once you've proved you can be trusted, we'll go from there. You've met Lily, I understand?"

I nodded. "Yes, last night."

"Lily can be careless, but she has learned what she may and may not do in this house. However, I suggest that if you are spending time with Lily, you keep an eye on her. She's impulsive, and that can lead to trouble, don't you think?"

I nodded. "Yes, definitely." It came into my head that maybe this old lady with her sharp eyes and fierce stare knew something firsthand about how being impulsive could lead to trouble. The image of her tumbling down the stairs came unbidden into my mind again.

"Well then," she said. "Your mother tells me your name is Alice."

I nodded.

"Alice. A good name. Although I suppose you can't help being curious, with a name like that."

I stared at her. How did she know I was curious?

"The Alice books were some of my favorites when I was a child," she went on. "I believe there are illustrated copies in the library. You may look at them." She had a rather grand air, as if she were a queen granting me a favor.

"You may call me Mrs. Bishop. And now I want my lunch." She dismissed me with an imperial wave of her hand. I noticed she was wearing several gold rings, including one with a large sparkling green gem. I wondered if it was an emerald.

I kind of backed out of the room with an awkward little bow.

Sheesh! She had me behaving as if she really were a member of a royal family.

Mom came out after me and closed the door, grinning.

"Not bad, kiddo," she said. "She's something, isn't she?"

I had to agree. A very sharp old lady. Not much that went on in this house would get past her. I'd have to be careful.

But one way or another, I was going to get into that locked room.

Chapter Eleven
SECRETS

"So," I said to Lily, who was balancing along the low stone wall of the terrace, "tell me about the ghost."

She and Mary had arrived at about two, as promised, and Mary had suggested that Lily show me around the garden while she went over some things with Mom. Lily and I had walked out to the middle of the lawn and stopped. Lily waved her arms in the air.

"This is The Garden," she said with a flourish, turning to me with one of her beatific smiles. "Lots of pretty flowers and grass. I think so."

I looked around. A long flower bed stretched the length of the terrace, nodding with pink, yellow and white flowers. The entrance with the two curved iron staircases I'd seen from the train led down to the terrace. A wooden slatted table stood just outside the kitchen, shaded by a huge dark green umbrella. Four wooden chairs were pulled up around it.

The sun was very bright. I put my hand over my eyes to protect them and gazed out at the lawn. Other lush flower beds stood here and there between the house and the edge of the hill.

Lily ran over to the two-foot-high terrace wall. She had a kind of galloping, lopsided run that reminded me of a new foal not quite steady on its feet. She climbed up and began walking along the top of the wall, her arms stretched out for balance and a frown of concentration puckering her forehead.

"I can go the whole way," she said. "I think so."

I stood and watched her. She was wearing yellow shorts and a short-sleeved green top, her hair in a ponytail with a yellow ribbon. She looked about six. Except she didn't. She looked sixteen and six at the same time.

After I asked her about the ghost, Lily looked at me, wobbled and then jumped down. She came right up close to me and put her finger to her lips.

"It's a secret," she whispered. "Don't tell!"

"I won't," I said. "But I think I saw her last night."

Lily looked over my shoulder toward the open kitchen doors. Mary's voice drifted out. Lily took my hand in hers and pulled me along the terrace, around the corner, and then began to run across the lawn. Her legs were longer than mine and I could barely keep up with her.

She headed directly toward a little summerhouse that stood at the edge of the hill, looking out over the fields and woods to the lake. She clattered up the wooden stairs, pushed open the screen door and pulled me in behind her.

It was round, with floor-to-ceiling screened-off windows, furnished with faded white rattan furniture. Lily flopped down in one of the chairs and grinned at me.

"Nobody can hear us. This is a good place for secrets. I think so."

"So tell me what you saw," I said.

Her eyes grew big. "A ghost. In the bed," she said in an exaggerated whisper, emphasizing each word. "In your room. Where you're sleeping."

"When?" I whispered back. I couldn't help myself: there was no need to whisper out here at the edge of the lawn, but her air of conspiracy was catching.

"Last week. After the nurse left. The one who smiled all the time. Mama and me slept over. It was fun. Mama said I could sleep in the green room, your room. I was excited because I like that bed. I got in and closed the curtains and I fell asleep." She stopped.

"Then what happened?"

"Then I saw the ghost."

"Were you still asleep when you saw the ghost?"

She shook her head. "Nope. I was awake. I woke up and there she was."

"She?"

"Yup. A girl ghost, sleeping with her head on the pillow.

She had red hair and, you know, those little speckles on her face. I think so."

"Freckles?"

"Yeah, freckles."

"So then what happened?"

"Well, I was staring at her. Wondering who she was. And why she was in my bed. And then her eyes opened. And she smiled at me and said—" Lily stopped and glanced outside. The lawn was empty.

"What did she say?"

Lily leaned in close to me and dropped her voice to a whisper again.

"She said, 'Hello, Bubble! It's not time yet.'" Lily sat back and waited for me to react.

"Bubble?" I said. "What does that mean?"

Lily shrugged. "I don't know. But that's what she said. I think so."

"Then what happened?"

"Nothing."

"What do you mean, nothing? Did you scream?"

"No. I turned over and went back to sleep."

"Weren't you scared?"

"No. I didn't think it was a ghost till the next day. Then I got scared. I've never been back in that room by myself."

"Did you tell your mom?"

She shook her head. "No. She would just say I was making it up. I think so. She always says that when I see ghosts. Or fairies."

"Do you see a lot of ghosts and fairies?"

Lily's eyes lost their focus, and she looked past me up into the sky, the way little kids do when they're making things up. "Sometimes. I think so."

She jumped up and bounded over to the door and opened it. She hesitated for a moment, a dark silhouette against the brightness of the garden beyond. Then she turned back to me and asked, "Do you want to see the swing now?"

The swing was on the other side of the lawn, hanging from a huge oak tree. I pushed Lily for a while, then she gave me a turn. Then we lay down in the grass and watched some white fluffy clouds drift slowly across the deep blue sky. It was almost too bright out there with the sun beating down.

"I went up in the attic this morning," I said.

Lily sat up. Her eyes were big.

"You're not supposed to," she said, shaking her head. "How did you get in?"

"The door wasn't locked," I said. "At least, the door to the stairs wasn't locked. The other door was locked."

Lily shook her head. "Nobody's allowed up there. Only Mama. And Mrs. Bishop. That door's supposed to be locked. Both doors are supposed to be locked. I think so."

"How come? What's so special about the attic?"

Lily put her finger to her lips again. "Secrets," she said. "Lots of secrets. I think so."

I sat up. She had that look she'd had earlier about the ghost, like she was brimming with something that wanted to spill out of her.

70

"Have you been up there?"

She did that looking around thing again, even though we were clearly alone and out of earshot of the house.

"Once. Mama forgot to lock the door to the stairs. I went up."

"Did she forget to lock the other door?"

Lily shook her head. "Nope. It was locked. But I tippy-toed across the big room and looked out the window. You can see forever. I think so."

I nodded. "I know. I did that too. But why is it secret?"

"Mama won't say. She says to mind my own business."

"I'm going to find out," I said, lying back down and gazing back up at the sky. The white clouds were multiplying and moving faster.

"How?" said Lily.

"I'm going to find that key."

"I know where it is."

I sat up again. "Where?"

"Mama has it. Mama has all the keys on a key ring. All the keys to everywhere."

"Where does she keep it?"

"In her purse."

"Does she take them home at night?"

"Yup."

"Does she carry them around with her while she's cleaning?"

"Sometimes."

"Okay, then we have to watch, and when she doesn't take them, we have to steal them."

Lily looked shocked. "Stealing is wrong. I think so. Bad girls steal. I don't steal."

"I saw you stealing the cookies last night when your mother wasn't looking."

She grinned. "That wasn't stealing. That was sneaking. I think so. I sneak all kinds of stuff when Mama isn't looking. Cookies. Candy."

"Taking the keys isn't really stealing. It's borrowing, because we're not going to keep them."

Lily frowned. "Borrowing? Not stealing?"

"If we were stealing, we wouldn't give them back. But we're just going to take them for a little while. So we can find out what's behind that locked door. It'll be fun. We'll find out the secret. You like secrets, don't you, Lily?"

She nodded, and laughed. "Secrets are fun. I think so."

Part Two

THE DREAM

Chapter Twelve
BUBBLE AND FIZZ

We didn't get a chance to "borrow" the keys that afternoon. After a while Mary called Lily to go home, and then I made macaroni and cheese for supper, with Mom supervising. She's been teaching me to cook this year and I can make a few things. Tuna casserole. Spaghetti. Roast chicken. I like cooking with Mom because it's one of the few times she just relaxes and lets all the other stuff go. She tells me stories about when she was a kid and learned to cook from her mom, my grandmother, who died last year. Mom had a hard time learning to cook, and she made all kinds of funny mistakes, like mixing up sugar and salt and leaving out ingredients and burning things. Her mother was patient with her, and Mom is patient with me.

I carried the dinner tray up to Mrs. Bishop, with Mom hovering behind me, and she made a point of telling Mrs. Bishop that I had cooked it myself. The old lady looked suspiciously at it, but after her first forkful, she nodded and said, "Not bad. I see you have potential. You may go now."

I backed out of the room again, dissolving into giggles in the hall with Mom.

I went to bed early. I was really tired, and a headache was hovering behind my eyes. It wasn't bad enough to take a pill, but I was happy to turn down the sheets and crawl into bed. Mom came in to say good night.

"Now, you're not going to wake up screaming tonight, are you?" she said with a frown. "I don't want to test Mrs. Bishop's patience. We need to stay here, Alice. For a while."

"I won't scream," I promised. "Have you heard from Dad?"

She shook her head. "I left a message at his hotel. They said he was out. I left the phone number but told him not to call unless it was urgent."

"Oh," I said in a small voice. "Don't you want to talk to him?"

"No. There's nothing to say at this point. Now forget all that and go to sleep."

She kissed me and left the room.

As if I could forget it. This whole thing still seemed unreal, like a strange dream that went on for days and days. Leaving Dad, the long train ride, the train crash and then the haunted house with the locked doors in the attic and the empty, sad rooms downstairs, the lawn with its too-bright light, Lily and

Mary-who-never-stopped-talking—and this strange, kind of floaty feeling that was somehow connected to the dull headache and the train crash. None of it seemed quite real. I felt the loss of my familiar life as if I were a boat that had been tied to shore and someone had cut the rope, and I was drifting, drifting into a wide lake that went on and on forever, with the faint call of a train far in the distance, echoing over the water.

I fell asleep without even thinking about the ghost.

* * *

Something woke me up again. A sigh? A movement? When I opened my eyes, it was just like the night before: the moonlight filtering in the open window, the curtains stirring in the warm summer breeze.

And someone beside me in the bed. Sleeping. That hum of another person's presence slowly bringing me to consciousness.

Again I felt my whole body freeze and my breath stop.

The ghost murmured something in her sleep, and I could feel her turning over. I summoned my courage from wherever it had fled to with my breath and, with a great effort, managed to turn my head to look at her.

Her eyes were open, staring into mine. Green.

I opened my mouth, and she swiftly put a finger to my lips.

"Don't scream," she said. "You'll disappear again if you scream."

The idea of screaming dissolved. She was real. Her finger felt warm, and I could feel her breath. She smelled faintly of roses.

"Who are you?" I finally whispered.

She took her finger away and grinned. Her eyes were dancing.

"I'm Fizz," she said.

"Are you a ghost?" I whispered. I still couldn't quite catch my breath.

She wrinkled up her nose. "I don't think so. Are you?"

"Me? You're the one who materialized in my bed."

"Your bed? This is my bed. *You* materialized in *my* bed."

I sat up. "How is this your bed?"

She sat up. "Because it's always been my bed. I've been sleeping for a long time, I know that, but now it's time to wake up. Where's Bubble?"

Bubble. That's what she had called Lily.

"Who's Bubble?"

"My sister. Let's go find her." She threw her legs over the side of the bed and slipped to the floor. She was wearing a sleeveless white summer nightgown with fine embroidery across the front, and her thick red hair was cut in a short bob that fell to her chin.

I scrambled after her and grabbed her arm. It was warm and soft. "Wait!" I said. "Tell me again. Who are you?"

She shook off my arm and turned to me impatiently.

"I'm Fizz. I live here. My sister lives here. My parents live here. I've been sleeping and—"

She stopped and frowned, as if she was trying to remember something. Then she shook her head. "I can't remember exactly, but I know I was sleeping for a long time. And then I dreamed that Bubble was sleeping in the bed with me, and she woke me up, but it wasn't time, so I went back to sleep. And then you were here and woke me up, and then you screamed the house down and you were gone, and I went back to sleep. And now you're here again. Only this time, thank goodness, you didn't scream. It's time to wake up. Come on. Let's go find Bubble." She headed for the closet.

I pulled at her arm again. "We need to be really quiet. We don't want to wake up the old lady."

"What old lady?"

"Mrs. Bishop. I woke her up last night and she was really cross. I promised not to wake her up tonight."

Fizz shook off my arm again. "You're nuts. There's no old lady here. But we do need to be quiet. Follow me."

And I did.

She turned to the right. I was dimly aware that there seemed to be more clothes hanging there than just my three sundresses, but I had no time to think about it as she pulled at one of the drawer handles on the built-in drawers and the whole thing swung to one side, revealing a small doorway.

"*Another* secret passage?" I squeaked.

"SHHH!" said Fizz fiercely. "Come on!" She grabbed my wrist and pulled me after her, through the doorway.

It was another bedroom, with two long windows hung with silvery curtains. The moonlight sparkled through them.

On the left was a large door, leading to the hall. I realized this must be the room between my room and the bathroom. I'd walked by the door a few times but hadn't yet looked inside.

A four-poster bed stood directly in front of us beside a fireplace. The bed curtains were silver, pulled back to reveal a lump just visible under a white bedspread. Fizz moved quickly over to it, jumped on the bed and gave the lump a shake.

"Whaaa?" came a voice, and the lump sat up. The light was dim, but I could see the tousled dark head of a girl wearing the same kind of cotton summer nightgown as Fizz.

"Wake up, Bubble!" said Fizz, "but be quiet."

Then she dug under the pillows and pulled out a small black flashlight. She turned it on.

Bubble looked about eighteen: a pretty girl with thick black curly hair and dark eyes. I thought I had seen her somewhere before. She was staring at me.

"Who's that?" she whispered to Fizz.

"A ghost," said Fizz.

Bubble stiffened and clutched at Fizz's hand.

"Don't worry, she's a friendly ghost," said Fizz, giving Bubble's hand a squeeze.

Bubble looked unconvinced.

"Here, touch her," said Fizz, pushing Bubble toward me. "She won't hurt you."

Bubble reached out her hand to my arm and I felt a feather-light touch. Her face relaxed a bit. "Where did you come from?" she asked.

"The city," I said.

"We've been to the city, haven't we, Fizz?" said Bubble, looking at her sister. "On the train. That's true."

"Yep," said Fizz. "We go every June for Mother's birthday and stay in a big hotel and see a show."

Bubble's eyes lit up. "We have so much fun! I like the city. That's true."

Bubble reminded me of Lily. She spoke like a little girl, but she looked almost grown-up. And she seemed to have the same habit of repeating a phrase. I looked around the room. It was mostly in shadow, with the flashlight creating a little bubble of light around the bed. There was something odd about the room, but I couldn't put my finger on it. The bed curtains fell a little stiffly and didn't quite touch the ground. The carpet felt a bit hard under my bare feet—I didn't sink into it the way I did in my room.

The girls' faces were lit up: they looked like girls in a painting, with their matching summer nightgowns and their bobbed hair rumpled from sleep.

Bubble was smiling at me. Then I realized why she looked so familiar. Of course, she was the older girl in the photograph I'd found in the desk. The one that was taken in the 1920s.

What was happening to me? Was I time travelling? Or was I seeing ghosts? Both seemed equally unlikely. I must be dreaming, that had to be it. Suddenly I felt very woozy.

Fizz was talking to me, but her voice sounded far away, and I couldn't understand what she was saying. Then I seemed to lose my balance and felt myself falling, falling—a long way down. Why did it take so long to hit the floor?

I sank into a soft bed that seemed to be full of pillows. Darkness filled the inside of my head and then—everything went blank.

Chapter Thirteen
THE SILVER ROOM

When I woke up, the sun was pouring in the window, and Mom was standing beside my bed.

"You slept in again, Alice," she said. "It's ten o'clock. Lily's here and she wants to play with you."

I sat up. My head was spinning. I groaned.

"Are you okay?" said Mom, looking into my eyes.

I nodded. The room came into focus again.

"Just sleepy, I guess," I said.

"Did that headache come back?" said Mom.

I was reluctant to answer her. "A little."

"Right," said Mom in her nurse's no-nonsense voice. "You're seeing a doctor. You may have a concussion after all. I should have taken you yesterday."

"But Mom, I'm okay—" I protested.

"You're showing two classic symptoms of concussion, Alice: an ongoing headache and sleeping more than usual. We're seeing a doctor and that's that. I think I can get Mrs. Bishop's doctor to take a look at you. He's coming this morning to see her."

She bustled out of the room. I knew there was no arguing with her, but I wanted to spend the day trying to get into the attic with Lily, not waiting around for a doctor.

I looked over at the closet. There was one thing I could do right now.

I slid out of bed and crossed the room, my feet sinking into the carpet. I opened the closet doors and turned to the built-in chest of drawers. What was it Fizz had done? Fiddled with one of the handles? I grasped the left-hand handle of the second drawer down. It was one of those brass loops that hangs from two little screws.

I pulled on it.

The drawer opened. There was a metal rod running from where the handle was attached to the back, set tight against the bottom of the drawer. I closed it again. I tried twisting the handle. Did it budge, just a little? I lifted it halfway up and then twisted again.

Bingo. There was a click, and then when I pulled, the whole chest of drawers slid toward me, opening a doorway to the room beyond. It moved smoothly, without a sound. Someone must have oiled the hinges recently.

That was something Dad pointed out to me when we were exploring that old house last summer: all the locks and door mechanisms had been oiled to open smoothly and quietly.

"It's these small details that show a house has been cared for," he said. "If you go into an old house that's been neglected, that's one of the first things you notice: doors and windows don't open and close properly because the hinges and locks haven't been oiled."

The door led into the back of a closet in the next room. The room itself looked much as it had last night, except brighter, with sunlight filtering in through the silvery drapes. The bed stood empty, with the curtains pulled back.

But they were different. I walked over, and this time my feet sank deep into the gray carpet. The bed curtains felt satiny smooth and they fell in puddles to the floor.

Weird. I walked over to the armchair by the fireplace. It was covered in a silky blue material with silver flecks. I sat down, sinking into the soft cushions. I looked around. This whole room felt different than the others in the house: the silver, blue and gray gave it a magical, luxurious quality quite unlike my peaceful green room or Mrs. Bishop's fresh blue and white bedroom. As if it had been decorated with someone in mind: a delicate, beautiful girl not quite of this world.

Bubble.

What was going on? Was I dreaming about the past because I saw that photograph? But why was this room exactly the same as it was in the 1920s, when Bubble and Fizz were girls?

It hadn't felt like a dream.

"Ahhh . . . lisss" came a soft, spooky voice behind me, dragging out the syllables of my name. "Ahhh . . . lisss!"

My heart started beating erratically. I leaped to my feet. Lily was peeking around the corner of the bed, smiling her radiant smile.

"Lily!" I cried. "You scared me!"

She laughed and came toward me. "I was trying to. Pretending to be a ghost."

I laughed, but it sounded a little forced even to me. "Well, it worked."

"You found the secret passage!" she said, coming over to me and brushing her hand over my hair. "And the Silver Room. Isn't it beautiful? I think so." And she spun around, her arms wide, taking it all in.

"Yes," I said. "It is. How did you know about the secret passage?"

"I found it from this side, one day when I was hiding from Mama. I hid in the closet and there was a hook."

"Show me."

She took me over inside the closet.

"See?" she said, taking my hand and placing it on the back panel. Sure enough, a little hook was there, hidden in the shadows.

"I found the hook and unhooked it. Then the wall moved and I was in your room."

"Pretty cool," I said. "Does your mother know about it?"

"I don't think so." She grinned, and then lowered her voice to a whisper. "It's a secret!"

"Lily!" called a voice from the hall. "I thought you were bringing Alice down for breakfast."

Lily looked at me, alarmed, then gave me a hard push through the secret passage and into my room. She shut the closet door behind us just as her mother opened the door to my room.

"What's taking you so long?" said Mary. "The scrambled eggs are getting cold."

Lily shrugged. "We're coming now, Mama. I think so." She looked the picture of innocence.

Mary gave her a sharp look. "I don't know what you two are up to, but Alice needs to eat her breakfast and get dressed, because the doctor is coming to see her and Mrs. Bishop in half an hour."

"We're not up to anything," said Lily, her eyes wide. "Just talking. I think so."

Mary shot her another look. "Right. Well, enough talking for now. Alice needs to get on."

Obediently we filed past her out the door and downstairs. She stayed behind.

Chapter Fourteen
THE OTHER DAD

D r. West was large and soft like a teddy bear, with thinning hair, glasses and a big friendly grin. He wasn't dressed like any doctor I'd ever met—he wore a floppy shirt with a pattern of palm trees and sunsets all over it and a pair of baggy shorts.

He came to see me after he looked in on Mrs. Bishop. Lily and I were sitting out on the terrace just beyond the kitchen window at the wooden patio table under the dark green umbrella.

"This is Alice," said Mom. I stood up.

"Hi, Alice," said Dr. West. "Hi, Lily!"

Lily got up and threw herself on him in a big hug. "How's my favorite patient?" he said to her, ruffling her hair.

"I got a new friend," said Lily. "Alice. She's really nice. I think so."

"I can see that," said Dr. West. "I just need to check her out, so why don't you go find your mom?"

"Can't I stay?" said Lily.

"Lily!" called Mary from the kitchen. "Come in here! Let Dr. West do his job."

Lily left, with a loving backward glance at Dr. West.

"So, tell me about these headaches," he said, sitting down in Lily's chair and looking into my face.

He did everything Mom had done that first night on the train and more—lifting my eyelids to stare at my eyes, asking me questions, making me follow his finger around with my eyes. Finally he turned to Mom, who had been sitting on the edge of one of the other chairs the whole time, watching.

"I think she does have a slight concussion, Mrs. Greene—"

"Oh, call me Ellie," she said quickly. "Everybody does."

He grinned. "Ellie. And please call me Sam."

She grinned back at him. There was a pause. I looked from one to the other. They were both grinning away, and something was passing between them, something I wasn't sure I liked very much.

"Yes, well," said Dr. West, clearing his throat. "Ellie. I think you were wise to have me take a look at Alice. It's not too serious, but just keep an eye on her, let her sleep as much as she wants, and she should probably stay out of the sun. Follow the usual precautions for concussion."

"Stay out of the sun?" I complained. "In the summer? Mom!"

"Or at least wear a hat. And sunglasses! The bright light will make her headaches worse. And if the headaches or the dizziness get bad, please call me right away. I'll be in every few days to see Mrs. Bishop, so it's no trouble to keep an eye on Alice."

A low buzzing came from the house. "Ellie!" called Mary from the kitchen door. "Mrs. Bishop is ringing her bell. Do you want me to go?"

"No, I will," said Mom. "Thanks, Dr. West—I mean Sam. I better go, she doesn't like waiting."

"No kidding," said Dr. West, and they both laughed, and that foolish look passed between them again.

After Mom went, Dr. West sighed and settled back in the chair. "I could stay here all morning," he said. "I love this house. And this garden. You're lucky, living here. They don't make them like this anymore."

"Where do you live?" I asked.

"Oh, just an ordinary little bungalow in Lakeport, up the hill from the railway station. My ex-wife and I bought it when I started my practice, and well, I've never moved. Couldn't afford a place like this anyway, and I'm on my own now, so even if I could afford it, there wouldn't be much sense in me living in a big house by myself."

"Mrs. Bishop does."

He laughed. "Yes, but she's Mrs. Bishop! Out of my class. Quite a character, Mrs. Bishop. To tell you the truth, Alice," he went on, leaning closer and lowering his voice, "I'm just a little bit scared of her."

I laughed. "Me too. Just a little." I liked him. And there was something familiar about him. Why was that? I'd never met him before.

He got up. "Back to work," he said. "It was good to meet you, Alice, and I hope you feel better."

"Um . . . Dr. West," I began. He was so nice. The kind of person you could tell anything to. "Umm . . . I was just wondering. Do concussions make you have funny dreams?"

He stopped his progress toward the kitchen door. "Dreams? Sometimes, I guess. Why?"

I hesitated. I didn't want to go much further than that. If I told him about Fizz and Bubble, he'd think there was something wrong with me. And he'd tell Mom.

"Well, I've been having some funny dreams since I got here."

"Alice," he said, coming back to me. "I understand you and your Mom are going through a difficult time right now."

"Oh. Did she tell you?" I was surprised. Mom is very private.

He blushed. "Uh . . . no. Actually, Mary did." He laughed. "Mary knows everything about everyone and she doesn't hesitate to pass it on. Look, I don't want to intrude, but sometimes when life is . . . um . . . challenging, shall we say, it shows up in our dreams. That could be what's happening to you."

"Oh," I said. I didn't see how dreaming about Fizz and Bubble could have anything to do with Mom and Dad breaking up, but I didn't say anything, because when he leaned over to talk to me, his face so concerned, I suddenly realized why he seemed so familiar.

He was the spitting image of the dad I'd imagined me and Mom going home to, when I was daydreaming on the train, the comfortable kind of dad who wore baggy pants and who lived in a little house on top of a hill.

Chapter Fifteen

BEHIND THE LOCKED DOOR

After Dr. West left, I sat staring blankly out at the lawn. *What was happening to me?* Was my imagination finally taking over my life? I imagined for months that Mom and Dad would break up—and then they did. I imagined a train crash—and then it happened. I imagined a different kind of dad in a house on a hill—a dad who was messy instead of ultra-neat, a dad who was easy to talk to and not always distracted by work, a dad who was home and not in LA—and then Dr. West shows up, just how I imagined him, and starts putting the moves on Mom.

Well, not really. All he said to her was "Call me Sam." But still—

"Alice?" came a voice at my elbow. I turned, and there was Lily, standing on one foot, frowning. "Do you feel okay? Mom says you're sick."

"I'm okay, Lily," I said. "Just a bit of a headache. Dr. West says I should take it easy."

Lily sat down beside me. "Mom says your brains got shaken up." She looked so concerned, I had to smile. I reached out to her and patted her hand.

"Don't worry, Lily, it's just a concussion. I know a couple of kids at school who've had them. They just rest for a while and then it's better."

"Does that mean you have to lie down?"

"Not right now."

"Good, because Mom left the keys in her purse in the kitchen. She's gone to dust the living room. So—" She smiled her angelic smile, reached into her pocket and drew out a bunch of keys.

"Hey!" I laughed. "You're pretty good, Lily!"

She smiled. "I borrowed them, like you said. Not stealing. I think so. We'll put them back after." She looked a little worried.

"Yes, we will, Lily. It's just borrowing. Let's go!"

We went quietly into the house and up the stairs into the dining room. When we rounded the corner into the hall, I could hear Mary humming in the living room. I tiptoed over to the door and saw her dusting the glass animals on the side table with a tiny little feather duster.

"Go!" I breathed into Lily's ear, and we climbed the staircase. A murmur of voices came from behind Mrs. Bishop's

94

closed door. Hopefully Mom would be busy with her for a while.

Once in my room, we closed my door tightly, then went into the closet. I turned on the light and closed the doors behind us.

"Just in case anyone looks in," I said.

Lily nodded, solemnly. "They won't know we're in here. I think so," she whispered.

The door at the end of the closet was locked.

"What?" I said. "This was open yesterday."

"Mama probably locked it," said Lily. "She always keeps it locked."

I started trying keys, one after the other. My hands were trembling. Lily put her hand over mine.

"Don't shake," she said.

I took a deep breath and kept trying keys. Finally one turned. We opened the door and Lily pushed past me, as if to rush up the stairs. I grabbed her shirt and held her back.

"Go slow," I whispered. "The stairs might creak."

She nodded and slowly, slowly raised one foot.

"Faster than that!" I said, laughing, and gave her a little push. I followed her up. A couple of the stairs creaked, but not very loudly. The walls were thick in this old house. I noticed there was still dust on the stairs. As far as I could tell, with Lily ahead of me, mine were the only footprints from yesterday, going up and down, with a few scuffs where I had fallen.

When we got to the top, Lily headed straight for the window on the opposite wall. I went after her and grabbed her shirt again.

"Tiptoe!" I hissed.

She raised herself on her toes and carefully placed one foot after another, arms outstretched for balance. I stifled another laugh and tiptoed along behind her.

We stood at the window looking out. The tops of the trees tossed in the wind, and we could see far, far away to the southwest, where a bank of clouds was gathering along the horizon over the lake. Beside me, Lily held her breath. I looked over at her.

"It's so beautiful," she said, her eyes filled with light. "We're on top of the world. I think so."

I looked back out. It did feel like the top of the world.

"Come on," I said, pulling at her arm. "Let's see what's behind that door."

The second key I tried turned. Lily and I locked eyes. But instead of opening the door, I froze. What if I really was making things happen with my imagination? What if there was someone held prisoner in there? Or worse, a dead body? Or maybe it was the portal to another world where Lily and I would be devoured by dragons, or—

Lily reached past me and pushed the door open.

We took a couple of steps in. We were standing in a large room that stretched the depth of the house, with a large half-circle window on one side identical to the one we had just been looking through on the other side of the attic. The walls were painted buttery yellow and a huge woven rug in dark blues and reds spread across the floor. A tall wardrobe stood in the far corner. There was nothing else there except—a dollhouse.

An enormous dollhouse. The biggest I had ever seen. Sitting right in the middle of the rug.

Lily gasped and slipped her hand into mine.

"A dollhouse," she said softly. "A secret dollhouse. I think so."

We walked over to it together. It was taller than me, taller even than Lily, with a peaked roof and two rows of windows across the front. The walls were gray-blue, and the front door had a little porch with two white columns.

"Lily," I said. "It's this house."

It was. It was an exact replica of Blackwood House.

Chapter Sixteen
THE DOLLHOUSE

We circled around to the back of the dollhouse. Each side had three tall windows and two chimneys. A half-circle window stood at either end of the attic. The back had that fancy porch I had seen from the train, with the two curved staircases going down. But there were no French doors leading out from the kitchen in the basement. In their place was a red door.

Otherwise it looked identical to Blackwood House.

Lily was peering in one of the second-floor windows at the back. "How do we get in?" she said.

I investigated and found some hooks on one side. I unhooked them, and the back wall of the house swung open.

Lily and I simultaneously caught our breath, and then let it out in an "ohhh . . ." of wonder.

Everything was perfect. Each floor was about fifteen inches high. At first it seemed to be a mirror image of the bigger house. The living room had the same furniture and color scheme, even down to the silver candlesticks on the mantel and a tiny shepherdess in a red skirt on a desk with curvy legs in the corner. The dining room had a long, gleaming table and dark-red velvet curtains. The hall was the same, with the chandelier and the curving staircase.

The basement kitchen was different: more old-fashioned, with no counters. Instead there was a long pine table with chairs, rows of kitchen cupboards and a big stove.

My room was the same, with the flowery wallpaper and the floating green bed curtains and—

"There's someone in your bed," whispered Lily, digging her fingernails into my arm. "The ghost!"

She was right. The curtains were partly open on this side and I could see a figure lying on the bed. I reached over, my hand trembling again, and gently pulled the bed curtains open.

A girl doll about nine inches long lay on the bed, her eyes closed. She had red hair and was dressed in a white cotton nightgown with embroidery along the top.

Fizz.

I just stared at it for a moment. I felt frozen, the way I felt when I woke up and she was beside me. The whole world seemed to have just stopped.

I swallowed. "How—?" I whispered, but my lips felt cracked and dry. I reached out and grabbed Lily's arm.

"Alice, are you okay?" Her eyes were big. "You've gone all white. I think so."

I took a deep breath. Then another.

"I don't know what's happening to me, Lily," I said.

"Maybe it's because your brain is shaken up," she said.

I shook my head. "No, I mean about the ghost. That doll—"

"She looks just like the ghost I saw," said Lily. She didn't sound at all surprised. "Same hair. Same nightgown. I think so."

I nodded. "I know. I saw her again last night," I said. "Her name is Fizz. And I saw another girl, in the Silver Room. The ghost took me through the secret passage."

Lily's head swiveled back to the dollhouse. There was a row of mahogany doors on the far wall, just like in my room downstairs.

Lily pulled open the doors to the closet. Clothes hung from the rail and there was a built-in dresser to one side. She started pulling at the dresser, but it didn't move.

"Wait," I said, then reached in. I grasped the small brass handle on the second drawer down and twisted it. There was a click and the dresser swung open, revealing the secret passage.

We looked at each other.

"It's just the same," said Lily. Then we leaned in closer so we could see through to the other room. I could see the bed, but not much more.

"Come on," I said, scrambling to my feet and going around to the front of the dollhouse. I found the hook along the corner and swung the front of the house open.

Again, we were looking into an exact replica of the front part of the house downstairs. The living room, the hallway, Mrs. Bishop's bedroom, the Silver Room.

The curtains were closed around the bed. Lily gently pulled them open.

A doll with curly dark-brown hair lay with her eyes closed under the white coverlet.

"Bubble," I breathed.

"Bubble?" said Lily. "That's what the ghost called me. I think so. She said, 'Bubble, it's not time yet.' What kind of a name is Bubble?"

"A weird name," I said, thinking about it. "A nickname, maybe."

Lily reached in and pulled the doll out from the bed. She ruffled her hair.

"She's bigger," she said, "than the other one."

I looked at the doll. "I think you're right." This doll was just about the size of a Barbie doll, only she looked more like a real person.

We went around to the back of the house, and Lily took the Fizz doll out of the bed. I was glad she did it. I didn't want to touch it.

The doll with the dark hair was definitely a couple of inches bigger than the other one.

"Her big sister," said Lily, sitting one down in a chair and making the other one stand behind her. "I wonder if they have other clothes."

She rummaged in the closet. "Look, here's a blue dress," she said. And then she took off the red-headed girl's nightgown and fitted the dress over her head.

I couldn't believe it. Lily was playing with the dolls. The ghost dolls.

"Let's find something for Bubble to wear," said Lily, and picking up the dolls, went around to the front of the house again.

"Hey, she's got a blue dress too," she said.

I went around and saw that several dresses hung in the closet in Bubble's room. Lily had the blue dress halfway on her already.

"Look," she said, holding them up. "Matching dresses! I think so."

With the dresses on, the dolls looked more real. The dresses were beautifully detailed, with drop waists and pleats . . . where had I seen dresses like that?

The photograph. The one in the desk downstairs.

"Holy God!" I whispered.

"That's swearing," said Lily, frowning at me. "You're not supposed to swear."

"Sorry," I replied. "It's just so weird, Lily, it's all so *weird*. I don't understand what's going on. These blue dresses," I pointed to the dolls, who were now lying side by side in their matching outfits. "I've seen these dresses before, Lily—in a photograph downstairs."

"What photograph?"

"You know that little desk in the corner in the living room? With a china girl in a red dress sitting on top of it?"

Lily nodded. "Yeah. I'm not supposed to touch her, ever. Ever."

From the expression on her face, I had the feeling maybe she had touched the china girl once and got into big trouble.

"I found the photograph stuck in the back of the drawer in that desk. And Bubble and Fizz were in the photograph, in these same blue dresses. I think they used to live here, long ago."

Lily looked down at the stiff, silent dolls she had just dressed.

"The dolls? They lived *here*? When? I never saw them."

"It must have been a long time ago, Lily. Before we were born."

I reached out a finger and touched the silky blue pleats on the Bubble doll's dress. "That style of clothes, and their haircuts—it's how people dressed in the 1920s—that's seventy years ago."

Her eyes grew big. "You mean they were real people, not dolls?"

I nodded my head. "I think so." Then I smiled. I'd echoed Lily's little chant.

"But then how did they get changed into dolls?" she whispered. "Did they do something bad? I think so. Did . . . did a witch put a spell on them?"

"I don't know, Lily," I said. "I don't understand. All I know is that there's a photograph downstairs of Fizz and Bubble, and they're real girls, not dolls."

"But I don't see how they got changed into dolls and stuck in the dollhouse. Did they die? Are they ghosts?" Lily picked up the Bubble doll and examined her carefully from head to foot.

"She doesn't look like me. Not one bit." She frowned. "Why did the ghost call me 'Bubble'?"

I shrugged. "Search me. Maybe she was expecting Bubble to wake her up and she didn't take a good look at you."

Lily laid the Bubble doll carefully in her bed, then picked up the Fizz doll, went around to the back of the dollhouse and laid that doll in her bed. My bed.

"Let them sleep," said Lily. She peered into the basement kitchen and touched a tiny, perfect kettle that stood on the stove. "I don't know, Alice," she said thoughtfully. "I don't think I'd want to be a doll forever and live in a dollhouse, would you?"

"No," I said. "But I'm not sure they know that they're dolls. I'm not even sure they *are* dolls. They seem like regular girls to me. I guess it might all be a dream."

"It's not a dream," said Lily firmly. "It's magic. Real magic. I think so."

I opened my mouth and then shut it again. Lily had a happy little smile on her lips and was looking into the distance with starry eyes.

Magic.

"Lilll—eee!" came a faint cry from somewhere deep in the house downstairs. "Lilleee!"

Mary.

Lily took a deep breath and opened her mouth, as if she was going to answer. I clapped my hand over her mouth.

"Shhh!" I said. "Don't say anything."

The call got a bit closer, then farther away. "Maybe she'll think we're outside," I whispered, and took my hand away from Lily's mouth.

"She'll keep looking," said Lily. "She always does. She'll think I'm getting into trouble somewhere. I think so."

"We better go down," I said. I hooked each side of the dollhouse closed.

We stood looking at it for a moment. It stood tall and quiet. A perfect house.

"It's the best dollhouse I ever saw," said Lily happily.

"I know," I said. "It's completely fantastic." I turned to her. "We gotta come back."

"Yup," said Lily. "For sure we gotta come back. I think so."

Chapter Seventeen
THE YELLOW DOG

Lily and Mary left after lunch, and Mom insisted I go and lie down to have a rest.

"Aww, come on, Mom," I protested. "Only babies and old ladies have naps after lunch."

"And people who have concussions," she said firmly, shepherding me up the steep stairs and into my room. "You've got to take it easy for a few days. Doctor's orders," she added as I opened my mouth to protest again.

She stood there and watched as I climbed up onto the bed.

"Can I at least have a book to read?" I asked. I had noticed some interesting old books in the toy cupboard by authors I liked, L.M. Montgomery and E. Nesbit.

"No books," said my mother crisply, whipping the green

afghan off the window seat and covering me with it. "You need to rest your eyes." She pulled all the bed curtains across so I was enclosed in a small green box. "One hour," she said, and then I heard her footsteps crossing the room and then the sound of the big door shutting.

Sheesh. How was I going to last an hour in here? It was stuffy and hot. I never took naps. I thought maybe I could wait for a few minutes, then creep through the secret passage into the next room, but what good would that do me? I'd be as much a prisoner in there as I was in here. I couldn't go back up to the attic because Lily and I had locked the doors and returned the keys to Mary's purse.

I needed to get hold of another set of keys. Mary was only here three times a week, and I was itching to get back up to the dollhouse again. There must be other keys in the house, somewhere. When Mom let me get up, I could go looking for them.

I sighed impatiently and turned over. This was boring.

I could get myself a book, but what if reading strained my eyes and made the concussion worse? That must be why Mom wouldn't let me have one. If I went ahead and read a book, I might damage my eyesight forever. And then I'd have to wear a blindfold all the time to keep out the light, and walk with a white cane and have a seeing-eye dog to lead me around. That would be fun. The dog, not the blindfold. I had always wanted a dog. A golden retriever with a red collar.

The heat and the stuffiness and the big lunch I'd put away were making me sleepy, in spite of myself, and my eyelids fluttered down and finally closed. I was drifting away when I thought I heard the sound of a train whistle far away, and then closer at hand, a dog barking. Then I was asleep.

* * *

Somebody was shaking my right shoulder.

"You sure do sleep a lot," said a voice in my ear.

I sat up. Fizz was sitting beside me on the bed, a big grin on her face. The bed curtains were still closed. The sun beat through the curtains on the window side. It was unbearably hot. Fizz was wearing a blue dress and her feet were bare. Outside a dog was barking.

"Whaaa . . . ?" I said. I felt groggy, the way you do when you wake up after sleeping for two hours in the afternoon.

Fizz laughed and jumped down from the bed. "Wake up! We're supposed to be meeting Bubble in the summerhouse." She pulled the dress off over her head and shook like a dog coming out of the water.

"That's way too hot for a day like this," she said, and skipped over to the closet. It was packed full of clothes. She plucked a sleeveless summer dress off a hanger and slipped it over her head.

I slowly lowered myself to the floor and picked up the blue dress she had left lying there. It looked just the same as the dress Lily had put on the doll in the dollhouse. I looked up at Fizz.

"I don't understand," I whispered. "The dollhouse—"

Fizz looked back at me and laughed again. "Come on!" she said, grabbing my hand. "Bubble's waiting." She pulled me toward the door.

"But—but—" I said, holding back. Her grip on my hand tightened.

"Don't be such a wet blanket," she said. "Just come!"

Wet blanket? That's what I felt like. A big heavy wet blanket. I stumbled along, but when we got to the top of the curving staircase, I wrenched my hand free.

"You're not pulling me down there," I said. "I'll come on my own."

Fizz looked at me for a moment, then smiled. "Okay, Ghost." She turned and charged down the stairs. I followed slowly, gripping the handrail.

The downstairs hall looked almost exactly the way it did in my waking world, and the glimpse I had of the grand living room was identical: silky sofas and elegant wing chairs, and the little desk in the far corner with the china shepherdess. But I only had time for a quick look as we hurried past to the big door at the end of the hall. Fizz grasped the doorknob, gave it a twist and a push, and we were outside, standing at the top of the curving iron staircases that led down to the terrace.

A big yellow dog with a red collar came bounding across the grass to meet us, barking. Fizz ran down the steep stairs and I followed, again holding the handrail.

Fizz and the dog threw themselves at each other and rolled around on the grass. I stood blinking in the bright sunshine and watched them.

A yellow dog with a red collar. The same dog I had imagined before I went to sleep. This was a dream. It had to be.

Chapter Eighteen
THE TEA PARTY

I shaded my eyes. The light felt too bright. From what Dr. West had said, I knew this was because of my concussion. Dream or no dream, I needed to get out of the sun.

The dog disentangled himself from Fizz and leaped over to me, placing his front paws on my shoulders and licking my face. I giggled and tried to push him away.

"Sailor!" cried Fizz. "Down!"

He paid no attention. She grabbed his collar and hauled him off.

"Sorry," she said. "He's still a puppy. Bubble and I are trying to train him, but he loves jumping up. Especially if he likes you. Come on!" She grabbed my hand again and started off running toward the summerhouse, Sailor leaping and barking beside us.

When we got to the summerhouse, Fizz turned to Sailor.

"Lie down! You know you can't come in."

The dog flopped on the ground, panting.

Inside, the summerhouse was in much better repair than the last time I'd seen it. The white rattan furniture was gleaming with fresh paint, and the blue-and-white cushions on the chair seats were crisp and new.

Bubble was sitting in the middle of the floor with a dolls' tea party in full progress. A flowery tablecloth was spread out and three dolls sat propped around the edge, each with a doll-size plate and teacup made of delicate white china in a blue-flowered pattern. Bubble had her own tiny plate and cup. There were two other empty places. A doll's plate in the middle was piled with little round shortbreads.

"Just in time," said Bubble, and she began pouring something out of the doll's teapot. She was wearing what looked like a cotton petticoat with eyelet lace ruffles. A blue dress lay crumpled on one of the rattan chairs, as if she had just pulled it off and thrown it there.

A blue dress. And Fizz had been wearing a blue dress when she woke me up. Lily had dressed both dolls in those blue dresses before we closed up the dollhouse.

"The dollhouse . . ." I said, trying to figure it out. "The dollhouse . . ."

Neither of them paid any attention to me.

"Time for tea," sang out Bubble, filling the cups.

"Sit down, Ghost," said Fizz. "Have some tea."

"My name is Alice," I said, sitting at one of the empty places. "I'm not a ghost."

"She doesn't look like a ghost, Fizz," said Bubble. "She's not even scary. That's true."

"But she is a ghost, Bubble," said Fizz. "She's from another world, aren't you, Alice?"

"Maybe . . ." I said slowly. "In the other world, I'm asleep, and I'm dreaming all of this."

Fizz went on as if she hadn't heard me. "In your world, maybe you're not a ghost. But in our world, you are."

"A friendly ghost," said Bubble, smiling at me as she passed me a teacup and saucer. "That's true."

The "tea" was a cloudy liquid with little bits of something floating in it.

"Umm . . ." I began, looking at it dubiously.

"Lemonade," said Fizz.

"Tea," said Bubble, glaring at her. Once all the dolls had their tea poured, Bubble passed around the shortbreads. They were small but delicious.

Fizz held out her teacup for more. Bubble filled the pot from a regular-sized jug.

"Oh, just give it to me," said Fizz impatiently, grabbing the jug and taking a long drink from it. "I'm dying of thirst."

"You're no fun," said Bubble crossly. "You should learn your manners, Fizz. That's true."

Fizz offered me the jug and I took a big glug from it.

"It's too hot for manners," she said.

"Well, at least April, May and June know their manners," grumbled Bubble, offering the dolls little sips of tea from their cups.

I sat watching her. Just like the last time I had seen her, she reminded me of Lily. She was obviously older than Fizz, but she talked and played like a little girl.

I yawned. It was a very peculiar dream. All mixed up with the dollhouse. And my headache. And this feeling like I wanted to sleep forever.

Bubble reached over and gave my arm a shake.

"Don't go back to sleep!" she said. "We want you to stay and play with us. That's true."

"But I'm already asleep," I said. I could barely keep my eyes open. "I'm asleep and dreaming. I'm having a nap on my bed, and Mom's downstairs. I'm dreaming about Bubble because she's like Lily, and I'm dreaming about Sailor because I thought about a dog before I fell asleep, and I'm dreaming about the summerhouse because I was in the summerhouse with Lily and—"

"And me?" said Fizz, leaning toward me, with a gleam in her eyes. "Why are you dreaming about me, Alice?"

"Because . . . because . . . because . . . you're the ghost," I said. "The ghost in my bed."

Fizz and Bubble both threw back their heads and laughed, like I'd made the biggest joke ever. April, May and June sat staring blankly at me, the way dolls do. Outside, Sailor, aroused by their laughter, began barking wildly.

"You're the ghost, silly," said Bubble. "Not Fizz. That's true."

Chapter Nineteen

INVISIBLE

In the midst of the laughter and the barking, the door to the summerhouse opened. A dark figure stood there motionless for a moment, silhouetted by the sunshine. It reminded me of the way Lily had stood in exactly the same place that morning, a dark shadow against the brightness beyond. Then the figure moved forward out of the dazzling light and into the summerhouse. A woman with dark hair swinging in a bob around her face, wearing a flower-bespeckled twenties-style dress with a drop waist.

I recognized her right away. The woman from the photograph.

She smiled a twinkly smile and said, "A tea party! And you didn't invite me! You sounded like you were having so much fun, I just had to come and see. But here's an extra place."

She moved toward me. But she wasn't looking at me. She was looking through me. I scrambled out of the way, and she sat down where I'd been sitting.

"Oh dear," she said, picking up the cup I had been drinking from a few minutes before. "Someone's been drinking from my cup. It's just like Goldilocks and the Three Bears." She laughed merrily and Bubble joined her.

I flattened myself against the wall, staring at her. Fizz glanced quickly at me and then away.

"It was me, Mother," she said, picking up the teapot and pouring more "tea" into the cup. "I was thirsty, so I drank your tea as well as mine."

Bubble giggled.

I felt weird. This woman couldn't see me. I was—invisible. I looked down at my hands. I could see them clearly. And Bubble and Fizz could see me. So why couldn't their mother?

I didn't like being invisible. I used to daydream about it sometimes, about how much fun it would be to sneak around and watch people and listen to what they were saying when they didn't know you were there.

But this wasn't fun at all. I felt the way I do sometimes if I'm in a room full of people I don't know. Like I don't matter. Like I'm not there.

Was I a ghost? Or was I dreaming?

"Well, this is just perfect," said the woman. "I love a tea party. But I came looking for you to tell you something. Mr. Inwood's come with a surprise for you."

"A surprise?" said Bubble, her face lighting up.

"Let me guess," said Fizz in a bored voice. "Something new for the dollhouse."

Her mother frowned. "Yes—something new. Something wonderful. Don't be so ungrateful, Fizz."

"I want to see it," said Bubble.

The woman stood up and held out her hand to Bubble. "Let's all go and see it. But put on your dress first, dear. You can't go running around in your petticoat. Even if it is hot."

She helped Bubble put on the blue dress while Fizz looked on, glaring at them.

"We *were* having a tea party, Mother," she said. "We were having fun. Why do we have to go inside where it's hot and stuffy to look at some stupid new thing that Mr. Inwood's made that we won't be able to touch or play with?"

"That's enough, Fizz," said her mother in a very different voice. "Don't spoil things for Bubble. She wants to see it and you're coming too, and you're going to be polite to Adrian."

"Daddy doesn't like him," said Fizz.

Her mother turned on her, and her face went very, very red. For a moment, I thought she was going to slap Fizz.

"Don't. You. Dare," she said, spitting each word out at her daughter. "Don't make trouble, Fizz. I've warned you before."

"Well, he doesn't," muttered Fizz.

Her mother took a deep breath. "Daddy and Adrian are very different people. They don't have a lot in common. But Daddy appreciates that Adrian is an artist, and Daddy is very pleased with what Adrian has accomplished with the doll-house." She said this as though she had said it before many times. "Now," she said, looking over at Bubble, who had been watching them, wide-eyed, "Let's all go together, remember our manners, and see what Adrian has made for you."

"For you, you mean," grumbled Fizz, half under her breath.

Her mother gave her a sharp look as she led Bubble out of the summerhouse. At the door, Bubble turned and whispered, "Remember your manners, Fizz," and stuck her tongue out.

Fizz returned the gesture, then looked over at me.

"You better come too, Ghost," she said.

I hesitated. I still had that uncomfortable feeling that I didn't quite exist, that I was somehow transparent. Fizz calling me Ghost didn't help.

"Wait," I said. "I want to ask you something."

She turned back.

"Why . . . why can't your mother see me?"

Fizz shrugged. "I don't know. Maybe because she's a grown-up. Grown-ups don't always see what kids see—haven't you noticed?"

She was right there. How many times had I seen things that my mother saw completely differently? And just in the last few days—the haunted house, the moon, the doll, the train accident?

"Yes, but—" I began.

"And anyway," Fizz continued, "it isn't her dream, is it? You say you're dreaming all this. In dreams you can see people who don't see you."

"Yes," I said slowly. "That true. So now you believe me that I'm dreaming? That this is all a dream?" I waved my arm around to include the summerhouse, the dolls and their tea party, Fizz. "And you're just part of my dream?"

"Well, I don't know about *that*," said Fizz, grinning, and she ducked out the door.

Chapter Twenty

THE PERFECT SUMMERHOUSE

Fizz was *so* annoying.

And yet I had to follow her, across the too-bright lawn, up the curving staircase and into the dark, shadowy hall. It felt deliciously cool after the heat outside. A grandfather clock standing near the opposite door began to strike. One—two—three chimes echoed through the house. The sound of the bells seemed to linger in the silence. There was a lovely smell of roses.

Fizz and I climbed the steep staircase to the second floor, then Fizz made a quick right turn into my room. Or was it her room? The mahogany closet doors stood open, and she ducked inside and started up the stairs to the attic.

But they were different from the last time I'd been here. There was no dust, for one thing. And the wooden stairs looked flat somehow, with no wood grain showing. When we reached the attic, I saw that it was no longer empty. In the light from the window at the far end I could see a few chairs, an old trunk and a lamp.

I only had a few seconds to take this in, because Fizz was disappearing through the door that had been tightly locked the last time I had seen it but now stood wide open. Voices were coming from inside the room. I stopped at the door.

"It's beautiful," cried Bubble. She was bending over an object at the far end of the room, on the other side of the doll-house, with her mother and a tall, thin man looking on.

"Don't touch it," said the man in a tight, worried voice, shooting out his arm to pull her hand back. He wore a light-colored summer suit and had unruly brown hair that kept falling into his eyes.

"Just look, sweetheart," said her mother. "You know the rules."

Fizz turned around to me and made a face.

"But what's inside it?" said Bubble, leaning down even lower to the floor.

Fizz and I moved closer.

"Your mother told me you like having tea parties in the summerhouse," said the man. "So I made you a summerhouse just like the one in the garden, and there's you and Fizz having a tea party in there with a little doll's tea set and—"

"There we are!" said Bubble. "And there's April, May and June! Fizz, Alice," she said, looking over her shoulder at us. "Come and see! He's made my dolls!"

The two grown-ups turned to us.

"Come and see, Fizz," said her mother. "Who's Alice, Bubble?"

"The ghost," said Bubble.

Her mother frowned. "You know there's no such thing as ghosts, Bubble. Fizz, have you been encouraging her again?"

Fizz sauntered over, and I hovered in the background the way a good ghost should.

"I don't need to encourage her, Mother," she said. "She's always imagining things all on her own, aren't you, Bubble?"

Bubble looked from her to me and back to her sister again. Whatever she saw in the expression on Fizz's face made her retract.

"Just pretend," she mumbled. "That's all. No ghosts. That's true. But look, Fizz, it's perfect! So tiny and perfect!"

Fizz crouched down so she could examine the summer-house. I slipped around to the other side of Bubble so I could see too.

Bubble was right. It was perfect. The summerhouse we had just come from had been recreated in miniature, with a screen door and a shady interior. Two girl dolls in blue dresses, one with brown hair and one with red, sat on the floor where a flowery tablecloth lay spread out. A tiny china tea set with blue flowers was arranged for tea for six, with three little dolls identical to the ones I'd seen in the summerhouse sitting obediently waiting for their tea. Behind them I could see rattan furniture with crisp blue-and-white cushions.

"Look!" cried Bubble suddenly. "There's Sailor!"

A toy golden retriever lay on the little rattan couch.

"That's wrong!" said Bubble. "He's not allowed on the furniture. He's not allowed to come to my tea parties. That's true. He messes everything up and drinks the tea and eats the cookies. That's true."

She reached her hand out to open the screen door, and the tall man yanked it back.

"Don't touch, Bubble!" he said sharply. "I'll get him."

"Sailor should be outside," complained Bubble, rubbing her hand where the man had grabbed it. "He's always outside. That's true."

The man opened the summerhouse door and, with a steady hand, extracted the toy dog, careful not to touch any of the dolls or furniture in the process. He laid the dog down just outside the screen door. "Better?" he said, looking at Bubble.

"I guess," said Bubble. She stood up and backed away from him. "You hurt me."

"Oh don't be silly, Bubble," said her mother. "Mr. Inwood barely touched you. I'm ashamed of you. He's made this beautiful summerhouse for you, with your dolls and the tea set, and all you can do is complain about Sailor. Say thank you."

"Thank you," mumbled Bubble.

"Fizz?" said her mother.

"Thank you, Mr. Inwood," said Fizz in a singsong voice. "Thank you for making us a beautiful toy summerhouse that we can't play with. And thank you for hurting my sister."

"Fizz!" snapped her mother. "I warned you!"

"It's all right, Harriet," said Mr. Inwood. He wouldn't look at Fizz, and he shifted from foot to foot uncomfortably. "I understand. It's difficult for them, but someday they'll appreciate that the dollhouse is not a toy."

"Then why do you say it's for us, if it's not a toy?" asked Fizz. "Why do you and Mother spend hours and hours talking about it and making things for it, and we aren't allowed to help or touch anything? It's your toy, not ours."

Her mother grabbed her arm and gave her a shake. "Fizz! That's enough. Go to your room this minute."

"Why should I?" yelled Fizz, stamping her foot.

Bubble stood looking from her mother to her sister, her lips quivering.

"Mama?" she said uncertainly, starting to cry.

Her mother dropped Fizz's arm and turned to Bubble. She put her arms around Bubble and gave her a hug.

"There, there, Bubble, it's all right," she said. "Fizz just lost her temper again. Let's all calm down."

"I don't like it when you yell," said Bubble. "That's true."

"I know," said her mother, looking over her shoulder at Fizz. "I'm sorry."

Fizz was still glaring at everyone.

"I'm sorry too," chimed in Mr. Inwood. "I shouldn't have

grabbed you, Bubble. It's just that the dollhouse is so special, and so precious, that if just one thing gets broken, it will take hours to mend."

"Wasn't going to break anything," grumbled Bubble.

"You know you can't touch, Bubble," said her mother. "Just like Queen Mary's dollhouse in England. No one can touch that. You remember when we saw it, Bubble? How we wanted one of our own?" She was smiling at her daughter now, dabbing at Bubble's tears with a lacy handkerchief.

Fizz had crossed her arms and stood watching them, frowning.

"Yes," said Bubble, brightening. "It was a beautiful dollhouse! That's true."

"And Mr. Inwood has worked so hard to make this one perfect too. We just can't touch."

Bubble nodded her head and hiccupped.

While their attention was on Bubble, I was curious to have another look inside the summerhouse. It was just as Mr. Inwood—Adrian—had said: everything was so perfect and small. The teacups, the plate of shortbreads, just as they had been in the real summerhouse. The shortbreads? I wondered if they were real. I stretched out my hand to touch them, glancing quickly at the grown-ups to see if they were looking my way. They weren't, and then I remembered that it wouldn't matter if they were, because they couldn't see me.

I was invisible. It was my dream. I could play with the dollhouse as much as I liked.

I gently touched one of the little cookies. They weren't real: they were made of plaster and stuck all together with glue so they wouldn't fall off the plate.

Not quite so perfect, I thought. Now if they were real little shortbreads you could actually eat, that would be perfect.

Looking past the cookies, I realized there was another doll standing in the shadows at the back of the summerhouse. I peered in, trying to see it more clearly.

It was a girl doll with a pale face and straggly brown hair wearing a sleeveless green top, jean shorts and bare feet. I looked down at my clothes and back at the doll.

It was me.

I felt that falling feeling again and the darkness closed in on me.

Chapter Twenty-One

BUTTERCAKES

A dog was barking outside.

I opened my eyes. I was lying on my bed with the green bed curtains closing me in and the afternoon heat beating through them. I struggled to sit up, then opened the curtains on the window side and got out of bed.

I went to the window and looked out.

A golden retriever with a red collar was racing back and forth across the back lawn, barking his head off.

I rubbed my eyes. I must still be dreaming. I stumbled out into the hall, where there was a sweet smell of roses, and then the downstairs clock began to chime: one—two—three chimes that rang out and then died away, leaving a whispering echo in the silent house.

The door opposite mine opened and my mother came out. Okay, not dreaming.

"Oh, Alice, good, you're awake. I need you to sit with Mrs. Bishop for an hour or two while I go to town to do my shopping. She's just woken up from her nap, and she needs some company."

She looked at me more closely. "Are you up to it? How are you feeling?"

I yawned. "I'm okay. How long was I sleeping?"

"A couple of hours. I decided to let you sleep. Can't hurt. Now go wash your face, and I'll bring you a glass of lemonade." She bustled down the steep stairs at a good clip. She must be getting used to them.

I turned to go into the bathroom. A dark-blue bowl full of white and pink roses sat on the little desk against the wall. I bent my head over and inhaled the candy-sweet smell. Then I went into the bathroom and splashed my face. I looked pale in the mirror, with dark shadows under my eyes. I could still hear the barking.

When my mother brought me the lemonade, I was sitting on my favorite perch on the window seat, looking out at the dog, who had flopped down on the terrace, his tongue out.

"Where did the dog come from?" I asked.

"Sam—I mean, Dr. West—left him here. He brought him for a visit with Mrs. Bishop—but then Sam got called to an emergency and had to leave in a hurry. Apparently, Mrs. Bishop likes the dog. I don't know why. With that big tail of his he could do a lot of damage to her antiques. Now that she's awake she wants me to bring him up."

"Can I help you with him?" I said.

"Sure. Come on."

* * *

The dog's name was Buttercakes.

I laughed when Mom told me.

She grinned. "I know. What kind of grown man calls his dog Buttercakes? Imagine calling him in the park!"

I laughed again. "I guess Dr. West has a good sense of humor."

"I think so," said my mom, with that foolish look on her face again.

"You like him, don't you?" I asked.

"Of course I like him," said Mom, becoming brisk. "He's a very nice guy. And a good doctor. What's not to like?"

I shrugged. "I don't know. I like him too."

We fell silent. Then Mom opened the kitchen door.

"Buttercakes!" she called, making a face at me as she did so.

After greeting us with more barking and a lot of jumping around, Buttercakes drank a big bowl of water and then Mom put him on a leash and said firmly to him, "Behave!"

Buttercakes looked solemn for a moment.

"Here, you take him," said my mother. "I'll come behind and make sure he doesn't knock anything over."

Buttercakes seemed to know that once he was in the house he had to calm down. He walked sedately up the stairs with me clinging tightly with one hand to the banister and the other to his leash.

Once we were at the top of the stairs, he pulled a bit at his leash and led me straight into the old lady's room. He put two paws up on the bed and his tail started wagging again.

Mrs. Bishop was sitting up in bed, wearing pink pajamas with blue flowers and a white hairband. When she saw Buttercakes, a wide smile transformed her stern old face.

"Hello, you foolish dog," she said, petting him. "Come to visit me, have you?"

She produced a dog biscuit from somewhere and Buttercakes gulped it down.

After a few more pats and endearments, and a couple more biscuits, Mrs. Bishop noticed me.

"Buttercakes, lie down and be good," she said, and the dog obeyed. "Alice, I understand you're going to be keeping me company this afternoon."

"Yes, ma'am," I said, standing a bit straighter.

"Your mother tells me you have a concussion," said the old lady.

I glanced back at Mom, who was standing at the door giving me an encouraging smile.

"Yes, I do. From the accident."

"And how are you feeling?"

"Umm . . . okay, I guess. I get headaches."

"Do you have one now?"

I didn't. The lemonade had woken me up a bit, and although I still felt a bit foggy, my head wasn't hurting at all.

"No. I had a sleep and that seemed to help."

"Well, you may be interested to know, young lady, that I, too, am suffering from a concussion. So, we have something in common, you and I."

"Does your head hurt?" I asked, forgetting to be scared of her for a moment.

"Sometimes," she replied. "Your mother and Dr. West have me on medication, so I think that helps. And I sleep a lot."

"Do you ever have funny dreams?"

Her eyes narrowed. "I certainly don't have dreams that make me wake up in the night and scream the house down, if that's what you're asking."

I glanced back at Mom. She gave her head a little shake.

"Just wondering," I mumbled.

"Well, never mind that." She turned to Mom. "Go away, Ellie. Alice and I can manage quite well on our own. You better put Buttercakes in the garden while you're gone, or he'll get up to mischief."

Mom and Buttercakes disappeared. Mrs. Bishop fixed her eye on me.

"Go to the window, then tell me when your mother's gone."

"Uh . . . okay." I went over to one of the tall windows that looked out on the front drive. After a couple of minutes, Mom came out, got into a dark-green car and drove away.

"Well? Is she gone?"

"Yes." I returned to her bedside. "Is that your car?"

"Of course it's my car. Whose car would it be?"

"I don't know, I just—"

"Never mind the car. Your mother seems to think I need a babysitter. Do you think I need a babysitter?" She glared at me.

"Umm . . . no. I think she just wanted me to stick around in case you needed anything. Not exactly a babysitter."

"I have a bell. I will ring it if I need you. Just bring me my reading glasses and you can go. I think your mother put them over on the dressing table earlier when she was tidying up. I'd like to know how they're going to do me any good way over there."

Obediently I went over to the dressing table, which had a large oval mirror in the center, with a smaller mirror on each side that you could move to different angles. A silver-backed mirror and brush and comb set lay on the polished surface, along with some pretty white china baskets. But no glasses.

"If they're not there, try the drawers," called Mrs. Bishop from her bed. I glanced back at her. The bed curtains hid her from my view.

There were three drawers with brass hoop handles.

I pulled out the middle one, and there were her glasses. And right beside them, a key ring full of keys.

Chapter Twenty-Two

THE KEYS

I glanced back toward the bed. I still couldn't see Mrs. Bishop, so she couldn't see me.

"Well?" she demanded. "Are they there or not?"

"Yes," I said, scooping up the keys and putting them in my pocket, then taking the glasses and shutting the drawer. "I'm just coming."

As I turned away from the dresser something pink caught my eye in one of the side mirrors. Mrs. Bishop's pajamas. The way the mirror was angled, there was a clear view of her sitting in bed. If I could see her in that mirror, then—she could see me.

I froze. My stomach started doing little jumps.

But she wasn't looking at me. She was gazing in the other direction, toward the window. Phew . . . That was close.

I shouldn't have risked stealing her keys like that. The only thing I can remember going through my head was, "Keys, locked doors, dollhouse," and then they were in my pocket. I'd get in so much trouble if she found out. Mom could get fired. We'd be homeless, cast out on the streets. Begging for food.

"Well?" Now she was looking my way. "What's taking you so long, girl? Bring me my glasses!"

"I . . . uh . . . I . . ." I stuttered, and then my body started working again, and I brought her the glasses, hoping the keys wouldn't start to jangle in my pocket.

She put them on, then gave me one of her sharp looks. "Are you feeling sick again? Do you need to lie down?"

"I . . . uh . . . yeah," I replied. I seemed to have lost the power of speech.

"Well, go on with you then," she said, picking up her book. "I'll ring the bell if I need you."

The hall was silent except for a distant tick-tick from the grandfather clock downstairs. The house seemed drenched in hot summer afternoon sleepiness. No one was here except for Mrs. Bishop and me.

I hurried into my room, leaving the doors open behind me so I would be sure to hear Mrs. Bishop's bell. The closet felt almost unbearably stuffy. At the door to the stairs, I fumbled with the keys, trying one after another. Finally I found one that worked. I climbed up the steep stairs, noting that they were dusty and the wood had a visible grain running through it. Not clean and flat-looking, the way the stairs were in my dream.

The attic was empty—no trunks or lamps. The heat shimmered in the light that streamed in the far window.

I still had the key that had opened the door clutched in my hand, and on impulse, I tried it in the lock to the dollhouse room.

Nothing. I tried the one right beside it, and the lock turned.

I stopped just inside the door and looked around at the room, trying to remember what else had been different in my dream. The dollhouse stood in the same place in the center of the room, tall and imposing. The walls, the rug, the wardrobe in the corner—everything looked the same.

But the room felt very, very hot. I glanced over to the window. Had it been open in my dream? Had there been a soft breeze slipping in, cooling things off? I couldn't remember.

I went over to examine the window. At first glance, it didn't look like the kind that could open. Identical to the window on the far side of the attic, it was a half circle of glass, taller than me and wider than I could reach if I stuck both my arms out on either side. On the lower part of the window was another half circle, like a sun, with white wooden sunrays radiating out to the top.

I took a step closer. A white-painted latch was visible on one side of the sun shape, blending in with the white bars so it was hard to see at first. I lifted the latch and the smaller half circle detached from the rest of the window and tipped forward, letting in a delicious breath of fresh air. It was still hot, but not as hot as the air in the attic.

I wiggled the latch a little. It moved smoothly and quietly. It must have been oiled recently. Someone had been up here at some point. But when? And who?

I turned back into the room. Something caught my eye on the floor to the left of the dollhouse and I caught my breath, unable to believe what I was seeing.

A doll-sized replica of the summerhouse sat on the carpet with a toy yellow dog lying in front. It had been hidden by the dollhouse when I stepped into the room.

How was it possible? Suddenly my head was spinning, and I sank to the floor and covered my eyes with my hands.

What was happening to me? Was this the concussion, making me see things that weren't there? Mixing up my dreams with reality? Was I going crazy? The house seemed to be rocking beneath me.

I took a few deep breaths and I felt a little better. Maybe it was the heat *and* the concussion that was making me feel so awful. I peeked through my fingers. The summerhouse was there all right.

The summerhouse had definitely *not* been there that morning when Lily and I had been here. Could someone have come up here and put it there while I was sleeping? But who? After Lily and I locked the room and tiptoed downstairs, we'd had lunch with Mary and Mom, they had left, and then I'd come up for my nap. There was nobody else here that I knew of, except for Dr. West dropping off the dog. Could someone have come through my room to the hidden staircase while I was asleep?

Possibly. But who? Mrs. Bishop had a cast on her leg and

couldn't move. And why would Mom do something like that without telling me?

Maybe Mrs. Bishop didn't want me playing with the doll-house. Like Adrian and Harriet in my dream, she might think the dollhouse wasn't for children. And that's why it was locked up and kept secret. Maybe Mom was in on it. Knowing how curious I am, Mom may have thought it was better to keep the dollhouse a secret from me.

But where had the summerhouse come from? All of a sudden like that, just after I was dreaming about it?

I stood up and went over to the window, gulping in the fresh air. Trees grew up quite close to the house, and I could see through a lattice of leafy green to the gravel driveway below. The leaves were motionless in the hot, still afternoon.

After a few minutes I felt better, and I went back to kneel beside the summerhouse and peer in.

The tea party was in full progress, just as it had been in my dream. The Bubble and Fizz dolls were seated on the floor with Bubble's three dolls, April, May and June. The tablecloth was spread with teacups, a teapot and a tiny plate of short-breads. But there was no ghost Alice doll standing at the back dressed in my clothes.

I reached out and touched the wooden roof. It was real. Solid. I pinched my arm. Okay, I could feel that. This was real. Not a dream.

I turned and looked back at the dollhouse. From where I was sitting on the floor, it looked enormous, looming over me. A brooding presence. A haunted dollhouse.

I gave myself a shake and stood up. I wasn't going to let my imagination get away with me, and I wasn't going to be scared of a dollhouse. I unlatched the back wall and swung it open.

The sweet smell of fresh-cut roses floated past me. I peered into the upstairs hall, and in the shadows, I could just make out a dark-blue bowl full of white and pink roses. I snaked my hand in carefully and pulled it out into the light.

The roses weren't real; they were made from silk, tiny and perfect. They didn't smell like anything. I must have imagined it. I put them back on the little desk in the hall and turned to my bedroom. The bed curtains were open and no doll lay on the bed.

Of course. The Fizz doll was in the summerhouse with Bubble.

I raised my eyes and looked at the dollhouse attic. I hadn't had time to notice it when Lily and I were up here before. But now I saw that a toy dollhouse that looked like a replica of this one stood in the middle of the attic room with its back wall open. A dollhouse within a dollhouse.

Two dolls stood on either side of it: A woman doll with dark brown hair and a flowery dress. A tall, skinny man with unruly brown hair, dressed in a light summer suit. At the woman's feet sat a miniature summerhouse with a small yellow dog stretched out in front.

I reached out a trembling hand and gently turned the little summerhouse so I could see inside. Tiny Bubble and Fizz dolls were having a tea party with even tinier April, May and

June dolls. And there in the corner, stood another. I lifted her carefully out.

The ghost Alice doll, with straggly brown hair, a green top and jean shorts lay in the palm of my hand. Tiny. Perfect. Me.

Chapter Twenty-Three
A MAGIC DOLLHOUSE

That feeling I got when I was running down the attic stairs the first time I came up here? When I lost my balance and for a moment I felt like I was going to fall? I hate that feeling. Weightless and falling and adrenaline jumping through my body. Whenever that happens, I always feel all trembly after, as if I really had fallen down. Mom says it's the body's natural reaction to a stressful situation, where the fight-or-flight response might be needed.

As I stood there in the hot attic, staring at the Ghost Alice doll in my hand, which along with the Adrian and Harriet dolls had apparently materialized in the dollhouse after I dreamed about them, I had an adrenaline rush, even though I was in no danger of falling. It swooped through my body and left me shaking.

Fight or flight, I thought stupidly. Which can I do? There

was no one to fight. Flight? Where would I go? I could run downstairs and hide under the covers on my bed, but then I might fall asleep and wake up to find Fizz beside me, grinning in that annoying way she had, like she knew something hilarious that I didn't.

I had nowhere to go and no one who could help me. Mom would say it was my concussion and have me in the hospital before I finished telling her. Lily might understand, but I couldn't see how she could help. She wouldn't know any better than I did what was going on.

Something weird and crazy was happening to me. It was more than concussion or bad dreams. I had to figure it out.

I looked back at the dollhouse. The dollhouse was the key. Carefully, I replaced Ghost Alice in the little summerhouse. Then I looked on the other side of the dollhouse attic. It wasn't empty, like the real attic outside this room. There were a few old chairs, an old trunk and a lamp. Just as there had been in my dream. I couldn't see down the stairs to see if they were dusty. Instead, I went around to the front and opened the wall to look in at Bubble's room, the first room I had taken any notice of after Fizz told me not to scream and led me through the secret passage.

I fingered the silver bed curtains. They were just a bit stiffer than the real curtains. I pressed my finger into the carpet. It wasn't as springy and deep as the real one. I remember noticing both of those things when I met Bubble in my dream.

What if . . . What if I was actually going *into* the dollhouse in my sleep? Was it possible?

I sat down on the rug and crossed my legs and stared at the dollhouse. I needed to be deliberate about this, like at school with a science experiment. Make observations. Draw conclusions.

I swallowed. Okay.

On the surface, the house I went into in my dreams was identical to the Blackwood House of my waking life. Except for a few telling details—the stairs with their lack of dust, the wardrobe full of clothes, the coarser curtains, the thinner rugs. And the material on the summerhouse cushions felt crisper and the colors brighter than the faded chairs I had seen in the summerhouse with Lily. Like they were brand-new.

Fabrics. I remembered how Dad always said good materials showed that a restoration was done right.

All of the fabrics in my dollhouse dream were not quite as fine as the real thing, as if it were harder to reproduce the high quality of the thick woolen rugs or the silky bed curtains. The wood on the attic stairs in the dollhouse wasn't the same fine wood as the real attic stairs. And they weren't covered in dust because in the dollhouse those stairs were used every day, and presumably somebody swept them.

The dollhouse closet was full of Fizz's clothes, whereas mine only held my three sundresses. And Fizz and Bubble were dressed in blue dresses the second time I dreamed about them, after Lily had changed the dolls out of their nightgowns and into their blue dresses. That was the biggest clue of all that they were in the dollhouse.

But. But. It was so hard to believe. Maybe I was just dreaming it all. After Lily changed the dolls into blue dresses, I dreamed about Fizz and Bubble wearing blue dresses. Things from the waking world often made their way into dreams.

But things from dreams didn't make their way back into the waking world. I looked back at the summerhouse on the carpet behind me. It wasn't here this morning. And I think I would have noticed the Harriet and Adrian dolls (and the summerhouse!) in the attic if they had been there the first time Lily and I saw the dollhouse.

Was it possible that whatever happened when I was in the dollhouse could be echoed in the real world afterward? And the reverse—if I made changes in the dollhouse in my waking world, would they be reflected in the dollhouse world when I went back there?

It was nuts. I had to be imagining it all. Finally my imagination had gone too far and taken me right inside one of my fantasies. And now I couldn't tell what was real and I was drowning in it. Maybe the concussion had pushed my brain over the edge.

Or—maybe it was a magic dollhouse?

Chapter Twenty-Four

FOUR GHOSTS

I would have laughed if I hadn't been so worried. I knew there was no such thing as magic. I'd come to that reluctant conclusion a few years ago. Despite my great desire to see fairies, have three magic wishes, find a cloak of invisibility and have the ability to fly, I had to admit that those were childish things and they just weren't going to happen. I could have them all in my imagination, but not in the real world.

But now this. And I *had* been invisible for a while. Neither of the grown-ups had been able to see me when I was in the dollhouse world. Maybe I'd stumbled into something.

A magic dollhouse? Really?

I could test it. Scientifically. I could do something to the dollhouse now, and then the next time I dreamed about it, see if whatever I had done was there.

A loud buzzing noise from downstairs made me jump. It took me a second or two to identify it. Mrs. Bishop's bell. She wanted me.

What could I do, quickly, that would be easy for me to check on in the dollhouse world next time I dreamed about it? My eyes fell on the bowl of roses in the upstairs hall of the doll-house. I picked them up and put them under Fizz's bed. Then I closed both walls, hooked them shut and went downstairs, locking both doors behind me.

I hesitated, wondering what to do with the keys. I couldn't keep all of them. They'd be missed. The bell rang again. I wiggled the two attic keys off the ring and shoved them under my underwear in the dresser. Then I stuffed the key ring back in my pocket and ran in to the old lady, just as the bell screeched out for a third time.

Buttercakes was barking wildly outside. I guess he didn't like the bell either.

"What on earth took you so long?" demanded Mrs. Bishop, glaring at me.

"Sorry," I said. "I was asleep."

"I thought my bell was loud enough to wake the dead," she retorted.

Wake the dead. I wondered if those people in the dollhouse were dead. Fizz. Bubble. Harriet and Adrian. Were they all ghosts?

"Alice!" barked Mrs. Bishop.

I jumped.

"Are you even listening to me?" She was looking very cross.

"Sorry, I'm . . . still waking up," I said.

"Well, finish waking up and pick up my book for me. I dropped it."

I glanced at the cover as I picked it up. A girl in a long, old-fashioned dress stood in front of a big spooky mansion. *Northanger Abbey* by Jane Austen. I opened the front cover. There was a name written at the top of the very first page in spidery old-fashioned handwriting: "Fiona Bishop."

"Well?" said Mrs. Bishop. "Why are you so interested in my book? Have you read it?" Then she answered for me. "Of course not, you're much too young."

"What's it about?"

"A very foolish young girl who goes to live in a house in the country and starts imagining all kinds of silly things about the people who live there," said Mrs. Bishop, a little smile turning up the corners of her mouth. "She's idiotic, but it's always been one of my favorites. I read it again and again, and it still makes me laugh."

"What kind of foolish things?" I asked.

"She has read too many ridiculous novels about men who keep wives locked up in secret rooms, and when she finds some rooms she's not allowed to enter, she creates an entire fiction about the man of the house, imagining that he was cruel to his wife and may have even caused her death. Total nonsense. She's the kind of girl who spends too much time in her imagination and finally couldn't tell what was real and what was not."

Mrs. Bishop's words rang through me. It was just as if she was talking about me. Locked rooms. A mystery. Not knowing what was real and what wasn't. Did she know? *Could* she know? Had she seen me with the keys after all?

She took the book from me and began turning the pages to find her place, that little smile on her lips, paying absolutely no attention to me.

"If you are a good reader," she said, "I can certainly recommend it. But the language might be a little difficult for you yet . . . How old are you?" She looked up at me. "Whatever's the matter with you, girl?" she asked. "You look like you've seen a ghost."

A ghost? I had seen a ghost! Or four! Five if you counted the dog. Was I like the girl in Mrs. Bishop's book, making it all up from my imagination? Or was all this craziness really happening?

Chapter Twenty-Five
THE PHONE CALL

"Well? What's the matter with you?" repeated Mrs. Bishop, fixing me with a fierce, penetrating look.

I struggled to return to what she had been saying to me before I started thinking about ghosts. "Uh . . . nothing. The book just sounds a little . . . um . . . scary."

"Scary! It's satire, my dear, not horror. You're much too young for this book if you can't understand that. Satire is making fun of things." She sighed. "I suppose that's why I like Jane Austen so much. She's light-hearted. I was a journalist for many years, and I had far too much seriousness in my life. Now that I'm older, I enjoy looking on the lighter side of life now and then."

"Mary said you were a journalist in England," I said, wanting to keep her on that subject so she wouldn't ask me any more questions.

"Mary!" snorted Mrs. Bishop. "That woman never stops talking."

I had to grin.

"I suppose she told you all kinds of things about my life and my business that she has no right to repeat?"

"No, not really, just that you had—um—oh!" I stopped, remembering that what Mary had said was that Mrs. Bishop must have picked up her bad language while she was a journalist in England.

Again, that piercing stare.

"Never mind, I can only imagine what she said to you. But the truth is, yes, I was a journalist for many years, and I ended up owning the newspaper I worked for. It was a man's world in those days—I daresay it still is. But I made my way and I accomplished nearly everything I set out to do. In my heyday I was what they now call an investigative journalist. Trying to right the wrongs of the world. I was fortunate, I suppose, starting out where and when I did. I moved to England as a young woman and started my career during the war, when there weren't enough men to fill the jobs, so they hired women instead. I got my start covering bombings in London, and you can't get any more closely acquainted with reality than that."

She shook her head, remembering. "After the war, I was always drawn to stories of injustice, and I was young and headstrong, and I believed I could make a difference in the world with my stories. And I think I did. Sometimes. Not always. But that's over and done with now." She sighed and gave herself a little shake, like she was shaking off the past. She looked over at me.

"And now I lie in bed reading Jane Austen. At least, I would be reading Jane Austen if you would leave me in peace and stop asking me questions."

She really was the grumpiest old lady I had ever met. She was the one who started talking to me! And how was I going to get the keys back in her drawer?

"I love your house," I said. "It's so beautiful. I was admiring your dresser, earlier, with the mirrors."

Her face softened. "Yes, it's lovely, isn't it? It belonged to my mother."

"I've never seen one like it," I said, glancing over at it.

"My mother was a very beautiful woman," said Mrs. Bishop. "She spent a lot of time in front of those mirrors, fixing her face. I never had much use for makeup myself, but having it there reminds me of her." She sighed again.

"Do those mirrors actually move?" I said. Maybe I could go over and move them so she couldn't see me and slip the keys back.

"Of course they move. That's the whole idea. So you can see the side of your face, or your hair."

"Can I . . . um . . . can I see how it works?" I asked.

"Oh, go and look at the thing, if you're that interested," she snapped. "You'd think you'd never seen a mirror before."

I walked over and sat down at the table. I started experimenting with the mirror on the left, the one I could see her in.

"Oh, I see," I called out to her. "Gee, I wish I had one of these."

There. I could no longer see her in the mirror. Quickly I took the keys from my pocket, slid the drawer open and placed them inside.

"You're too young for makeup," said Mrs. Bishop.

I returned to her bedside.

"Too young for makeup and too young for Jane Austen, I'd say. So what are you good for?"

"I could bring you some lemonade," I offered. "And some of Mary's cookies."

I smiled at her, and she glared at me again.

"Go on then," she said. "I could use a little snack." She turned back to her book.

* * *

When Mom came home with the groceries about an hour later, I was out in the garden, lying in the shade of a big oak tree with Buttercakes. I'd thrown a stick for him for a while, and when we both got tired of that, we stretched out in the grass together. I figured that was close enough to hear Mrs. Bishop's buzzer if she rang it again. I was glad to be out of the house for a while. It was giving me the creeps.

While I was helping Mom unpack the groceries, Dr. West came by to pick up the dog. Mom was all kind of giggly and blushing, and he was making jokes and watching her laugh. Honestly, she'd only been away from Dad for a couple of days. What was wrong with her?

He was kind of cute, I guess, with his rumpled shirt and big smile. He had lovely eyes, warm and twinkly. Even I couldn't help liking him. He took a close look at me and asked me how I was feeling. He asked it not just like a doctor, but like he really cared how I felt.

I looked away and mumbled, "Fine."

"She had a long sleep this afternoon," said Mom. "I'm sure it did her good."

He turned his easy smile back on her and she giggled. Mom. My Mom. Sensible, practical Mom, giggling because a man smiled at her.

Maybe she liked him because he was so different from Dad. The opposite, really. Dad always had a little frown between his eyes, thinking about work, I guess, preoccupied with his building developments, finances, deals—whatever it was that kept him away from us day after day after week after week—Mom was right. He had kind of removed himself from our family life over the last couple of years. He never made it to my choir concerts or student-parent night or even my birthday. There was always a crisis he had to deal with, usually out of town. We hardly ever went antique-hunting anymore. When he was home, I had to really work to get him to turn his attention to me. Even then, I always felt his itch to get back to what was really important, his work.

But he was my dad. I missed him. I wasn't going to forget him as quickly as Mom seemed to be doing.

As Dr. West and Buttercakes were lingering by the front door, the phone rang in the study and Mom told me to get it.

"Mrs. Bishop's residence," I answered, the way Mom had told me to answer the phone in Blackwood House.

"Alice?"

"Dad?" Just when I'd been thinking about him, he called.

"How's it going, Alice?"

"Oh—fine," I said.

"You okay?"

"Yeah, sure. How . . . how are you, Dad?"

"Oh, fine," he said.

Silence. This was hard.

"Dad, when are you coming back? When will I see you?"

There was a pause. "I don't know right now. Your mother doesn't want to see me for a while, and there's a bit of a crisis here with the new development in LA."

Another pause.

"But Dad—" I said. "I miss you." There was a catch in my voice, and I felt like I was going to cry.

"I know, honey, I—I miss you too," he replied. "I just don't know when I'll be back. But I will see you, promise."

How many times had he said that. "I'll be back on the weekend, promise," or "I'll be back for the concert, promise," or "I'll come to the cottage, promise."

"Promise," usually meant the opposite. He wouldn't be back on the weekend, he wouldn't be there for the concert, he wouldn't make it to the cottage. I choked and handed the phone to Mom, who was standing just behind me with a grim look on her face.

I fled.

Chapter Twenty-Six
THE TRUTH

I was afraid to go to sleep that night.

I lay in bed, trying to keep my eyes from closing. It had cooled down a bit, and a breeze was ruffling the bed curtains. I had left the closet light on and the closet door slightly open so the room wasn't completely dark. The crickets were humming outside, a high-pitched, ringing sound. Then I heard a train whistle, far away, but getting closer.

If I went to sleep, I would dream about the dollhouse. I didn't want any more of that. I just wanted to be home in my own bed in my small bedroom with Dad and Mom down the hall and the city noises of cars and sirens outside my window. I didn't want adventures and haunted houses and grumpy old ladies telling me what to do. I didn't want anything exciting. Just ordinary, boring everyday life again. The way it used to be.

Except it wasn't. I could be back there, but most likely Dad wouldn't be. He was hardly ever home anyway. I sighed and turned over.

"I thought you'd never fall asleep," said a voice from the window.

I sat up. In the light from the closet, I could just make out the figure of someone sitting in the window seat. Fizz. She stood up, made a leap toward the bed and landed half on top of me, laughing.

"I didn't. Fall asleep," I protested, untangling myself from her.

"Oh yes you did. Otherwise you wouldn't be here." She flopped down on the pillow beside me.

I reached over and turned on the bedside lamp. She was wearing the same sundress I'd last seen her in.

"You know what's going on with me, don't you?" I said, watching her face.

She grinned.

"Yup."

"Then tell me. I'm sick of you giving me hints and acting so superior. Tell me what's happening to me."

Her eyes narrowed and she stopped smiling.

"You tell me."

"I'm in the dollhouse, right?" I said, fingering the silky green bed curtains that weren't quite as silky and fine as they were when I was awake. "These are dollhouse curtains, this is a dollhouse bed, and you're nothing but a doll."

"Wrong," said Fizz, sitting up. "I'm not a doll. This isn't a dollhouse. This is a real house. I was sleeping, sleeping for a long time, and then you appeared in my bed and woke me up. You're a ghost. You come from somewhere else."

"Yes! I come from the outside world, and this dollhouse is inside the attic in the big house."

She shook her head. "Nope. If this is a dollhouse in the attic, how come we can see the moon out there, and trees, and grass and sky?" She pointed out the window.

She had me there.

"Wait a minute," I said, jumping off the bed and looking under it. I pulled out the bowl of roses. Their sweet smell filled the room.

"I can prove this is a dollhouse. I put these under the bed in the dollhouse in the attic today, and here they are. That proves I'm going into the dollhouse when I'm asleep. It's some kind of magic dollhouse."

Fizz threw back her head and started to laugh. She had a loud, distinctive, infectious laugh, and soon she was laughing so hard she had to bury her face in the pillow. So as not to wake up the other dolls in the dollhouse, I guess.

I wanted to slap her. I went and opened the door to the hall and started yelling.

"Wake up, everybody! Wake up! I know you're all dolls."

Fizz sat up and tried to speak through her laughter.

I started slamming the door and yelling some more. She jumped out of bed and pulled me away from the door.

"Stop it," she said. "They won't hear your voice, but they

will hear the door slamming. Stupid. I keep telling you, you're a ghost. Haven't you figured that out?"

There was the sound of a door opening in the hall. Fizz leaped for the bed, switched off the light and pulled the covers up to her chin, just in time. Her mother burst into the room and switched on the overhead light.

"What's going on, Fizz? Why were you slamming the door?"

Fizz opened her eyes. "Whaaa?"

Harriet stood over her daughter. She was wearing some marvelous satiny-blue nightgown that rippled down over her body from her shoulders to her ankles. The last time I'd seen her, she'd been dressed in daytime clothes, in the attic with Mr. Inwood. Time must have passed here. Of course. It was night now and it had been afternoon then.

"Fizz! What's wrong with you?"

I stood with my back to the wardrobe, watching.

Fizz blinked. "I was asleep. What's going on?" She was very convincing.

"Your door—it was slamming. Didn't you hear it?"

"I heard you come in."

"You know very well that's not what I meant," snapped her mother.

"Maybe it's a poltergeist," said Fizz helpfully.

"Don't you poltergeist me, young lady," said her mother. "I don't know what you're up to, but you can't fool me. I've had it with your nonsense. The sooner you're off to boarding school the better. I don't want to hear one more peep from you tonight, you understand?" She glared at Fizz, who threw the covers over her face.

Harriet stomped out, turning off the light as she went. I moved slowly toward the bed and switched the bedside lamp on.

Fizz sat up, trembling. "She can't wait to get rid of me. I hate her."

She covered her face with her hands for a moment and took a few deep breaths. Then she brushed away some tears and looked at me.

"What are you staring at?" she said. "Don't you ever hate your mother?"

I thought about it. "No. Not really. I get mad at her. But sometimes . . . sometimes I hate my father," I said very quietly.

"Why?" asked Fizz. "What does he do to you?"

"Nothing." I shrugged and sat down on the bed beside her. "He's just never around. He's always working. He makes my mother cry, and he acts like he doesn't care about us."

"My dad works a lot too," said Fizz. "But when he's around, he's so much fun. He plays with me and Bubble and chases us around the house and gets down on all fours and barks at Sailor and acts like a little kid."

"He does sound like fun," I said sadly. "My dad used to play with me when I was little, but he never seems to have the time now. That's why we're here. Mom wants a divorce I think . . ."

"Divorce?" said Fizz. "Really? You don't think they'll make up?"

"Not this time," I replied. "I hope they do, but Mom is fed up. And now she's flirting with Dr. West—"

"Who's Dr. West?"

"This doctor guy," I said gloomily. "I mean, I like him, and I even sort of imagined him before I saw him, the kind of dad I'd like to have, kind of funny and easygoing and always there, but Mom and Dad only split up a couple of days ago. I don't understand grown-ups."

"Me neither," said Fizz. "My mother's always flirting with Adrian. Mr. Architect, Mr. Don't-touch-my-dollhouse-with-your-dirty-little-hands Inwood."

"Oh," I said, thinking back to the two of them in the attic. "You think she likes him?"

"Oh yeah, she likes him all right," said Fizz. "And he's in love with her. You can tell the way he looks at her. His eyes go all dreamy, and he stutters, and he falls over things when she's around. It makes Dad mad, but Mother just laughs it off. She likes having men in love with her. It's sickening."

"Don't you want to go to boarding school?" I asked. I'd read a few books about girls in boarding school and it sounded like fun.

"I don't know. Maybe. Anything would be better than those two gushing about the dollhouse day after day. But I'll miss Bubble. And Dad. And Sailor." She fell silent.

A faint breeze stirred the curtains at the window.

"About the dollhouse," I said. "You were going to tell me what's going on."

She looked at me. "Do you really want to know?"

I felt suddenly cold. She had a calculating look on her face, as if she was weighing up my courage.

"Of course I want to know," I snapped.

Fizz reached out and took my hand, pulling me onto the bed beside her.

"Brace yourself," she said.

"Oh stop being so dramatic," I said. "Just tell me!"

"Well . . ." she began, her eyes big. "Has something happened to you recently? Some kind of accident?"

"Yes," I said slowly. I didn't like the sound of this. "I was in a train accident and hit my head."

"Is that all?" asked Fizz. "Have you been feeling—at all strange?"

I was getting more uncomfortable.

"Well, yes. I've been having headaches and I feel kind of dizzy sometimes. I have a concussion."

"I think you got more than a concussion in that train crash," she said softly. "I think you died."

Chapter Twenty-Seven

A VERY BAD DREAM

Fizz sat watching me, sitting as still as if she were a statue. I stared at her. I was icy cold now, and I couldn't quite catch my breath.

"You're lying," I said. "This is your idea of a joke."

"No." She shook her head. "It's not funny. You're just not ready to hear the truth."

"It's not the truth," I said. "I have a concussion. I have headaches. I have weird dreams, and the dollhouse . . . I keep dreaming about the dollhouse, that I'm inside it, here, with you."

Fizz leaned toward me. "You've made up this story about the dollhouse because you don't want to face the truth," she whispered. "You're a ghost."

I drew away from her. "No. I'm not a ghost. I'm not dead!

I'm living in Blackwood House with my mom and Mrs. Bishop, and I'm just dreaming all this about the dollhouse."

"You're still half in the other world . . ." said Fizz, in a gentle, singsong voice as if she was telling me a story. "You can't accept that you're dead. I've done a lot of reading about ghosts. A lot of ghosts are like that. They think they're still alive. But every time you let yourself go to sleep, that's when you're dead. And for some reason you've come to our house. You'll be nothing but a ghost here until you realize that you're dead, that you died in the train accident."

I began to scream. "I'm not. I'm not. You're lying! You're horrible! You're the ghost, not me! I'm not dead!"

I pushed her away and fell out of bed, all tangled up in the sheets.

"No!" I yelled, "No!" as I thrashed about on the floor, trying to free myself. Somehow the sheets had wrapped themselves around my head, and everything was dark and breathless for a moment until I managed to peel them away and struggle to my feet.

The room was lit by faint moonlight. Fizz was nowhere to be seen. I stumbled into the hall, calling my mother, bursting into her room.

It was dark. I could see a shape in the bed and I threw myself on her.

"Mom, Mom, wake up! Tell me I'm not dead! Mom!"

The figure stirred and muttered and then sat up and grabbed me by the shoulders.

"Alice! Alice! Calm down."

She turned on the light.

It was Mom. I began to sob.

* * *

I cried for a long time. I kept saying I wasn't dead, and Mom kept hugging me like I was a little girl and telling me of course I wasn't dead, I'd just had a bad dream. Then Mrs. Bishop's buzzer went off, and Mom pulled herself away and said she'd just be a minute and went in to Mrs. Bishop next door.

I sat on her bed, hugging my knees, my sobs slowly quieting. I hiccupped.

I was alive. I could feel every part of my body. I could feel the warmth in my mother's bed where she'd been lying. I could smell the sweet night smell of trees and grass coming in the open window. I could hear Mrs. Bishop complaining next door and Mom trying to placate her.

I was alive. Of course I was alive. But why did Fizz say I was dead? And was I just dreaming about going into the dollhouse? Or was I really going into it every time I fell asleep?

Mom came back. She rolled her eyes.

"Mrs. Bishop is fit to be tied. Let's go down and make her some hot chocolate."

She sat down on the bed beside me.

"Are you okay, sweetie?" she said, a frown creasing her forehead. "You scared the wits out of me."

I gulped. "Just a bad dream," I said. "A really, really bad dream."

"Come on," she said, standing up and reaching out a hand to me. "Come downstairs and we'll talk about it."

I followed her through the shadowy house, holding her hand like I was five, looking over my shoulder for ghosts as we went. Downstairs, the kitchen looked ordinary in the overhead light.

Mom put some milk in a saucepan to heat up and then sat down across the table from me.

"Alice," she began. Then she stopped and took a deep breath. "Alice, look. I know you're upset about me bringing you here and messing up your summer. I know you're worried about me and Dad and what's going to happen."

"What is going to happen, Mom?" I whispered. "Are you going to get a divorce?"

She didn't answer me right away, but just sat there looking at me, her eyes filling with tears.

"You are, aren't you?" I said. She nodded.

"Your dad and I talked about it on the phone tonight. It's no good, Alice. This has been coming for a long time. Your dad—your dad—well, you know he loves you."

I nodded my head, although I really didn't know, not anymore.

"He just—he's just so distant now. He's never around, and I can't rely on him for anything. I can't take it anymore. I'm sorry, honey." Her tears spilled over, and she wiped at her eyes with the back of her hand.

"We'll work things out so you'll get to spend some time with him. Later in the summer."

I felt the world dropping away from me, the way it did in the kitchen when they were fighting on my last day of school.

"I don't want you to get a divorce," I whispered. "I want Dad to come home. I want it to be like it used to be."

Mom came around the table and put her arms around me.

"So do I," she said. "But it's not going to."

There was a gurgling sound from the stove, and she let go of me and went to see to the milk, which was starting to boil over. I watched her take it off the heat and stir cocoa and brown sugar into it.

"I think that's why you're having these bad dreams," she said, glancing over at me. "Because you're upset about me and Dad. We just have to get through this next bit. It's going to be hard for everyone."

"But the train accident," I said. "I remember it."

"Alice, there was an accident. But it wasn't a bad one. You hit your head and were out for a few seconds, that's all. I was with you the whole time." She came over and brushed my hair back off my forehead and smiled at me. "You're not dead, honey. You're very much alive. Now, help me bring this cocoa up to Mrs. Bishop."

Mom took the tray with cocoa and a plate of cookies and I went up behind her. The house seemed to whisper around me.

I stood at the door and watched Mom hand Mrs. Bishop her drink. She was sitting up in bed with her glasses on, glaring at me.

"You've woken me again, young lady," she said. "I don't appreciate it. I thought the house was on fire, at least."

"Sorry," I mumbled.

"Your mother tells me you get carried away with your imagination," she continued. "I suggest you stop that."

"I would if I could," I protested. Mom gave me a warning look.

"When I was your age, there were enough troubles in the world without imagining more," she went on, taking a dainty sip of the hot cocoa. "I grew up between two world wars, and I survived the Depression, the Blitz, and food rationing in London in the 1950s," she said, taking a large bite of an oatmeal cookie.

I said nothing.

"And I did it all without waking up the house screaming with nightmares!" she ended, glaring at me some more. "Don't let it happen again."

I turned and went into Mom's room, where I got into her bed and started in on my cocoa and cookies. When Mom came in a few minutes later, I was lying under her covers.

"Okay," she said. "You can sleep here with me tonight. But tomorrow it's back to your room."

Part Three

THE PARTY

Chapter Twenty-Eight
THE ROSES

When I woke up, the sun was beating through the window of Mom's bedroom, and I was alone. It was hot. I had slept in. No dreams. No dollhouse. No Fizz.

I could hear a vacuum humming downstairs. I got up, went to the bathroom and then went down the hall staircase in my bare feet, yawning. It was getting a little easier to navigate the steep curves every time I did it, but I still hung on tight to the banister.

The vacuum noise was coming from the study. I poked my head in, and there was Mary in shorts and a tank top, vacuuming in the corner beside the fireplace. She hadn't heard me, so I left her to it and went downstairs to the kitchen.

Lily was sitting at the kitchen table by the window, her tongue sticking out as she concentrated on something she was drawing.

"Boo!" I said, and she jumped. Then she saw it was me and grinned.

"What are you drawing?" I said, leaning over her shoulder to look.

She had drawn three little figures in dresses with their legs stuck out, like they were sitting on the ground, and one bigger figure to the side, also sitting down. In front of them were teacups and saucers.

Despite the heat, a shiver trickled down the back of my neck. Why was Lily drawing a scene from the dream I had yesterday afternoon? The sense of unreality I had in the attic the day before came rushing back.

"Is this a . . . teapot?" I asked, pointing to a larger object on one side. My voice squeaked a little on the word *teapot*.

"Yup," answered Lily, putting her head on one side and looking at it. She reached forward and added a little squiggle to the handle. "It's me and my dolls. Having a tea party. I think so."

Weird. I gave my head a little shake, trying to clear it.

"Do you like tea parties, Lily?" I asked.

She nodded. "I love them. I have a really pretty tea set, with blue flowers on it," she said, lifting her pencil again and starting to draw little flowers on one of the teacups.

The same pattern as Bubble's tea set in the summerhouse.

"Where did you get that pretty tea set, Lily?"

"Mrs. Bishop gave it to me."

Mrs. Bishop?

"She said it should be played with and not just sit in a cupboard. It's really old, and one of the cups is chipped."

"And . . . and are these your dolls?" I asked, watching as she moved on to another teacup and began to decorate it.

She nodded her head. "Lucy and Ruby and Jane. They love tea parties too."

At least they weren't April, May and June, like Bubble's dolls.

I took a deep breath. Lily kept on adding flowers to the teacups, sitting back after each one to admire her work.

It was like dreaming backward. Back at home, I had noticed that sometimes things from my daily life would appear in my dreams, transformed in some way, but here at Blackwood House, things from my dreams were making their way into the daytime world. Unless I was dreaming the daytime world and the dollhouse world was the real one—

"What's wrong, Alice?" asked Lily, looking at me in concern. "You look funny."

"Umm . . . I *feel* funny, Lily. Weird things have been happening to me lately."

"Oh?" she replied, looking interested. "Like what?"

"Well . . ." I hesitated. "I've seen the ghost again, the one in my bed."

"Oh! Is she scary?"

"No. Not exactly. But I see other ghosts too. And some of them can't see me."

"Oh . . ." whispered Lily. "That is scary. I think so."

"Kind of. And I think—"

I hesitated again. Lily was staring at me with a look that was half-curious, half-apprehensive. I wanted to tell her. I wanted to tell someone. I needed to tell someone. I didn't want to scare her too much, but—

"I think I'm going into the dollhouse at night, and that's where I see the ghosts." It came out in a rush.

Lily put down her pencil. Her eyes were big. "You go into the dollhouse?"

I nodded. "I think so."

She jumped up. "That sounds like so much fun. I want to go too."

I guess I didn't need to worry about scaring her. I shook my head. "I don't know how to get you there. I don't know how I get there myself. I just have these dreams. But I tested it. I found Mrs. Bishop's keys and went up to look at the dollhouse, and I put a bowl of roses under the bed, and the next time I dreamed about the dollhouse, they were there."

"Let's test it some more," said Lily. "Let's go right now!"

"Okay," I said. "But I have to eat my breakfast first, and we have to time it right so our mothers don't catch us."

By the time I finished my toast and peanut butter, we had a plan. We'd tell our mothers we were going to go for a walk to Potter's Pond for a swim, a place Lily went to all the time. But instead of going swimming, we'd sneak back into the house and up to the attic.

I wasn't so sure about how we'd get in without being seen, but Lily assured me we could do it.

"It's easy, Alice. We just play the invisible game."

"The . . . what?"

"The invisible game. I play it all the time. Pretend I'm invisible. I just hide and stay very, very still." She froze in place for a moment. "Like that. And listen." She tipped her head to one side. "Then creep along quiet as can be." She tiptoed around in a circle, then stopped and flashed that big, beaming grin. "Mama never sees me. Easy peasy. I think so."

When my mom appeared a few minutes later, and we asked her about the swimming, she gave me a searching look and asked about my headache. Once I told her I felt fine, she said we'd have to check with Mary.

We all trooped upstairs to the study, where Mary was vacuuming.

Mom asked her about Potter's Pond.

"Oh, it's fine, the kids all go there," said Mary. "It's only about a fifteen-minute walk, down a shady road allowance, no cars or anything. And the pond isn't that deep. I let Lily go with her friends all the time. They'll be fine."

"Well—" said Mom, undecided.

"Mom, you know I'm a good swimmer. I've been taking lessons for ages."

"It's not even over their heads, Ellie," put in Mary. "Nothing to worry about."

"Oh, all right," said Mom finally. "But before you go, I need to ask you something. Come upstairs for a minute."

I went along, Lily trailing behind me.

Mom stopped in the hall beside the little table. "Yesterday I put a bowl of fresh roses here from the garden, and now they've disappeared. Did you move them? Mary hasn't seen them."

I froze. "Umm—Umm—"

Lily was giving me a funny look.

"It's all right if you did," said Mom kindly. Way too kindly.

"I—I think they might be under my bed," I blurted out.

"What on earth—?" she said, but then stopped herself and got all nursey and kind again. "Let's have a look, shall we?" she said, and went into my room.

Lily and I made desperate faces at each other and then followed her.

Mom was on her knees, pulling out the bowl of roses. She looked up at me.

"Now, why would you do that, Alice?"

"They smelled good," I said, thinking as fast as I could. "I wanted to smell them while I was going to sleep, and I thought you wouldn't let me bring them into my room, so I hid them and then forgot about them."

Mom was having a hard time keeping her face unconcerned. "Alice, if you want roses in your room, we can get you roses. But they won't be doing anybody any good under your bed."

"Okay. Sorry."

"Are you sure you're up to this expedition with Lily this morning?"

"I feel fine—honest. I think it would do me good. You know, fresh air, stuff like that."

Mom put the roses on my bedside table and then came over to me. She reached out and smoothed my hair off my face.

"Alice, remember the talk we had last night?"

I nodded.

"I know it's hard for you right now. Just come to me if you need anything—like roses—or anything. Okay?"

I nodded. I wished I could tell her. But I couldn't. If she was worried now, what would she be like if I started talking about ghosts and magic dollhouses?

"Okay," she said. "You can go. But if you start getting a headache, come straight home. And wear your hat and sunglasses. Lily, you take care of Alice, okay?"

Lily nodded solemnly. "I will."

Once Mom left us, I went and touched one of the roses.

It was real. The candy-sweet smell wafted up to me and the petal I touched fell off. Lily came and stood beside me.

"Tell me about the test," she said, frowning. "You put the roses under the bed in the dollhouse?"

"Yes."

"Not in the real house?"

"Yes. I mean no, not in the real house."

"But they were under your bed in the real house?"

"Yes. You know what this means, Lily?"

"What?"

"This proves that stuff I do in the dollhouse can happen in this house too. It works both ways. Whatever I do in the dollhouse can happen in the real house, and whatever we do to the dollhouse in the real house happens there too."

Lily looked completely confused. "I don't understand, Alice."

"Okay, so I put the roses under the bed when I was playing with the dollhouse. Next time I dreamed I was in the dollhouse, there they were, under the bed. But they were also under the bed in the real house, where Mom found them. And remember how you dressed the dolls in blue dresses?"

Lily nodded. "Yup."

"Well, the next time I saw Bubble and Fizz, they were both wearing those dresses."

"Wow!" said Lily, her face lighting up. "This is so cool. A magic dollhouse! I think so. Come on, let's go!"

Chapter Twenty-Nine
SNEAKING

After we assembled swimsuits and towels and snacks, we said loud goodbyes to Mom and Mary and headed down the driveway.

Once we were out of sight of the house, Lily hauled me behind some bushes and then led me in a roundabout fashion into the back garden. By dashing from one tree to another and edging along the side of the house, we managed to get right up to the kitchen door without being seen. Lily had obviously done this before.

"We're invisible!" she whispered as we stood with our backs to the wall outside the kitchen. "I think so."

There was no sound from within. Lily peered around the corner of the door, then beckoned me to follow her. On tiptoe we went into the kitchen and up the stairs to the dining room.

She opened the door just a little and we listened. It was very quiet. Mary must have finished the vacuuming.

Lily put her finger to her lips. "Wait," she said. We listened some more.

A low, murmuring sound was coming from the living room. Like someone talking to themselves, or maybe singing.

Lily stifled a giggle. "Mama," she breathed at me. "She sings while she's dusting."

We made our way silently through the dining room, and Lily peeked through the doorway. She gave me the all clear, and we went swiftly around the corner and up the stairs.

"Come on, baby, light my fire," sang Mary in the living room, her voice rising a bit.

Trying not to giggle, we climbed nearly to the top of the stairs, but then Lily made me crouch down and we listened again. I could hear voices rising and falling softly a few rooms away.

"It's okay," whispered Lily. "Your mom's with Mrs. Bishop. I think so."

In a flash we were through the hall and into my room, closing the door softly behind us. I retrieved the keys from my underwear drawer, and we crept upstairs as quietly as we could. The stairs creaked a few times, but not too loudly. We made our way into the dollhouse room and shut the door.

"There!" said Lily, a look of triumph on her face. "I told you! It's easy to be invisible! I think so."

I laughed, a little uncomfortable. I remembered how it had felt to really be invisible, which wasn't anywhere near as fun as pretending.

Together we walked over to the dollhouse. Lily stopped dead when she saw the summerhouse on the other side.

"Where did that come from?" she asked. She sank down to her knees and peered inside.

"It was just here when I came up yesterday." I sat down beside her. "It's another thing that happened in the dollhouse world and then happened here. I dreamed I was in the summerhouse with Fizz and Bubble and—"

"A dog?" asked Lily, picking up Sailor. "He looks just like Buttercakes. I think so."

"Yes, that's their dog, Sailor."

Lily looked back into the summerhouse. "The dolls have dolls," she said delightedly, putting out a finger to touch one of them. "Having a tea party. Just like I do with my dolls. And look!" she added, picking up a tiny teacup. "This is the same as my tea set, Alice! The very same! I think so."

"I know. I think the set you have is the one they had when they were alive—years ago, when the photograph was taken. It must have been here in the house all that time."

I watched for a moment as Lily inspected the tea set, picking up each little cup and saucer, the cream jug, the sugar bowl. I smiled.

"The sister doll, Bubble, she's a lot like you. She likes tea parties. In my dream I was in the summerhouse with them having a tea party, and then Harriet, their mother, came in, but she couldn't see me. It was like I was invisible. Really invisible. Then we all went up to the attic, and there was a guy there, Adrian, the guy who made the dollhouse, and—"

Lily whispered, "Alice! Were you actually invisible? Not just pretend?"

"Yes. Well—at least, Bubble and Fizz could see me, but their mother couldn't."

"What about the man? Could he see you?"

"Adrian? Mr. Inwood? No."

Lily frowned. "What about the dog? Sailor? Could the dog see you?"

"The dog? Oh—" I thought about it. "Yeah. He could."

Lily nodded wisely. "Dogs can see stuff. I think so. Sometimes Buttercakes looks like he's watching fairies flying through the air. Or ghosts passing through the room. I think so."

"But I'm not a ghost, Lily."

"No. But the kids could see you. And the dog could see you. But the grown-ups couldn't. So maybe you were . . . a ghost."

I frowned. She had a point. But since everyone could see me in this world, maybe I was only a ghost when I was in the dollhouse world. Because I didn't belong there. That was more or less what Fizz had said to me in the summerhouse. Before she decided I was dead.

Lily jumped up and bounded over to the dollhouse.

"Never mind about ghosts. Let's play with the dollhouse! Do you think the other dolls will be here? The grown-up dolls?"

"They were yesterday," I answered, and opened the back of the dollhouse.

But the Harriet and Adrian dolls weren't in the attic.

"Wait a minute," I said. "Last time I dreamed about the dollhouse, everyone was sleeping."

We circled around to the front of the dollhouse, unhooked the front wall and peered into the front bedroom.

"Oooo," said Lily in a whisper. "There's someone in the bed."

Carefully, she reached under the canopy of the four-poster bed, which was hung with dark-blue velvet curtains, just like Mrs. Bishop's bed. Her hand came out with the Harriet doll in it, still dressed in her slinky satin nightgown.

"Wow," breathed Lily. "She's so pretty. But where's the man doll?" she asked, looking around the bedroom.

I frowned. "I don't know. He doesn't live there, so he probably went home."

Lily went back to the summerhouse and pulled out the Bubble and Fizz dolls.

"Let's put them in the sitting room," she said. "Sitting on these fancy chairs. I think so. And let's take their clothes off."

"What?" I said, as Lily began stripping the dolls.

"It will be funny," she said. "They will all be bare naked." She giggled.

"No," I said, laughing, and I put out a hand to stop her. "Let's just put them in different clothes. I don't want to see everybody naked if I go back again."

"Do you think you will go back?"

I shrugged. "Seems like every time I go to sleep I dream about the dollhouse."

"I wish I could go," said Lily, absent-mindedly removing Harriet's nightgown. The doll had lacy underwear underneath.

"WOW!" said Lily. "Fancy undies."

"Come on, Lily, let's find some new outfits for them."

"Okay," she said.

There was a closet in Harriet's bedroom, and Lily started rooting through it for clothes.

"She has the best dresses," said Lily happily, holding up a sapphire-blue gown and an emerald-green one. "And all the shoes to match!"

I left her to it and wandered over to the tall wardrobe on the other side of the attic room. I was curious as to what was in there.

There were two doors and a little key in a lock. I turned it and opened them up.

The wardrobe was filled with shelves, and the shelves were filled with shoeboxes. They all had labels neatly printed: Dishes. Linens. Doll clothes. Dolls.

I started taking them down and opening them up.

The one labeled Dishes had various bits of doll-sized china in it, little knives and forks, some pots and pans. The one labeled Linens had carefully folded sheets and towels and curtains, all dollhouse size.

I opened the one labeled Extra Dolls. There was one Barbie-doll-size shape wrapped in white cotton, like an Egyptian mummy. I unwrapped it.

My breath stopped. My heart began to hammer wildly in my chest.

The doll had curly black hair that fell just over his ears. He was wearing jeans and a T-shirt. The doll's face—the doll's face was Dad's face.

Chapter Thirty

PLAYING

"I can't decide," called Lily, bringing a pile of sparkly dresses over to me. "They're all so beautiful, Alice."

"Oh . . ." she said as she saw what I held in my hands. "Another doll. Who's he?"

"Umm . . ." I hesitated. "He's . . . he's my dad," I said finally.

"Your dad? How did he get here?" said Lily, reaching over my arm and picking it up. "He's got nice hair. I think so."

Lily turned him over and inspected all his clothes. Then she lay him carefully down on the rug and tilted her head to one side, staring at him.

"Why?" she said finally. "Why do you think there's a doll that looks just like your dad?"

"I don't know," I said. "I think I'm going crazy, Lily. I think this is a dream. I think that bump on my head did something to my brain and—" My voice was rising.

Lily reached out and grabbed my hand tight.

"You're not dreaming. I'm here." She kept holding my hand, and I tried to slow down my breathing. The Dad doll shimmered through the tears that had gathered in my eyes. It looked so much like him, as if it was going to start to speak any minute.

Finally Lily spoke.

"It's magic," she said solemnly. "I think so. A magic dollhouse. Magic dolls."

Magic again. That sounded better than me losing my mind or being dead. A lot better.

"It's just—" I said. "It's just—so hard to believe in magic. Real magic."

Lily shrugged. "I don't think so. Magic is everywhere. You said that when you change things in the dollhouse, they change in the real house too. That's magic."

I gave in. I couldn't argue with her. "Okay, so it's magic. A magic dollhouse."

A magic dollhouse. That I could go into in my dreams. Where I could do things that then happened here.

She reached past me and picked up the Dad doll again, watching me to make sure it was okay.

After a moment she said, "Your dad looks nice. I think so."

"He is nice," I said, with a gulp. I felt like I could start bawling any second. "He's great. I really miss him."

"Where is he?"

"In California," I said shortly. "Working. He's always working."

"My dad went away too," said Lily. "A long time ago. I think so. I don't really remember him."

We sat there in silence for a while. I concentrated on not letting any tears spill out of my eyes.

"Is your dad going to come back?" asked Lily.

"I don't know," I said, giving up on the pretense and wiping away the tears. "Maybe. But just to visit. He and my mother are—" I took a deep breath. I didn't want to say it. "They're getting a divorce." My voice broke halfway through saying the word *divorce*, and it came out in a squeak, and now I was really crying.

After a minute or so I felt a hand gently patting my back.

"Don't cry, Alice," said Lily softly. "It'll get better. I think so. Use my hanky," and she pushed a rumpled handkerchief into my hand.

I wiped my eyes and blew my nose.

Lily was looking at the Dad doll again. Suddenly her face lit up and she turned to me, grabbing my arm.

"Oh! Oh! Oh, Alice, I have a great idea!"

"What?" She was starting to bounce up and down with excitement.

"What if—what if your dad came back? What if we *made* him come back?"

"How would we do that?"

She held the doll in front of me.

"If we put your dad in the dollhouse, maybe he will come to visit you. In the real house. Like the roses. I think so."

"I don't know, Lily, it's not the same. People are different than flowers. You can't just make someone appear out of nowhere. My dad's in California."

"But it's a magic dollhouse," said Lily. "Magic can do anything. I think so."

Her face was glowing with the wonder of her brilliant idea. I didn't want to make that look go away.

"Yes, but Lily, the thing is, I don't know how this works. He might not come here. He might turn up in the dollhouse world, in my dreams."

"But then you'd see him, right? That would be good. I think so."

She looked at me with her shining eyes, and I suddenly wished more than anything that I was Lily and not me. She was just so happy.

I had no idea why there was a Dad doll or why there was a Ghost Alice doll here in this spooky, weird attic, along with the dolls of the people who must have lived in Blackwood House seventy years ago. It was all crazy. Or . . . magic. I liked Lily's explanation a lot better than my own.

I smiled back at her. "Okay, Lily, let's do it."

She jumped up, radiant, clapping her hands.

"Oh goody. We gotta find him something better to wear. I think so. Something . . . fancy." She started pulling more boxes out of the wardrobe and looking through them.

"Hey!" she said, holding up a box labeled Extra Clothes. "Maybe we'll find something in here." She pulled out a black suit and tie. "This might fit your dad."

I looked down at the doll. I wasn't too keen on undressing my dad, even if he was just a doll. I pushed it into Lily's hands.

"You do it," I said, and went over to stand by the window.

"It's all right, he's got underwear on," sang out Lily, giggling. "I like dolls with underwear. All dolls should have underwear. I think so."

A car was pulling up outside. The front door slammed, and then I heard voices outside. Through the trees, I could just see the edge of the driveway below. There was a blue car there, and Dr. West was leaning against it, talking to Mom.

I couldn't quite hear what they were saying, but Dr. West was beaming at her.

I stood watching them for a while. Mom was beaming back and waving her hands around a bit, the way she does when she's telling a story.

Those two were getting way too friendly. It would be a really good time for Dad to come back. What if—what if Lily was right and the magic dollhouse could bring him here?

"Okay," said Lily, coming up beside me. "He looks very handsome now."

She handed me the doll. The suit was a little wrinkled and old-fashioned looking, but it definitely made a better impression than the jeans and T-shirt.

"Okay," I said, taking him from Lily. "Where should we put him?"

Chapter Thirty-One

DOLLHOUSE FURNITURE

Lily frowned. Then her face cleared.

"At the front door," she said. "He can ring the bell, and your mother can answer it, and there he'll be! I think so."

I shrugged. "Okay." I stood the doll at the front door.

"Let's dress them all up now," said Lily, pulling at my hand. "Let's dress them up for a party. And then when you dream about the dollhouse again, you can go to a party!"

I smiled at her. Maybe . . . maybe I could just play along with her. Let everything else go and just play, the way she did.

"Oh! and maybe I could come too," she said, her face brightening up again. "If I stay overnight, we can go together!"

"I don't know if it works that way, Lily . . . I mean, it's my dream, and how could you get into my dream?"

"I could, if I sleep with you in the magic bed. I saw the ghost there. I'll see her again. I think so. Easy peasy!"

She made it all so simple. I gave in. "Okay. Why not?"

"We're gonna have so much fun," she said, then she pulled the Fizz and Bubble dolls out of the summerhouse and handed them to me. "Try some of the mother's party dresses on them. I bet they'll fit."

We dressed the dolls, Lily murmuring to herself as she wrestled the Harriet doll into a long, sparkling dress. I dressed Bubble in the sapphire-blue gown. It fit perfectly. I reached for the green one for Fizz. It would go with her red hair, but it was going to be big on her.

Lily had the Harriet doll in the dress now. It was silver, with all kinds of little silver baubles sewn on it that glinted in the light. Lily had the doll lying on its back with the dress hiked up a bit as she fitted a pair of silvery slingbacks on the doll's little feet. Lily handed me matching shoes for my two dolls.

"They were in the cupboard with the dresses," she sighed happily. "Don't you just love matching shoes?" She watched as I fitted the shoes on the dolls' feet. "Now they're all ready for the ball. Where should we put them?"

"How about in the living room? That's about the fanciest room in the house."

Lily sat Harriet on a sofa in the living room, spreading out her skirts around her. I placed Bubble in a chair near her.

"I can't wait for the party!" said Lily. "Let's go ask your mother if I can sleep over."

"But we're supposed to be swimming," I said. "Would we be back yet?"

"Maybe not. But soon. I think so."

"Well, let's just play for a while and then go."

Lily decided the furniture in the living room should be moved so they could dance at the party, so we cleared a space in the section of the room closest to the front door, putting the couch and chairs back against the walls. As I placed the pale-yellow silk couch beside the two blue armchairs, I ran the tips of my fingers over the material. Soft but not quite as soft as the ones downstairs.

"Why is the furniture the same?" I asked suddenly. "Why is all the furniture the same as in the real house?"

Lily shrugged. "Because they made it the same."

I shook my head. "No. If it's true that Adrian built the dollhouse, he made it years and years ago, in the 1920s. But the big house is still the same as the dollhouse. The same furniture. The same curtains. Why hasn't the big house changed?"

Lily shrugged again. "I don't know."

"When did Mrs. Bishop buy this house?"

"Last summer. I think so."

"And what about before that? Who lived here?"

"Nobody. Mom worked here but nobody ever lived here. I came with her sometimes."

"And was all this furniture here then?"

Lily nodded solemnly. "Yes. But it was covered in sheets! All of it! It was spooky, Alice. It looked like rooms full of ghosts. Sometimes Mama and me would take off the sheets and shake them out. Then she cleaned the furniture and then we'd put the sheets back."

I frowned. "So Mrs. Bishop bought the furniture with the house?"

Lily shrugged again. She had obviously lost interest. "I guess. Let's make them dance."

We borrowed the Dad doll and made him dance with each of the others in turn. I had to dance the girls and she danced Dad.

"Swirling their skirts." She hummed one of those classic waltz tunes that are always playing at skating rinks. "Pum pum pum pum pum, pum-pum, pum-pum."

I played along. It was fun.

"They're so sparkly," sighed Lily happily. "So sparkly and beautiful."

And they were.

A car door banged outside. I jumped up and went to the window, just in time to see Dr. West's blue car chugging out of the driveway.

"I guess that's long enough," I said. "We should try and sneak out now."

We shut up the dollhouse, leaving the dolls sitting in the living room in all their finery and the Dad doll outside the front door. Then Lily led the way and we successfully sneaked downstairs and out the door that looked over the terrace, then circled around to the front door as if we were coming back from swimming.

* * *

Mom and Mary were both fine with Lily staying over that night, but Mom wanted me to have a big rest first in the afternoon. Mary and Lily went home after lunch, promising to return before supper.

The last thing I wanted to do that afternoon was go to sleep. I was afraid. Maybe tonight, with Lily, it would be different, but that afternoon I didn't want to dream about the dollhouse again, and see Fizz with her knowing smirk, telling me I was dead.

But lying in my green curtained bed in the summer heat, I couldn't keep my eyes open. After catching myself drifting off a couple of times, I got up and moved over to the window seat and made a little bed for myself there in the cushions. Maybe, just maybe, if I wasn't in that bed, I wouldn't dream of the dollhouse.

Chapter Thirty-Two
BALL GOWNS

I woke what seemed like a long time later. I sat up and pulled back the window curtains.

Late afternoon light flooded the room. The curtains felt soft and silky under my fingers. I took a deep breath of the warm, flower-scented air.

I was awake. In the real house. I could hear voices drifting up from the terrace. My mom and Mary, and Lily too.

I walked carefully around my bed, pulling back the curtains. No sign of Fizz. Of course not. She was in the other house. The dream house. The dollhouse.

I headed downstairs, touching the highly polished dark wood banister and feeling the lush carpet on the stairs. The real house, large, solid and reassuring.

"There you are," said my mother. "Sleepyhead!" She was sitting under the umbrella on the terrace with Lily, who jumped up when she saw me and came running over to give me a hug.

"I thought you'd *never* wake up," she said. "I brought some dress-up clothes. For later . . ." She tried to wink at me but only managed to screw up her face and blink both her eyes at me at once.

"Lily, what a silly face," said my mother, laughing. "You can play dress-up after supper. Right now, I want you and Alice to make a salad while I get the hamburgers ready for the barbecue."

* * *

After supper and dishes, Lily and I went up to my room, where she showed me what she'd brought.

"Ball gowns," she said, pulling a long, billowing apricot dress out of a pillowcase. It was strapless with a cinched-in waist.

"Wow!"

"And this one—" added Lily triumphantly, producing a turquoise dress of much the same style from another pillowcase. Both dresses seemed to have yards and yards of some kind of stiff lace petticoat underneath that made the full-length skirts stand out like huge bells.

"Lily, they're—they're amazing!" I said. "Where did you get them?"

"Mama bought them for me at the thrift store. She says they were bridesmaid dresses. I think so. I call them my ball gowns."

"Will they fit me?" I asked. I was a lot smaller than Lily.

"Let's try." She held out the turquoise one to me, and I took off my shorts and top and slipped it on.

"Safety pins," she said, pulling and tugging at the back. "All we need is safety pins and then you and I will be ready for the party!"

With a box full of safety pins Mom found in a kitchen drawer, Lily managed to remake the dress on me so it didn't fall off. I didn't think Mom would let us wear them to bed, so we took them off, and I got into my nightie and Lily put on her pj's. Then we went to the library to look at books until it was time to go to bed. I found Mrs. Bishop's copy of *Alice's Adventures in Wonderland* and started reading it to Lily. She sat close beside me on the leather couch, transfixed by the story, her mouth open. It was one of the few times I'd seen her sit perfectly still.

Mom sent us to bed early, and we waited quietly for about half an hour to make sure she wasn't going to look in again. Then we crept out of bed and got dressed.

"This way, when we wake up, we'll be all ready for the dance!" whispered Lily, twirling in the pretty apricot dress. The color suited her and it fit perfectly. She jumped on the bed. "I don't know how I'm going to go to sleep!"

After a lot of fluffing and arranging of the big skirts and petticoats, we settled into the bed. I didn't think I'd be able to go to sleep either, after my long nap. But I soon found myself yawning. Lily was so excited that she took a long time to calm down, wriggling and chirping away about this and that.

I closed my eyes and let her words wash over me. It was nice to have her there beside me. It made everything a little less scary.

Eventually she grew quiet. I could feel myself starting to drift away. Then Lily spoke again, her words coming out one by one as if she was very tired.

"Last time . . . I was sleeping . . . in this bed . . . was when . . . I saw . . . the ghost. I think so. But . . . as long as you're here . . . I'm not scared."

"Not scared," she repeated. "Not scared at all. Coming to the party . . ." Then her voice died away.

She must be asleep, I thought. I wonder . . .

* * *

Somebody gave me a shake.

"Wake up, Alice!"

"Lily?" I opened my eyes.

"Nope," said Fizz.

I sat up. Fizz was sitting on the edge of the bed, the curtains open to the moonlight coming in the window. Lily was nowhere to be seen.

Chapter Thirty-Three

SPARKLY AND BEAUTIFUL

"Who's Lily?" asked Fizz. "And why are you wearing that evening dress?" She peered at it. "It looks a little big for you."

I looked down and saw that I was still wearing the pinned-up turquoise bridesmaid dress.

"I might ask you the same," I said, and then Fizz noticed what she was wearing. The sparkling green dress that I'd dressed the Fizz doll in earlier, when Lily and I were playing in the attic.

"Oh," said Fizz, frowning. "This is Mother's dress." She wriggled a little and pulled up one strap, which had slipped down over her shoulder. She laughed. "I guess it's too big for me too!"

She jumped off the bed and twirled around. The dress shimmered in the moonlight. Then she came back and plopped down on the bed again.

"So who's Lily?"

"Lily's my friend. In . . . in my other world." I was a bit nervous about saying this, in case Fizz started talking about me being dead again, but she just looked mildly curious. "Lily wanted to come into the dollhouse with me in my dreams, so she's sleeping over, and we got dressed up for a party."

"Well, funny thing," said Fizz, jumping up again and going over to the walk-in closet. "There *is* a party tonight. But I have better dresses for both of us."

I suddenly became aware of sounds drifting up from downstairs: music playing, people talking, glasses clinking.

Fizz dived into the closet and I followed. Besides now being stuffed with her clothes instead of my sundresses, the closet also held the two zippered-up dress bags I'd noticed in the big house. Fizz unzipped the first one and pulled out a glittering midnight-blue party dress with a drop waist in the style of the 20s.

"This is too small for me now, but I think it's about your size," she said, tossing it in my direction. Then she reached in and pulled out a dark-green dress.

"My new party dress," she said, slipping off her mother's dress. "My father brought it back from the city for me to wear tonight. It's Mother's birthday."

She looked older in it, more sophisticated. She added a

little silver headband then turned to see how I was getting on with her old dress.

It fit me perfectly. The spangles on the soft, dark-blue material twinkled like a starry sky. I had that feeling I get sometimes with a new dress—that I was suddenly pretty. I twirled for her.

"Here," she said, rummaging around the drawer where she found her headband, then handing me a dark-blue one. "This matches that dress."

We stood side by side and looked in the mirror.

"Aren't we fine?" said Fizz, grinning. "Not that anyone will be able to see *you*, except Bubble of course, but still, I think we make a pretty pair, don't we?"

I grinned back at her.

"Let's go to the party," she said, and led me out of the room.

As I paraded down the curving staircase behind Fizz, walking slowly and holding my long skirts in one hand and the banister in the other so I didn't trip, I wondered about Fizz.

Last time I saw her she was trying to convince me I was dead, a ghost, and all this was the real world. But today she didn't seem to be giving it another moment's thought. She'd been a bit curious about Lily, but then dropped the subject. Her party was more important than anything in my world, which I had the feeling she didn't quite believe in anyway. It was as if she could only focus on one thing at a time, and then her mind jumped away to something else.

We walked down the stairs and into the party noises—a woman laughing, a murmur of voices, a guy on a scratchy recording singing a song about a girl he loved with a sunny, funny face. The crystal chandelier hanging from the ceiling shimmered and a warm golden glow spilled into the hall from the living room.

Fizz and I stopped just outside the door. The entire living room was lit by a series of candlesticks lined up on the mantelpieces, and the party dresses Lily had chosen for Harriet and Bubble twinkled in the dancing light.

They were both exactly where Lily and I had placed them in the dollhouse, but there were other people there too. Harriet, all in silver from head to toe, glittered on the white silk couch, talking to an older man with white hair. He wore a tuxedo with a snowy white shirtfront and was laughing at something Harriet had just said.

Bubble sat on a green wing chair near them, wearing the sapphire-blue gown that made her look much older than the matching outfits she usually wore with Fizz. Wearing grown-up clothes, Bubble looked so much like her mother in that uncertain light that they could have been twins. Bubble was listening to her mother's story and smiling happily.

Lily had been right. It was sparkly and beautiful. Just the way a party should be.

Fizz, who seemed to have forgotten all about me, glided into the room and sat down in the opposite wing chair to Bubble, just where Lily had put her in the dollhouse.

A man I recognized as Fizz's father from the photograph stood on one side of the fire, facing Adrian, the architect, who stood at the other. Both were in immaculate tuxedos and scowling at each other. They looked like two bristling dogs squaring off for a fight, and for some reason, this made me want to laugh. If what Fizz told me was true, they were both jealous of each other. Adrian because he was in love with Harriet, and Bob because Adrian was spending too much time with his wife.

Bob broke away from the scowling contest first and turned to Harriet with an expansive smile.

"Time for some bubbly, darling?" he said. "And a birthday toast?"

"Yes, please," said Harriet.

He strode over to a side table where a large bottle of champagne stood in an ice bucket surrounded by wide-rimmed wine glasses. With a flourish, Bob held the bottle at arm's length, and then he paused, making sure that every eye in the room was on him. Satisfied, he turned back to the champagne, and with a sudden upward swing of his arm, he slashed a gleaming knife against the neck of the bottle.

Bubble and Harriet shrieked as the glass broke cleanly, the top of the bottle flew across the room and the champagne bubbled up in a fountain over Bob's hand.

Bob quickly poured the frothing champagne into a glass and held it out to Harriet.

"Happy birthday, sweetheart," he said.

She rose and took it from him, and he kissed her. Something green on her finger flashed in the candlelight as she raised the glass to her lips.

A large, sparkling emerald ring. Where had I seen an emerald ring recently?

"You're such a show-off, Bob," she said, laughing. She turned to the older man on the couch. "How many times have you seen him do that trick, Fred?"

The man was also laughing and shaking his head. "I couldn't count."

"But Adrian's never seen it, have you, Adrian?" said Harriet, bestowing a dazzling smile on the architect.

"No," he said, coming forward into the family circle. "It's very impressive, Bob. Dangerous, but very impressive."

"Not dangerous when you know what you're doing, Adrian," said Bob smoothly. "Which I do." Then he turned away from him and poured two more glasses and held them out to his daughters.

"Bubble and Fizz," he said, grinning. "Tell me. Come on, tell me!"

"Oh, Daddy, really," said Fizz, rolling her eyes. "Do we have to go through this every time?"

He laughed. "Yes, you do! Come on. Bubble?"

Bubble was dancing on her tiptoes in front of him, laughing.

"I'm Bubble because I'm happy and bubbly, and I remind you of your favorite drink, champagne! That's true." She held out her hands and he gave her a brimming glass.

"That's my girl," he said. "Now, Fizz?"

She rolled her eyes and said quickly in a singsong, bored voice, "I'm-Fizz-because-I'm-always-popping-like-the-fizz-in-your-favorite-drink-champagne."

Bob handed her the glass, grinning. Both girls held out

their glasses to their mother. "Happy Birthday, Mother," they said in chorus, and took a drink.

So that was where their odd names came from. Champagne. I'd had my first taste of champagne last New Year's, when Dad had actually been home, and he and Mom were getting along for a change. Getting along so well that they decided I could have a little glass of "bubbly," as Mom called it. It was the most wonderful drink I had ever tasted. The fizz and the bubbles went right up into my eyeballs and made me giggle.

"Aren't they a bit young to drink?" said Adrian.

His words dropped into the happy room like dead weights, bringing all the laughter to a sudden halt. There was a brief, echoing silence and then Bubble piped up.

"I'm not too young. I turned twenty-one last April. That's true."

Another uncomfortable silence.

Bubble certainly looked twenty-one tonight, but everyone in that room knew that she was just a little girl in every other way. Adrian had brought unwanted attention to the fact that Bubble was childlike, and likely to remain so. By doing so, he had embarrassed himself and everyone else. His ears turned a fiery red.

Chapter Thirty-Four
INTO THE DARK

Bob shot one quick, dirty look at Adrian, then he ruffled Bubble's hair and smiled down at her.

"So you did, sweetie, so you did. And we all had a drink together on that occasion in this very room to celebrate your birthday," he added, shooting another dirty look at Adrian.

"And I'm not too young either, Adrian," piped up Fizz. "I've been drinking since I was four," she told him. "Champagne's my favorite, but there's nothing like a martini. Cheers!" She raised her glass to him with that superior smirk I knew so well and drained the remaining champagne in one gulp.

"Oh, stop it, Fizz," snapped her mother. "You're as much of a show-off as your father."

Fizz winced as if she'd been slapped. Harriet flashed a rather forced smile on Adrian.

"It's quite harmless, Adrian. Bob and I give the children wine with Sunday dinner and champagne on special occasions. One glass only. We've done it for years. We think it helps them develop a responsible attitude to alcohol."

Fizz jumped in. "Like yours, I suppose?"

Everyone froze. For the second time in five minutes, it seemed like all the air had been sucked out of the room.

Harriet turned to her daughter and spoke slowly, enunciating each word. "What do you mean by that?"

"Just what I said," replied Fizz. "You're ever so responsible with your drinking, aren't you, Mother?" She began counting on her fingers. "Sherry in the morning when Adrian comes to show you some new little treasure he's made for the dollhouse; Scotch in the afternoon when you're talking to Adrian about the dollhouse; martinis before dinner when Adrian is here to talk more about the dollhouse."

Each time she said "Adrian" she made it into a bigger sneer than the time before.

Adrian was starting to look like a rabbit caught in the headlights, his eyes darting this way and that. Harriet flushed.

Bob laughed. "Really, Adrian," he said with a wide grin. "Drinking all day with my wife when I'm away in the city? Sherry? Scotch? Martinis? Shocking."

Adrian opened his mouth as if he was going to say something but then closed it again.

"Don't encourage her, Bob," said Harriet, sitting back as if Fizz's words hadn't bothered her at all. "You know what she's like. It's all lies."

"Not all," said Fizz.

"A complete exaggeration," said Harriet. She took a careful sip of champagne. I could see that her hand was shaking, just a little. "As you very well know, Bob, Adrian and I have a drink together now and then when he visits to discuss the dollhouse. Fizz is making trouble the way she always does. Now she's trying to ruin my birthday dinner, but I'm not going to let her."

With an air of rising above such petty concerns, she smiled a bit too brightly at her husband. "Darling, perhaps you should finish pouring the champagne?"

Bob held her eyes for a moment. Her smile slipped.

"Yes," he said finally. "I'm neglecting my duties." He poured drinks and handed them round to Fred and Adrian. Then he picked up his glass and raised it to her.

"To my lovely and beautiful wife, Harriet," he said. "Happy Birthday!"

Adrian and Fred both echoed the "Happy Birthday" and they all drank.

"Excellent champagne!" said Fred.

"Only the best for Harriet," said Bob. "Always. Only the best. The best clothes, the best jewelry, the best—" He paused, and turned to Adrian. "The best architect. You know, when I hired you, Adrian, four years ago, I chose you because you were the best architect money could buy."

Adrian swallowed nervously. "Well, I wouldn't say that—"

"Oh, I would," replied Bob. "Definitely. I wanted my wife to have the best dollhouse in the world. Better than Queen Mary's.

The best. And you must be congratulated, Adrian, because you have created it for her. The very best dollhouse."

"Hear, hear," said Fred, raising his glass. "To the dollhouse!"

Everyone held their glasses aloft and repeated, "To the dollhouse!"

The dollhouse.

Now they were moving around in the candlelight, talking to each other, drinking more champagne, laughing. The dresses swirled and sparkled, the light bouncing off them. The colors started to blend together, and I felt suddenly dizzy, like I was going to fall.

I closed my eyes and clutched at the doorway to steady myself. Everything was rocking as if I was in a small boat on a tossing sea.

I turned blindly into the hall. I needed to get back to bed.

The sounds of the party started to fade away as I slowly climbed the stairs. My dress kept getting in the way of my feet, threatening to trip me. When I got to the steepest curve of the stairs, I sank to my knees, hoping to crawl the rest of the way.

The doorbell rang. Harriet's voice rang out clearly from the living room. "Now who could that be?"

I was dimly aware of a figure moving from the dining room across the hall to the front door. The door opened and then I heard a muffled voice saying, "Alice. I'm looking for Alice." I tried to speak, but the shadows were gathering around me like a thick, heavy blanket, and soon I was engulfed in the darkness, unable to move or see. For a moment, everything went very still, and it was as if I winked out of existence. I had the sense of teetering on the brink of a vast dark abyss. And then there was nothing. Nothing at all.

* * *

It seemed like a very long time later when suddenly out of nothingness and nowhere my head started hurting again, and then I could feel the stairs under me. I began to pull myself up the last few feet to the upstairs hall. It was completely dark, and I could no longer hear any sounds of the party, or from the person at the front door. I crawled along the hall, thinking I would find my mom's room, but I had no sense of where I was. I turned to the left and came up against a door that gave way when I pushed.

"Mom?" I whispered. I crawled through the doorway and into the room, which was as dark as everywhere else. Shouldn't there be a moon somewhere? or some stars? or a nightlight?

I stumbled to my feet and moved slowly through the empty space, my arms stretched out ahead of me, like those sleepwalking zombies you see in the movies. Surely Mom's room wasn't this big? I just kept going and going, one foot after another.

"Mom?" I whispered again.

Then I heard a noise behind me. A kind of rustling, then a fumbling, then a small "click."

A soft light spread around me. I was facing a fireplace.

"What on earth are you doing in my room, young lady?" came a piercing voice from the direction of the light.

I spun around to see Mrs. Bishop in her grand four-poster bed, sitting up among the bedclothes, her white hair disheveled, staring at me in outrage.

Chapter Thirty-Five
THE GROUCH

"This is the third night in a row you've woken me up," said Mrs. Bishop. "That's three times too many. I repeat, what are you doing in my room? And why are you wearing an evening dress?"

My head began to clear. Even though the old lady was glaring at me, and I knew I was probably in big trouble, it was so good to see the light again, as well as another human being, however grouchy.

I stood up and approached the bed. "I don't know," I said. "I guess—I guess I was sleeping, and then I woke up and I was here."

Mrs. Bishop narrowed her eyes. "Sleepwalking? You're trying to tell me you've been sleepwalking?"

"I . . . I don't know. I never have before. At least, I don't think I have."

"And the dress?" Mrs. Bishop was staring at my outfit with a strange expression on her face. Disapproval, I thought.

I smoothed down the midnight-blue party dress Fizz had lent me over my knees as I sat down on the chair beside Mrs. Bishop's bed. The dress was a little the worse for wear since I had crawled up the stairs in it.

There was a glass of water on Mrs. Bishop's bedside table, and without thinking, I took a long drink from it.

"Lily and I were playing dress-up," I said, putting the glass back. "I guess we fell asleep in our dresses."

She glared some more. "Well, this has got to stop," she said briskly. "I don't sleep well at the best of times, but if I'm woken up at—" She glanced at her bedside clock. "Three o'clock! Well, I'll never make up the sleep. I'll be out of sorts all day tomorrow."

"Aren't you always out of sorts?" I said it without thinking. Something about being alone with Mrs. Bishop in the middle of the night had made me forget to watch what I said. I held my breath and closed my eyes for a second, waiting for a blast from her.

A kind of snorting sound made me open my eyes and look at her.

She was laughing.

"You've got your nerve," she said. "Aren't you afraid of me?"

I thought about it. "Yes. But I forgot to be, for a minute."

"Well, you should be afraid," she said. "I could fire your mother first thing tomorrow morning and have you out on the streets with nowhere to go."

"I don't think you'd do that," I said. "I think you're more bark than bite."

She laughed again. For such a crusty old lady, she had an unexpectedly pleasant laugh. "Maybe. But I used to have senior editors at the paper shaking with fear after just one look from me."

"I guess you're a bit of a bully, then," I said. I don't know what came over me. Words just kept coming out of my mouth.

"Yes. I probably am," said Mrs. Bishop. "I have high standards, and I expect people to meet them. Very high standards."

"Does my mother meet your standards?"

"Yes. She's a very good nurse, and she treats me with respect."

"What about Mary?"

"Mary is an excellent cleaner. She talks too much, but she can also keep a secret if she has to."

"What secret?"

Mrs. Bishop shot one of her razor-sharp looks at me. "Never mind what secret. You're getting me off topic. We were discussing what we are going to do to stop all this nonsense in the middle of the night."

I sighed. "I wish I could stop it. I have the strangest dreams."

"So do I," said Mrs. Bishop. "Dr. West says it's the concussion, but I'm not so sure."

"What do you dream about?" I asked.

"Oh, this and that," she replied, picking at something on her crisp blue sheets. "Mostly the past. People who are long gone. But you're too young to dream about the past."

"I guess," I said uncertainly. I *was* dreaming about the past, just not my past. At least, I thought I was.

Mrs. Bishop was watching me intently, as if waiting for me to say more.

"I suppose you miss your father," she said, finally.

I sighed again. "Yes. I do. But for months now he hasn't been around much."

"Still," said Mrs. Bishop. "He is your father."

"Yes," I said. "I just wish Mom and Dad would figure out a way to stay together. I don't think they've tried very hard."

"Sometimes things happen that we don't like, but there's nothing we can do about them," said the old lady. She wasn't looking at me now so much as past me, and I got the feeling she was thinking about something specific. Something she wasn't very happy about.

"Like your broken leg?" I asked.

She started and looked back at me, as if she'd forgotten I was there. "Oh—yes. Certainly. Like my broken leg. That was unfortunate."

"How did it happen?" I asked.

She shook her head. "I wasn't paying attention. Thinking about something else when I was coming down the stairs, and I slipped."

"The big stairs. You fell down the big stairs."

She narrowed her eyes. "How do you know that? You're a very curious Alice, aren't you?"

"They're so steep. I'm scared every time I go down them. And the taxi driver said—" I stopped.

She jumped on it. "What did Ben Johnson say? Honestly, that man! He can get more drama out of the tiniest little thing—"

"Not so tiny," I said. "He said you lay for a long time after you broke your leg, all night, and if Mary had come any later you would have died."

A red flush spread over her pale cheeks. "See what I mean? Nonsense! I was in no danger. Uncomfortable—yes, but I knew Mary would be in the next morning. That man exaggerates everything."

"I guess it was lucky that you fell on one of Mary's cleaning days," I said.

"Lucky? Lucky?" She narrowed her eyes. "Do you think it's lucky that I'm lying here in bed for weeks, unable to do anything for myself, unable to walk around my own house? That I have to have strangers living here to take care of me, including a very rude little girl?" She glared at me. "I think I've had enough of your curiosity for one night, Miss Alice." She raised her voice. "Ellie!" she yelled. "Ellie, your blasted child has woken me up again. Ellie!"

In a moment my mother came stumbling into the room.

"Whaaa? Mrs. Bishop? Alice?" She looked at each of us in turn. "What's going on?"

"Sleepwalking," snapped Mrs. Bishop. "She blundered in here and woke me up. I think you should send her to a psychiatrist. She's obviously very disturbed."

"Alice?" said Mom, her face creased with worry.

"Oh, don't pay any attention to her," I said crossly. "She's just a grouch."

"Alice!"

"Well, she is." I flounced out of the room.

I went back to my room. The bed curtains were closed. I peeked in and there was Lily in her party dress, fast asleep with an angelic expression on her face.

As if she could feel my presence there, suddenly she opened her eyes.

"Hi, Alice," she said sleepily. "Is it time for the party?"

"It's all over," I said. "It didn't work. I went to the party, but you didn't."

Her face fell. "I missed it? I wanted to go to the party!"

"Sorry," I said, collapsing onto the bed beside her. Suddenly I was very, very tired.

Chapter Thirty-Six
THE HOSPITAL

Mom bustled in at that point.

"Alice," she began. "Oh, hello, Lily, you're awake too. Why on earth are you two wearing those dresses?"

"We were going to go to a party," said Lily, pouting. "We were supposed to go, but then Alice went without me. I think so."

"Lily!" I said.

"Well, you did," she replied.

"Never mind that," said Mom, sitting down on the bed and stroking the hair back from my forehead. "Alice, I'm going to take you to the hospital."

"Mom!"

She was quiet, but firm. "I'm sorry, Alice, but you're showing more symptoms of concussion, and we need to get you checked out properly. Dr. West said if there were any changes, we should go to Emerg., and sleepwalking is definitely a change."

"But Mom—"

"No arguments, miss! Get your clothes on. Lily, get out of that dress and into your pj's. I'm calling your mother to come and stay with you and Mrs. Bishop."

She was in bossy nurse mode and she wasn't going to budge. She turned and went to make the phone call. Sighing, I slipped off the dress and found my shorts. Lily was very quiet, shooting worried looks at me as she got changed.

"Are you real sick?" she said, finally, sitting on the bed with her knees drawn up, hugging them.

"I'll be okay. Don't worry." I pulled a T-shirt over my head.

"But you're going to the hospital!" she said in a small voice. "People only go to the hospital when they're real sick! I think so."

I went over and gave her a hug. "Don't worry," I said again. I couldn't think of anything else to say. All kinds of scary thoughts were racing through my head, and my stomach kept doing little flips.

What would they find at the hospital? Brain damage? Was that why all these weird things kept happening to me? Was it all in my head?

Would I have to have an operation? Would Dad come back and stand with Mom at my bedside, would that finally get them together, watching their only daughter die?

Tears started to my eyes as I pictured them, clinging to each other while I lay white and unmoving on the bed.

No. I couldn't think about that.

"It'll be okay, Lily," I said in a shaky voice.

Mary got there amazingly quickly, and soon Mom and I were driving through the darkness to the hospital. At 2:30 in the morning, the Emergency Department at Lakeport Hospital was pretty quiet, and it didn't take us long to get in to see the doctor, who just happened to be Dr. West.

I felt a rush of relief as he walked into our cubicle with his easy grin. He put his arm around my shoulders and gave me a squeeze.

"So, what's been going on, Sunshine?" he asked.

"Bad dreams," I said, tears filling my eyes. "And headaches."

"And sleepwalking," put in Mom.

"And . . . and I'm dizzy a lot," I added.

He arranged for some tests. I had a CAT scan, which was kind of scary, because I had to lie really still on this table that moved inside a big white metal ring. They took my blood, looked in my eyes with a light and asked me questions.

And all the time I thought about what had been happening to me.

Being in the dollhouse world wasn't like any dream I'd ever had before. Things had a logic that they never have in dreams. All my senses were working: I could feel the silk of the bed curtains on my fingers, and I could smell the bowl of roses. In my regular dreams I could see and hear things, but I never experienced my other senses so vividly, the way I did in the dollhouse. If I did feel my body in a dream, it was more general, like my legs feeling really heavy and not being able to take a step. And although time seemed to have moved on each time I went to the dollhouse, while I was there it progressed in the usual way and didn't jump all over the place the way it did when I was dreaming.

It couldn't be a dream.

But then what was it? Fizz said I was dead. That couldn't be true either . . . could it? Nobody knew what being dead was like. Maybe it was like this: a lot like life, only even more confusing.

Something must be wrong with me. Maybe they could find out in the hospital.

The tests took a few hours, and in between, I dozed off. No dreams. Thank goodness.

It was mid-morning when Dr. West came in and told Mom she could take me home.

"Don't worry," he said. "It's a slight concussion, just as we thought. No permanent damage. No bleeding. She just needs to take it easy."

"But my dreams," I said. "They seem so real. They're scaring me."

Mom and Dr. West exchanged glances. He sat down on the edge of my bed and gave me a friendly look.

"Your mother tells me you have a very good imagination, Alice," he said.

"Yes, but—"

"Sometimes a good imagination can be a bad thing," he went on. "It can scare you, if you let it run away with you."

"Yes, but—"

"Your mother tells me this has happened before, that you've got carried away with ideas about things that haven't actually happened."

"Yes, but this is different." I finally got the rest of my sentence in. "Before, I would always realize eventually that it was just one of my daydreams. Like this one time, Mom was late coming home, and I thought she had an accident and died, and I was thinking about how things would change, and I almost believed it until she walked in the door, and I realized it was all just in my head. Remember that, Mom?"

She nodded grimly.

"But this time, I can't tell what's real. There's no difference between being asleep and being awake. I don't know if I'm day dreaming or night dreaming or if it's really happening."

"What is it you're dreaming about?" asked Dr. West.

Uh-oh. I couldn't tell them about the dollhouse. If Mom found out that I had stolen the keys and gone into that room, I'd be in the worst trouble of my life.

"Your mother said something about a doll and a ghost?"

"Um . . . yeah. That kind of thing. Ghosts."

"It's a spooky old house, I'll give you that," said Dr. West. He glanced over at my mother, who was looking on with a worried frown. He lowered his voice. "She said one night you dreamed you were dead?"

"Yes," I said, fear filling me up again. "That's what I'm afraid of. That I died in the train accident, and I'm a ghost too!"

"Oh for goodness' sake, Alice," broke in my mother. "There was no train crash. Just a little bump."

Dr. West put up his hand to stop her. His glasses were slipping down his nose, and he had the kindest eyes. He took my hand and smiled. At that point, even my heart gave a little pit-a-pat, and I could see why my mother liked him so much.

"Look," he said. "Like I said before, you and your mother are having a hard time right now. If you want to talk to someone—to a counselor, or even just to me—just say the word."

I shook my head, unable to speak.

"That's fine too," he said, giving my hand a squeeze. "But remember, the offer is always open. Any time. And meanwhile, just take it easy, stay out of the sun, and try and relax." He winked at me.

He was cute. He really was cute. What would it be like if he was my dad, as I had imagined on the train? If he was there every night for Mom and me, cooking on the barbecue, making little jokes, listening to every word we said with that sweet expression on his face? And Buttercakes nearby, knocking things over with his big tail. Dr. West would never be too busy or too preoccupied to come to my choir recitals, help me with my projects, take a walk in the park.

"Alice?" said Mom.

I surfaced from the vision of happiness with Dr. West and Buttercakes. Mom was frowning.

"You're off again, aren't you?" she said. "In la-la land."

Dr. West laughed. "I'll just have a word, Ellie, and then you two can go home and catch up on your sleep."

He and Mom went out into the hallway. I could hear them muttering away. Talking about me, no doubt. Or else setting up a date. Yikes. A date! But would it be so bad if they did?

I sighed. I was very tired. All I wanted to do was sleep.

All the way home I kept nodding off. The sun was so bright, glaring in the windows of the car. The day was already hot and stifling. I thought about getting back to my room, climbing into bed and sleeping for a long, long time. With no dreams. Definitely with no dreams.

When we finally turned off the road and started up the steep road that led to Blackwood House, Mom was yawning too.

"We'll both need a nap," she said. The car reached the top of the hill, and as she steered it around the circular drive in front of the house, we noticed a man standing on the doorstep. He had his back to us and his hand up as if he was about to knock on the door.

"Now who could that be?" asked Mom, irritated.

Something about the back of his head looked familiar. He was wearing a rather wrinkled black suit.

"Oh my God!" said Mom and hit the brakes hard. At the sound of the screeching brakes, the man turned to look at us.

"Dad!" I scrambled out of the car and threw myself into his arms, tiredness and concussion and Dr. West all forgotten.

Chapter Thirty-Seven

MONEY ISN'T EVERYTHING

I started to cry. I couldn't help myself. It was so good to feel his arms around me and smell that comforting Dad smell that was only his. A mixture of soap and his peppery aftershave. Though there was a whiff of musty clothes, too, coming from the suit.

Dad nearly lost it too. I could hear a crack in his voice as he murmured, "Ally. Ally-Bally." My nickname from when I was little. He hadn't called me that in a long time.

I stood back, crying my head off, and he managed to come up with a handkerchief from an inside pocket in that remarkable suit. It looked just like the one Lily had put on the Dad doll, wrinkles and all. And he'd been knocking at the front door, just where I had placed the Dad doll, outside the dollhouse.

A faint memory came back to me of leaving the party in the dollhouse, climbing up the stairs, feeling dizzy . . . and someone at the door asking for me. Dad?

Freaky weird. Had I brought him there? Had I brought him here? Me and Lily? And the magic dollhouse? I'd wanted him so badly . . . and here he was. Almost as if I'd wished him here.

Like when I thought of the perfect dad on the train, and then the next day Dr. West, Sam, showed up. Could I make things happen? Just by wanting them?

I blinked at my dad through my tears, afraid he would disappear.

"Stephen?" said Mom. She looked as if she might lose it too. "What on earth are you doing here? And where did you get that ridiculous outfit?"

Dad actually laughed.

"I know. It's crazy . . . but I kind of like it. It's vintage, honey. The airline lost my baggage and all I had was the clothes on my back. I got it at a little secondhand store in Lakeport, near my hotel."

"Your hotel?" asked Mom.

"Yeah. More of an inn, really, but it's not too bad for such a small town." He smiled at me and ruffled my hair.

"But, Stephen, why are you here?" Mom was getting desperate.

"Oh," he said, as if he suddenly realized what she was asking. "I'm . . . uh . . . well, I have a lot to tell you, Ellie. Can we . . . um . . . go inside? It's awfully hot out here."

Mom pulled herself up. "Stephen," she said in her sternest nurse voice, "this is my place of work. I can't be bringing our family problems in and parading them around. Mrs. Bishop would not appreciate it and it's not professional."

"Mom! Give him a chance!" I pleaded. "Mrs. Bishop already knows about you and Dad, and I've been waking her up every night with my nightmares, so I think the least you could do is let Dad come in for a drink of water and—" I was getting worked up again and the sobs were coming back.

"Alice," said Mom quickly. "It's okay. Take a breath."

I took a couple, trying to stop that hiccupping kind of crying that was about to take over.

"You need to rest," she said. "Okay, Stephen," she said coldly, "you can come in for a few minutes, but Alice and I have been in the hospital half the night and we need some sleep." She pushed past him and opened the door.

"Hospital?" bleated Dad, putting his arm around my shoulders and looking into my face with concern as we followed her into the cool, dark hall. "Are you okay, Ally? Was it the concussion Mom told me about? From hitting your head on the train?"

"She's fine," said Mom over her shoulder. "It's a slight concussion, just as we thought. But we had to go through a battery of tests to confirm it, and we haven't had much sleep."

"That's a relief," said Dad, and then stopped in his tracks. "WOW!" he said, gazing at the splendors of the hall. "A preserved Georgian. A genuine, well-preserved Georgian." He spun around, his face alight with enthusiasm. "This place is incredible, Ellie! Do you have any idea how rare it is to find a house this old in such impeccable condition?" He was walking up and down, taking in the details of the door moldings, the wide floorboards, the curving staircase.

"Yes, Stephen," said Mom crossly. "I do know. It's rare, it's wonderful and it's beside the point. We're tired. I'm going upstairs to check on Mrs. Bishop and Mary, and you can look around until I get back, then we're going down to the kitchen and you can tell me what you're doing here." She humphed up the stairs.

Dad and I looked at each other and made the same oh-my-god-she's-scary face we used to make whenever Mom would get mad and start bossing us around. We hadn't made that face for a long time. Then we laughed.

It felt so good to have Dad back. I mean, really back. The old Dad, the one who cared about us.

"Come on, Ally," he said, taking me by the hand. "Give me the five-minute tour."

I took him through the rooms downstairs, and he was even more impressed than I had been the first time I saw it.

"You know, it's a marvelous house, one of the loveliest Georgians I've ever seen," he said, turning round and round in the living room. "It's been well cared for, and as far as I can tell, there have been no major changes made to this house since it was built. That's very rare. It must have been in the same family. But what's so amazing to me is the furniture. It's vintage 1920s, perfect in every detail. Someone went to a lot of trouble to create this look."

I looked around. He was right. Someone had gone to a lot of trouble, but not to create this look—someone had gone to a lot of trouble to preserve it. But who?

"Lovely," said Dad, running his fingers over the white silk couch, where Harriet had been sitting the night before. "Oh, there's some sign of wear," he said, leaning forward to examine the seams in the upholstery. "But very little. Almost like a time warp. I'd say this house looks pretty well exactly the way it did in the 1920s."

I could confirm that. At least, I think I could. If the life I was observing in the dollhouse was real, and not a dream. But that brought me back to my dilemma. My head was starting to ache again.

"Has it been in the same family?" he asked. "Do you know?"

I shook my head. "Mrs. Bishop bought it last year. No one lived here for a long time before that."

Dad examined one of the doorframes. "Uninhabited." He nodded his head. "That makes sense. This wood has been cared for recently. But before that—" He walked over to the window and gently touched the silky curtain. "I'd say it was all shut up with blackout curtains on the windows for a very long time indeed. Light is the biggest enemy for fabric. Someone must have come in, opened things up, repainted the walls and given the wood floors a gentle sanding and some new stain and here we are. In a beautiful recreation of a 1920s interior."

He sighed happily. "What a treasure. You know, Ally, I've spent too long with modern buildings." He leaned in for a closer look at the molding on the mantelpiece. "Older buildings were always my passion. I would have loved to go into the restoration business, but—well—the money just wasn't there."

"Money isn't everything," said Mom from the doorway. She was leaning tiredly against the doorjamb, as if she couldn't hold herself up anymore.

"No," said Dad. "No, Ellie, it isn't."

"Come on," she said with a sigh as she pulled herself upright again. "Lily's gone to a friend's house, and Mary is fine to stay with Mrs. Bishop for the morning. Let's go have some coffee and we can talk. Alice, straight to bed."

"Mom!"

"You heard me."

"But this affects me as much as you," I protested. "You act like it's all between you and Dad and I have no say in it."

"Let her come," said Dad. "You both need to hear what I've done. It will only take a few minutes, and then she can go to bed, and you and I can talk some more."

"Fine," said Mom. "I'm too tired to argue."

Chapter Thirty-Eight

THE ROCKET

At first Mom wanted us to sit outside, under the umbrella on the patio, but it was way too hot. So we sat at the kitchen table. Mom and I were ravenous after the long night at the hospital, so she brought out muffins, cheese, jam, coffee and juice. I dug in.

"You don't look too sick," said Dad doubtfully as I slathered butter and jam on my third muffin.

"She's not that sick," said Mom impatiently. "It's been a rough few days for everybody, Stephen, and Sam thinks it's the stress as much as the concussion that's affecting her."

"Sam?" asked Dad.

Mom looked away. "Dr. West. He's Mrs. Bishop's doctor and he's been watching Alice too. Luckily he was on duty last night. He was a great help."

"He has a dog called Buttercakes," I added. "And he comes nearly every day to check on Mrs. Bishop, doesn't he, Mom?"

"Yes," she said shortly, concentrating on buttering her muffin.

"Hmm," said Dad, looking from me to Mom and then back again. "Well, that's good news. I'm glad there's been someone to keep an eye on you, Alice. I was worried sick about you when Mom told me you had a concussion."

He cleared his throat and took a deep breath.

"Honey . . . Ellie . . ." He didn't seem to be able to get the words out.

"What?" she said.

He sighed. "This is harder than I thought it would be."

My heart sank. Was he going to tell us he was moving to California? That he had another family there? That he was abandoning us forever? That he had got a quickie divorce in Reno? I had heard about that in a movie.

Mom was also feeling the strain.

"Stephen!" she yelled. "For God's sakes, just tell us. What the hell are you doing here? Last time we spoke you said you'd be in LA for a month, and we agreed that we were going to both get lawyers and start the divorce proceedings. Why are you here?"

She was standing up now, shouting and stamping her foot. I figured she had pretty well forgotten about not bringing our family troubles into her workplace.

Dad held up a hand. "Ellie, calm down. Just calm down. It's okay. It's going to be okay." His voice trembled, like he was going to start crying. "I quit, okay? I quit my job. I want to be with you and Alice. I don't want a divorce. I don't want to lose you. Nothing in my work is that important. I just didn't realize it." And now he was crying, and Mom was standing there staring at him. My insides started twisting. I'd never seen him cry before.

"You quit? You quit your job?" she said, as if she didn't believe him.

He started to laugh, so he was laughing and crying at the same time. "I did, Ellie, I really did! It's crazy, I know, but I did."

"But how can you just quit? I mean, what about all your projects? How can you just leave?"

"Well, I can't just leave," he said, swiping away the tears on his cheeks. "I have to give them six months' notice. That's in my contract."

"Right," said Mom, snatching up her plate and mine, even though I hadn't finished my muffin yet. "Right. Same old story, Stephen. You're always saying it's only going to be another few weeks, or next spring, or next year, and that time never comes. I don't believe you." She turned her back and headed toward the sink.

Dad jumped up and caught her by the arm. "Put those down, Ellie. You're not listening to me." He took the plates and returned them to the table.

"Just sit down and listen," he said.

Mom sat down and crossed her arms and looked at him the way she looked at me when I said I'd do the dishes later, promise, right after my TV show.

"I have quit, Ellie. My job is over. At least, it will be. By Christmas I'll be done, and I'm going to find something to do that doesn't take me away from you guys. I promise."

Mom looked unconvinced. But I felt this leaping, soaring hope inside me that was sparking like those engines at the bottom of a rocket. If only he meant it this time, if he really meant it, if he kept his promise and quit his job and came back to us. If only—and then the feeling of dread about our family breaking up that had been growing inside me for months would just fall away like the structure that held the rocket in place and the whole hopeful, happy rocket would lift up and shoot away into infinite space. We'd be a real family again. Not broken. But could it be true? Could it really be true?

Dad went on. "After we talked on Monday, I couldn't concentrate on work. I didn't sleep a wink that night. I couldn't believe that I was going to really lose you. I thought about everything you said, and I realized that you were right. I haven't been there for you, and I haven't been there for Alice. So the next morning I called Ted and told him I was quitting. I wanted to walk away right then and there, but he pointed out that if I gave them six months, I could finish my projects, train my replacement and avoid a lawsuit for breach of contract. So I agreed, and he gave me till next Monday to come back here and fix things with you. Then I have to be back in LA. But it's going to happen, Ellie. I've really quit and this time I won't let you down."

Mom's lower lip was trembling. She stood up.

"I think, Stephen, that it might take a bit longer than till next Monday to 'fix' what is wrong between us." She gathered up the plates again. "Alice and I have to rest. Leave the number of your hotel on the kitchen table and I'll call you later." She brought the dishes to the sink.

Dad just sat there, staring at her.

"Alice!" said my mother sharply, turning to me. "Upstairs. Now."

Part Four

THE TRAIN

Chapter Thirty-Nine
SLEEPING

I slept for hours. At first I didn't think I'd be able to. My head was full of questions about Dad and Mom. Would she give him a chance? Would he really change, like he promised? Could we be a family again? A happy family?

Mom didn't look like any of those things were going to happen when she marched me into my room and stood over me as I lay down on the bed. It was too hot to get under the covers.

"Sleep," she said, as if she expected to be obeyed immediately. "And no dreams or sleepwalking or anything else. Just sleep." She turned away.

"But Mom," I said. "What about Dad?"

She stood with her back to me for a moment. Then she gave a big sigh and turned back.

"This is between your father and me, Alice. I know it affects you. I know it's hard for you. But it's your dad and me who have to figure it out. Just leave it, okay?"

Her stern, determined expression had dropped away. Now she just looked tired and sad. I felt a wave of doubt sweep over me. Maybe it was too late for Dad to fix it.

"Okay," I said in a small voice, and she left.

I lay in my little green world inside the curtains, closed my eyes and worried about Mom and Dad for a while. But then I thought of how he'd looked when I saw him standing on the step in the wrinkled suit, and I smiled. It was so good to have him back. And no matter what he said about how he got here, I knew deep inside that the real reason he was here was because I had wished him here, and I had placed the Dad doll on the dollhouse steps. The magic dollhouse. Finally something good had come out of it.

And it wasn't a dream. Dad was really here.

* * *

I drifted away. I slept for a long, long time. Now and then sounds filtered through heavy layers of sleep. The murmur of voices. Faint, faraway music. A train whistle, blowing sharp and lonely, rising and falling as the train approached, passed and then faded away into the distance.

I dreamed that I had been sleeping in that floating green bed for years and years—decades—sleeping and dreaming while the world went on without me, waiting for the time when I would wake up and everything would be right again.

* * *

When I woke up, the first thing I was aware of was the heat. That thick, heavy heat where it's hard to take a breath. Then, for a moment, I didn't know where I was. Or who I was. I had that stunned, just-run-over-by-a-truck feeling that some-times comes after a long afternoon sleep.

Then it all came back to me. The haunted house. The magic dollhouse. Dad.

I sat up. The bed curtains were closed around me. Maybe that's why I was so hot. Mom must have come in and closed them while I was asleep.

I pulled them open and went over to the window. I must have slept for a very long time, because the light was begin-ning to fade. The sky beyond the trees was filled with that strange, metallic light that comes before a storm.

I tiptoed to the door, opened it and listened.

All was quiet. They must have let me sleep through supper. I wondered if they would leave me a little while longer, because I needed to go up to the dollhouse. I wanted to take the Dad doll and put him somewhere that would make him stay here with us, that would force him and Mom to make up.

But where? If I put the Dad doll in the front bedroom in the dollhouse, maybe he'd turn up in Mrs. Bishop's room in the real house, talking about architecture with her, and she would want him to stay.

It was lame. I knew it was lame. Or what if I put him in Mom's bed? I giggled. But the way things were between them, that would probably make her really mad.

I'd figure something out.

I fumbled under my underwear in the dresser for the keys, then quietly unlocked the door at the end of the closet. I went carefully up the stairs, trying not to make a sound. In the attic, the fading afternoon sunlight was slanting in the far window, falling in dusty paths along the floorboards. Even though I was eager to get to the dollhouse, I couldn't resist tiptoeing across to look out.

Under the tinny, darkening sky I could see the lush summer countryside rolling into the distance and the train tracks snaking between the hills. I saw the train at the same time I heard its whistle—and the dream was suddenly there with me again. I clutched at the memory, feeling it about to disappear again.

I had dreamed that I was lying in the green-curtained bed, sleeping for years and years, hearing the train whistle . . . but there, it was gone. I couldn't remember anything else.

Something about the dream was pulling at me. Something very sad. Something very wrong. But I couldn't quite put my finger on it.

I turned back into the attic and crossed silently to the dollhouse room. The key turned easily and I was in.

The room felt hushed and still. In the dim light the dollhouse dominated the room, a huge, dark bulk.

As I started toward it, I tripped on something, and before I could catch myself, my arms were flailing and I fell with a thud.

So much for being quiet.

I sat up and listened, holding my breath.

There were no sounds from downstairs. Relieved, I looked to see what it was that had tripped me.

Train tracks. I had tripped over the tracks for a model train. They ran in a wide circle around the edge of the room, encircling the dollhouse. I stood up and followed them to the other side. In one place the tracks ran up and down over a bridge. In another they ran through a woodlot of toy trees. Along the far wall they ran by a little wooden train station. I crouched down to read the lettering on the station wall.

"Lakeport."

It was identical to the station where Mom and I had disembarked from the train from the city the night of the accident.

Chapter Forty

ALONE

I sat back on the floor with a soft thump.

The tracks hadn't been here yesterday afternoon. Where had they come from? Had Adrian added the tracks and the station as his latest surprise for Harriet? And just like the summerhouse, once the tracks were set up in the dollhouse world, they were echoed here, in the real world.

Because . . . because both worlds were slowly lining up? Adjusting to each other? Coming closer?

A shiver slithered down the back of my neck. Everything was so quiet. As if we were waiting for something—the big house, the dollhouse and me. The storm?

I gave myself a shake, stood up and went over to the dollhouse. I unlatched the back and looked in.

The living room was empty. No party, no dolls in their best clothes. Where were they?

I looked through the other rooms, and there was no sign of them. All the rooms were empty. The only doll I found was the Fizz doll, lying in the green-curtained bed by herself. Asleep.

I went around to the front of the dollhouse. The Dad doll was gone. I unlatched the side and swung it open.

Bubble's bed was empty, and so was her mother and father's bedroom across the hall. There was no one in the study, no one in the basement.

I crossed to the cupboard and pulled out the box labeled Dolls.

It was empty.

Whoever had set up the train must have taken the dolls away. I started pulling out all the other boxes in the cupboard, getting more and more puzzled as my search came up empty.

The clothes were there, the extra furniture was there, the linens for the beds and the dishes and knick-knacks—all of them were there, but no dolls. No Bubble, no Harriet, no Bob.

And no Dad.

But they weren't all gone. Fizz was still here. Asleep in her bed.

I had a bad feeling about all this. I had a sudden urge to go running downstairs and find Mom and Dad and Lily. I wanted to see them and touch them and make sure that they were real. And that I was real. And that everything that had been happening with the dollhouse was just some crazy hallucination from my concussion.

I stood up. I must have got up too quickly, because I had a sudden moment of dizziness so strong that I sank back down to my knees and closed my eyes. It must be the heat. The air was thick and I had a hard time breathing, the way you do just before a summer storm breaks. The attic seemed twice as hot as the rest of the house. I had to get out of there.

I got to my feet and lurched across the room. I left the boxes on the floor and the dollhouse standing open. I didn't even lock the door—I just stumbled toward the stairs.

Then I stopped myself. These stairs were dangerous. I had to go slowly. I held tight to the railing and took them slowly, one step at a time.

When I got down into the second-floor hallway, it wasn't quite so hot, and I took a deep breath. But everything still had that suffocating weight of the coming storm.

I went to Mom's room and opened the door. "Mom?" I whispered.

There was no answer. I tiptoed in and stood at the open bathroom door, looking into Mrs. Bishop's room beyond. The curtains were closed and the room was dim. I could just make out a motionless figure in the bed.

Mom must be downstairs. I crept back into the hall and began to descend the curving staircase.

The house seemed unnaturally quiet. Hushed. Waiting for something.

I popped my head into each of the downstairs rooms, but no one was there. Mom must be in the kitchen. I started down the stairs to the basement, calling, "Mom?"

The kitchen was deep in shadows. I flipped the light switch beside the door, but nothing happened.

"Mom?" I said uncertainly.

No answer.

Where was she? She wouldn't have gone off and left me sleeping with a storm coming and Mrs. Bishop helpless in her room. The vision I had had in the attic, of everyone gone except me, came back. My uneasiness increased.

Maybe she was outside. I crossed to the door, pushed it open and went out into the garden.

Night was falling quickly, and I could only just see the outline of the trees at the far edge of the lawn, where the land dipped down into the railway cutting.

There was no one in the garden. A flash of white near the summerhouse caught my eye.

"Mom?" I called.

No answer.

I headed across the lawn. My bare feet sank into the soft grass. The summerhouse was wrapped in shadows. I slowed my steps.

"Mom?" I called out again.

No answer.

I stopped. A thread of fear twisted up my spine. If it was Mom I had seen, why didn't she answer? If it was someone else, why didn't they answer?

I had the strongest feeling that there was someone or something in that summerhouse that I didn't want to see. I wanted to turn around and run back to the house as fast as I could, up the stairs, into my room, close the curtains, put my head under the pillow and make it all go away.

And in that moment, thinking about my bed, my dream came back to me in full.

I had dreamed I had been lying in my bed, sleeping. Sleeping for years and years, while the world went on around me. All alone in my little green world, waiting to wake up. Lonely. With a train whistle in the distance, getting closer.

How long had I really been asleep? A few hours? Or a few years? In the dream, it had been decades.

Standing in the darkening garden with the summerhouse and its secrets looming ahead of me, I began to feel very cold inside. Cold and scared. What was happening to me?

And then from far, far away came that high-pitched, haunting call of a train whistle blowing.

Chapter Forty-One

LEFT BEHIND

And just as I was standing there, listening to the mournful cry of the coming train, with fear rising all around me in the stifling heat, my knees weak, my heart pounding—the door to the summerhouse creaked open.

A figure in white stood there. It was too dark to see their face, but whoever it was raised an arm and beckoned to me.

I couldn't move. I tried to speak, but it came out as a high-pitched squeak. "Who . . . who's there?"

A laugh rang out through the darkness. A familiar, taunting laugh.

Fizz.

"Fizz?" I said, peering into the shadows. I took a step closer.

She broke away from the doorway and came over to me. She was wearing the same white sleeveless nightgown that she had been wearing the first time I saw her, and her feet were bare, like mine.

"Did I scare you?"

"Yes," I gasped, feeling the breath starting to flow back into my lungs. "Yes, you did scare me! I thought you were a ghost."

She laughed again. "We've been through all that, Alice. You're the ghost, not me." She put a friendly arm around me and drew me toward the summerhouse. I could feel the warmth from her body.

"I don't understand," I said, dazed, as we went in. "I thought I was in the real house, not the dollhouse. I saw Mrs. Bishop in her bed, but everyone else is gone."

"Mrs. Bishop?" said Fizz, fumbling with something.

"The old lady. I told you about her before."

There was a snap of a match and a thin streak of golden light sprang up. Fizz had lit a candle that was sitting on a little rattan table with a glass top. For the first time I could see her face clearly. She looked very tired, with her curly hair frizzled from the heat.

"Oh yeah," she said. "The old lady. In the other world."

"But this *is* the other world, Fizz! This is the real world, not the dollhouse. Why are you here? Everything feels wrong. I had this awful dream like I was asleep for years and years and everyone had forgotten about me and gone away, and there was a train and—"

Just then the train whistle hooted again, closer now.

"There's always a train," said Fizz. "We live beside the train tracks." She sighed and curled up on the rattan sofa.

I picked up the candle and went over to her. I held the candle high so it illuminated the flowered sofa cushion. The material was bright and new, not faded the way it was in my summerhouse.

"Oh," I said flatly. "I guess I'm in the dollhouse after all. But the kitchen—"

The kitchen had been so dark I hadn't been able to tell if it was the old kitchen or the modern kitchen. If I had woken up in the dollhouse, then the train tracks were in the dollhouse world, not mine.

But why was Mrs. Bishop here, sleeping in her bed? Or was that her? All I had seen was a lump—someone was sleeping there, but not necessarily Mrs. Bishop.

The train whistle hooted again, much closer, and now I could hear the engine rumbling as it drew closer. Or was it the sound of distant thunder? I gave an involuntary little shiver. I don't like thunderstorms.

"That's the eight-thirty freight train," said Fizz. "I'm waiting for the nine o'clock passenger train from the city."

I put the candle back on the table then sat down beside Fizz.

"Why are you waiting for that train?" I asked. We seemed to be in our own little bubble of light, with the darkness spreading around us.

"Mother and Dad and Bubble are on it," said Fizz. "They've been gone for three days. Mother's birthday trip."

"I thought you were going with them," I said, remembering the party. "I thought it was a family tradition, that you all went together."

"Yes," sighed Fizz. "It is. This is the first year I've missed."

"How come?" I asked.

She shrugged her shoulders. "Mother and I had a huge fight. After the party. She said I was making trouble on purpose, telling Dad lies about her and Adrian drinking all day. I told her . . ." She stopped. She seemed to be having trouble with this part of the story.

With a deep breath, she continued. "I told her that if she wanted to have an affair with Adrian, she should be more careful if she didn't want me to notice and tell Dad. That I loved him and didn't want her hurting him. That Adrian was a jerk, and if she wanted to get a divorce and marry him, don't expect to ever talk to me again. That—" She broke off, unable to continue, tears choking her.

"You said all that to your mother?" I asked. "Is it true? Is she really . . . um . . . having an affair? With Adrian?" I made a face. "Eww."

"I know," said Fizz, starting to laugh through her tears. "He's such an idiot. He may be a famous architect, but he's not very smart. And he's mean to Bubble."

"But does your mother really like him?"

"She does! She laughs whenever he talks, and she bats her eyes at him, and they're always whispering in corners. I . . . I even saw him kiss her once." She dissolved in tears again.

"Yuck," I said, and put my arm around her. "Maybe she'll come to her senses."

Fizz shook her head. "I don't think so. She and Dad were fighting about it before they left. She told him she didn't want me to come on the trip, and I said I didn't want to come anyway, and Dad said she was breaking up the family, and it just went on and on with them yelling, and my mother crying, and poor Bubble was so scared. Finally Mother said she wouldn't go at all, and then Dad had to persuade her, and then she only agreed to go if I stayed home." Fizz jumped up and started pacing.

"She's so mean! She didn't used to be like this. Before the dollhouse, before Adrian, she was fun and played with us. She took us places. We went to England on a family trip, and we had so much fun. I loved England. I just loved it. I loved all the old buildings, and the castles and the beautiful cathedrals. And that's when we saw the dollhouse. Queen Mary's dollhouse."

"What was it like?"

Fizz smiled, remembering. "It was fantastic! Bubble and Mother and I went crazy for it. It's about the size of our dollhouse, only it's a palace, right? It's the Queen's palace, so she has these fancy cars in a garage in the basement, and these big rooms with paintings and crystal chandeliers and a knight in a suit of armor and painted ceilings—oh, it was wonderful. There were even bottles with real wine in them and real books that were specially written for the dollhouse by famous writers."

The memories were dancing across her face . . .

"And then Mother and Bubble and I begged Dad to build us one. We begged and begged!" She laughed. "All the way home on the ship, every meal, we talked about the dollhouse and how marvelous it was and how we wanted one of our own. Dad thought we were all nuts, but he finally gave in and said we could have one. But it had to be done right, with an architect, like the Queen's dollhouse, and it was going to be very expensive, and we kids had to be really careful with it.

"When we got home, Dad got Fred—Mr. Brock, he's a lawyer—to help him find an architect. And they hired Adrian. There were weeks and weeks of planning, and Dad had the special room built in the attic for it. The dollhouse took so long to build that Bubble and I got impatient. We thought it would never be finished. But Mother worked with Adrian and they hired people to make the furniture and the dolls and the clothes and made it all exactly like our house.

"But after a while it seemed that Adrian and Mother were creating the dollhouse for themselves, not for us. Bubble and I would get in trouble if we touched things. It was a work of art, they kept telling us. Not a toy.

"And now Adrian just keeps coming up with more ideas as excuses to see more of Mother, like the summerhouse, and the model train—"

"Train?" I asked.

"Yeah, that was his latest, just before they left on the trip. He brought a model train and set it up around the dollhouse, with a real little station that looks just like Lakeport. Mother was wild about it."

The train I had seen in the attic. The train and the station. That was Adrian's work. I had been right about that.

Fizz clenched her fists. "I hate that dollhouse. If I could, I would just smash it to bits. And I hate Adrian. If it wasn't for him and that stupid dollhouse, we'd all still be happy. And I would have gone to the city and seen *Funny Face*."

"Funny face?"

"It's this great Broadway show. Bubble and I've been looking forward to it for months."

"Your father agreed with your mother, then, that you should stay home?"

She nodded unhappily. "He came and told me he was sorry. That it was a hard time for the family. That he'd take me to see *Funny Face* on my own, later in the summer, before I go to boarding school. So I said okay, and I've been here all by myself with Betsy for the last three days. Boring. So boring."

"Who's Betsy?" The name sounded familiar, but I couldn't remember where I'd heard it before.

"Betsy is our housekeeper. She's been with us ever since Bubble was a baby, and she's really nice, but not much fun. Anyway, tonight they're coming home," she said, brightening. "On the nine o'clock passenger train. I'm going to wait out here till it comes. I'm going to go to the edge of the garden and see if I can see them as they go by. Bubble said she'd look for me and wave. They should be back here by about twenty past nine."

"But it's so dark," I said. "How will she see you?"

Fizz frowned. "It's the storm. It shouldn't be this dark."

And just at that moment, there was a brilliant flash of lightning and a crash of thunder.

Chapter Forty-Two

THE CRASH

For a moment the summerhouse and the two of us were lit in stark relief and then it was dark again, with just the candlelight flickering over our faces.

"Phew! That was close," said Fizz.

"Not even time to count 'one, one thousand,'" I said, shaken. "That means it struck less than a mile away."

A faraway train whistle called.

Fizz's face lit up with a smile. "That's them. Come on!"

She darted out the door. I blew out the candle and followed her uncertainly into the dark garden.

A thin yellow light ahead of me bounced over the grass.

"It's okay, I've got a flashlight," called Fizz over her shoulder.

Fine for her, but I was still stumbling in the dark, trying to catch up.

A jagged fork of lightning zigzagged down from the sky almost at the same time as another bang of thunder. I screamed and threw myself on the ground, covering my head with my hands.

I heard Fizz's footsteps pounding back to me.

"Oh, don't be such a baby, Alice," she said, pulling me to my feet.

"It was close!" I protested. "Just over those trees."

"It wasn't that close," she replied, heading back toward the edge of the garden, pulling me along behind her. "It probably hit somewhere near Lakeport."

I didn't feel safe. Mom had drilled it into me, if you're out in a thunderstorm, first of all, don't be! And if you're caught, lie down on the ground. Whatever you do, stay away from trees.

And here I was with Fizz, running toward the trees that ringed the garden.

"Fizz, I think we should go in," I said, pulling back.

The train whistle called out again, much closer.

"No!" said Fizz, holding my hand even tighter. "The train will be here any minute. We've got to see them. I told Bubble I'd wave."

She hauled me into the long grass at the edge of the hill. Below us, I knew the ground gave away steeply, but now it was just a bowl of darkness.

Fizz flicked the light down the hill. Bushes and trees appeared and then vanished as the light moved on. Something silver glinted at the bottom of the hill.

The train tracks.

The train whistle called again. Fizz had let go of my hand and was jumping up and down with excitement. "It's coming!" she said.

I turned to look at her and realized that the light was better, because I could see her now, her hair, frizzy from the humidity, standing out like a halo around her head, her silhouette outlined against the sky behind her. Where was the light coming from?

I looked behind her, and there, sailing up over the top of the house was a bright, full moon. The house loomed up behind us, just as it had that first time I'd seen it from the train, so very much a haunted house, with its blank windows staring out, the vines creeping up the walls, the elegant staircases curving down from the door—

But it had been a few days since the full moon. Was dollhouse time as different as that? Up until now, whatever time it was in the real world had been reflected in the dollhouse world. When I fell asleep in the afternoon, I woke up in the afternoon in the dollhouse. When I fell asleep at night, I woke up at night in the dollhouse. So why was there a full moon now? It should be growing smaller, not shining out in a perfect silver dollar circle against the black night sky.

I had no time to try to figure it out. The train whistle screamed in our ears, and the train roared as it thundered into sight. Its bright white headlight cut into the darkness just a little way down the track, moving fast.

Fizz grabbed my arm. "Watch the windows," she shouted in my ear. "She said she'd be waving."

The lighted windows on the train came into view. I could see vague shapes inside, but the train was going too fast to see anyone clearly.

"There she is! There she is!" cried Fizz, jumping and waving madly. I just caught sight of someone inside waving their arms, but then the car flashed by us and she was gone.

Fizz turned to me, laughing, and was about to say something when there was a white flash of lightning and an almighty clap of thunder, both at the same time.

I screamed and reached out to grab hold of Fizz. But just as my hands made contact with her arms, there was an even bigger crash of sound and my hands closed on nothing, and the whole world seemed to turn upside down, and the train, clearly visible now in the moonlight, jerked up in the air and came down with the cars all piled up like toy blocks spilled out of a box.

Then Fizz was gone, my hands closed on emptiness, and my head snapped forward and hit something hard. Everything folded into deep black.

Chapter Forty-Three

BLOOD

Everything was very dark, and all I could think about was how my head hurt. It felt like it was going to explode. A terrible, unbearable pain beat like a pulse behind my eyes.

Then I began to hear noises around me. Someone was crying as if their heart would break. Someone else was groaning. Someone else was screaming.

I opened my eyes. I might as well have kept them shut, because it was still very dark. I seemed to be lying wedged between two seats, and there were people around me: some still, some moving. Was I inside the train? How did I get here? Last thing I remembered was standing on the hill with Fizz, watching as the train leaped into the air and fell to the ground with an almighty crash.

But here I was.

I struggled to sit up and then managed to pull myself to my feet, my head pounding. It was hard to keep my balance; the floor seemed to be sloping all in one direction, so even though I thought I was standing upright, I kept feeling like I was going to fall backward. Then some lights flickered past the windows, and someone with a flashlight was at the door at the end of the train car, peering in.

The light passed over several people who were starting to move. I saw a man with his eyes closed and blood pouring down his face. That's where the groans were coming from. A little boy of about four was stuck between two seats, and he and his mother were both screaming. The light flickered over a woman sitting in the seat across the aisle from where I was standing. She was the one crying, her head buried in her hands. There was something familiar about her, but the light passed on before I could figure out what.

The person with the flashlight went immediately to the aid of the screaming child and his mother, and I took a few steps toward the door.

I could still hear the woman sobbing. My head was spinning with the pain, and I just wanted to get out of the train car, but something made me look back at her. In the flickering light from the conductor's flashlight, I saw that the woman was bending over someone beside her.

And then I heard my name.

"Alice!" sobbed the woman.

I held on to a seat and made my way back. There were lights coming from outside now, flashlights raking across the windows. I could hear people yelling.

The woman was rocking back and forth, crying. Beside her was the crumpled figure of a girl. A girl with light-brown hair matted with blood.

Then the woman looked up, not at me, but through me. Her face was streaked with tears. It was my mother.

The whole world tilted again, and I closed my eyes as I lost my sense of up and down. I felt myself sliding into the darkness that was eating everything up around me.

Then there was nothing. For a long, long time.

Chapter Forty-Four

WRECKAGE

When I came to, the first thing I was aware of was the harsh, bitter smell of scorched metal. The second thing was that my nose was full of grass. The third thing was that my head still hurt.

I sat up. Below me was the twisted wreckage of the train, smoking in the pale moonlight.

I shook my head, trying to clear the clouds of confusion away. What had just happened? I felt like I had been unconscious for a long time, but now I was back at the moment I left, just after the train crashed and the cars flew up in the air.

Fizz and I had fallen to the ground together with the impact of the crash. She scrambled to her feet with a sob and took off down the steep embankment, half running, half flying, then skidding and sliding to the bottom. She nearly careened into a train car, stopping herself just before she hit it. This car and the one ahead were still upright on the tracks, but the next one in front was lying crookedly, half on the tracks and half off, swaying as if it hadn't quite finished falling yet. And the cars ahead of that one were lying in a tangled heap of metal.

I was up in a second, my head and my confusion forgotten.

"Fizz!" I yelled. "Stop!"

She paid no attention and took off running toward the mangled cars at the front of the train, where Bubble had stood waving at Fizz as the train whipped past us, just before the lightning struck.

I slithered down the bank. Stunned-looking people were emerging from the cars that were still upright. Some had blood on their clothes. Some fell to the ground, moaning.

Suddenly there was a loud screeching noise followed by an explosion that was even louder than the thunder had been. Billows of black smoke poured out of the mangled mess up ahead, and bright orange flames began licking into the air.

Fizz hesitated for just a moment, then took off again, straight toward the fire.

A man in a conductor's uniform caught Fizz as she ran and swung her back.

"Don't go any closer, kid. You'll get hurt."

I caught up to them, panting, and then the crooked train car teetered and fell with a squeal of metal. The boom reverberated through the air and the ground shook.

Fizz struggled to free herself from the conductor. He gave her a shake.

"You can't go over there," he said. "You'll get killed."

"I want to get killed!" she howled. "My whole family was in one of the front cars!"

"I'm sorry," said the conductor. "We'll get a rescue crew in there as soon as we can. But you can't risk your life."

He turned and looked right through me, shouting out to some people behind me who were jumping down from the nearest train car. Apparently I was just as invisible to the conductor as I was to Harriet's mother and father, and Adrian.

The noise of people crying and calling out questions began to swell around us. The moon lit up the scene with a cold, bright light. What had been hidden in shadows before now stood out in ugly detail: the shocked faces of the people stumbling around me, the blood on their clothes, the twisted limbs of some of the people lying on the ground. The seared, broken metal of the train cars that were piled up on top of each other, the smoke and flames rising from the wreckage. I didn't want to see it. I closed my eyes tightly, but I couldn't block out the sounds.

People calling for their loved ones, shouting for help, crying. And a familiar voice, very close to me, was yelling furiously.

"Let me go!" cried Fizz. And then she screamed, "Bubble!"

I opened my eyes. Fizz was still trying to free herself from the conductor's strong grip. He gave her another shake.

"You're not going over there," he said. "That's final."

A crowd was gathering around us, drawn to the conductor and his flashlight. A man lurched forward and grabbed the conductor's sleeve. He was wearing a three-piece suit smeared with blood, and his eyes were unfocused. "What happened?" he demanded, swaying from side to side.

The conductor turned to him, keeping tight hold of Fizz as he did so.

"Far as I can tell, lightning struck a tree and it fell over the tracks. There was no time to stop. It's a terrible mess. We need to get help."

"There's a telephone at my house," said Fizz, who had stopped wriggling. "Up the hill."

"Go!" cried the conductor. "It's the only thing you can do now to help your family. Go and call for help."

He let her go and bent down to help a woman who was crawling toward him, blood on her face and blouse.

Fizz stood frozen, staring down at the woman.

"Go!" yelled the conductor, looking back at her. "As fast as you can!"

Fizz spun around and began running up the hill. I followed.

Chapter Forty-Five
THE TELEPHONE

We scrambled up the hill, sometimes on all fours where it was steep, grabbing at branches to haul ourselves up. My still-pounding headache slowed me down, and by the time I got to the top of the bank, Fizz was far ahead of me, pelting across the lawn.

The thunder had moved a little farther away and I could hear it rumbling in the distance. But the night was still hot and thick around me, and I felt as if the world, like the floor of the train car, was tilting slightly. Crossing the lawn, I started to have that nightmare feeling when you need to run but your legs feel so heavy that each step feels like wading through thick mud.

There was a light in the kitchen. Fizz ran toward that and burst through the door. By the time I got there she was out of

sight, but I could hear her footsteps pounding up the basement stairs and into the dining room.

When I caught up with her in the front hall, she was standing by a little desk holding an old-fashioned telephone in her
hand. Her hands were shaking too much to get her finger in
the dial. She looked up at me, her face grimy with tears in the
soft light from the lamp on the desk beside the phone.

"Alice," she whispered, "I can't make it work."

I took the phone from her and stared down at the dial. Somehow, I didn't think they had the 911 number for emergencies
in the 1920s.

"What's the number for police?" I asked.

"Just dial the op-op-operator," she stuttered.

I didn't know what she was talking about.

"O!" she shouted. "O for operator!"

I dialed it and after a couple of rings a woman came on the
line.

"Operator! What number please?" she said in a singsong
voice.

Fizz grabbed the phone from me.

"Help!" she yelled. "Help us please! There's been a terrible
train crash. Near Blackwood House, Lakeport."

"Oh my God," cried the woman. I could hear her voice crackling out of the receiver. "Just hang on, honey. I'll get help there
as soon as I can."

Fizz put down the phone and turned to me. She was shivering and crying. I put my arms around her and held her.

The front door banged open and a woman who looked remarkably like Mary came rushing in. Her hair was disheveled, her face streaked with tears. She flew over to Fizz. I stepped aside, and it's a good thing I did, or I would have found out what it was like to be invisible and have someone pass right through me. She fell upon Fizz and scooped her up into her arms, talking the whole time.

"Fiona, Fiona, thank God you're all right! I heard the crash when I was down the road taking a little walk in the moonlight, and I came running back, and when you weren't in the house, I thought you had gone down the bank to see the train and . . . Oh, Fiona—" and she was crying and hugging Fizz, and Fizz was crying and hugging her back. But why was she calling her Fiona? If I could just think for a minute, I knew that was important somehow.

"It was their train!" sobbed Fizz. "Oh, Betsy, you know it was their train. I saw Bubble waving at me through the window just before it crashed."

"I know, I know," replied Betsy.

"We called for help," gasped Fizz. "Alice had to do it because I was shaking so much—"

"Alice?" said Betsy. "Who's Alice?"

Fizz opened her eyes and glanced quickly over Betsy's shoulder at me.

"Nobody, I was confused. I phoned. Help is coming. But Betsy, do you think they're all right?"

"I don't know. We can only pray that God spared them."

As I stood there, watching them clinging to each other, I couldn't get over how much Betsy reminded me of Mary. And then I remembered something Mary had said about her family cleaning houses around here for over a hundred years, and I wondered if she could possibly be Mary's grandmother.

And then it came back to me. My first day here, Mom had said that Mrs. Bishop called her Betsy a couple of times. Why on earth—

My thoughts were interrupted by the loud sound of someone banging at the door at the back of the hall. Then it was wrenched open and a man called out, "Can you help? There are wounded people coming up from the crash. Can you help?"

Betsy and Fizz went to meet them.

"Bring them in the kitchen door, downstairs," said Betsy. "It's easier that way, without the stairs."

The man turned back outside, and Fizz and Betsy disappeared into the dining room.

I was left alone in the hall. I could hear the far-off wail of sirens and a clamor of voices downstairs.

I couldn't help. An invisible person does not make a good nurse. And I didn't want to see any more. The images of people broken and dying and dead were seared into my memory already, frozen like flash photographs, illuminated by a cold white light.

I shivered, although the air was still so warm and muggy around me. I headed toward the stairs and began to climb. I wanted nothing but to get back into my bed and sleep, and wake up in my own world, with Mom and Dad fighting and maybe getting a divorce and maybe not getting one. I could go swimming with Lily, listen to Mary talking her head off, and laugh at crotchety old Mrs. Bishop bossing everyone around. All of that was familiar and safe, so much safer than the dollhouse world where Fizz's whole family had been wiped out in a train crash.

Because all of them had died. I was sure of that. They were too near the front of the train when it hit the tree and flew up in the air. Bubble and Harriet and Bob. All gone. Winked away. Just like that.

Fizz knew it and so did I, the moment it happened.

* * *

I gave an involuntary sob and stopped, just at that turn of the stairs where it got so steep and scary. I was suddenly so tired that I didn't think I could lift my foot to the next step. My head began to spin, and I sat down quickly near the wall side of the stairs, not wanting to lose my balance and fall. I closed my eyes for a moment and took some deep breaths.

This is the dollhouse, I told myself. This is a dream. It's not real.

But the train crash hadn't felt like a dream. Standing on the hill with Fizz when the lightning struck and watching the train cars heaving and toppling over, and the people screaming—that hadn't felt like a dream. And waking up inside the train in the dark where Mom was crying as if her heart would break, and someone who looked just like me was lying still and covered in blood beside her—that hadn't felt like a dream either. It was all too real—and strangely familiar. I'd experienced that train crash before, the night we came to Blackwood House.

As I sat on the stairs, transfixed by the possibility that I had been right all along and our train crash had been far worse than Mom had told me, the world split apart again.

Another bright burst of lightning accompanied by an almost instantaneous crash of thunder rent the air and the dark hall jumped into sharp relief—the thickly carpeted stairs, the polished banisters, the paintings, the chandelier—then it was all swallowed up in a deeper darkness.

The electricity must have gone off. I held my breath. Then, with a mighty swoosh, came another sound: the rhythmic, clattering noise of a torrential downpour.

The weather had finally broken and it was raining.

My first thought was how much more difficult the rain would make it for the crash victims and their rescuers. At least it wasn't raining the other time. The time with Mom.

I couldn't figure it out. I had such clear memories of being in a horrendous crash that first night and yet—and yet I also remembered waking up afterward with everything being okay. No one was hurt too badly, and the train wasn't tipped over. Mom wasn't crying, and the train started up soon after. How could I have both memories? Which one was true?

The pain in my head was grinding away. The bloody images from both train crashes were bouncing through my brain, till I couldn't tell which was which. Poor Fizz. All her family—dead. Everyone I had met in the dollhouse—dead. All ghosts.

The rain was drumming on the ground and the windows and the roof, encasing the house in a torrent of falling water. Like Niagara Falls, I thought. Thunder rumbled in the distance, moving away.

I dropped my aching head into my hands and held it.

A thought stirred, deep in my cotton-batten brain, and it slowly rose to the surface.

Maybe they weren't all ghosts. Fizz wasn't killed in that crash. It happened in the 1920s. She would be an old lady by now if she was still alive.

A very old lady.

Suddenly the house seemed very quiet. I couldn't hear any voices from outside or from the basement. No sirens.

I stood up. It was very dark. I gripped the banister and climbed the last few steps to the hall.

I groped my way into Mom's room and fumbled on her bedside table until my hands closed on a candlestick. I'd seen it there the morning after I slept in her bed. It was the old-fashioned kind with a dish and holder underneath, like the one Wee Willie Winkie carried in my old nursery rhyme book.

I felt around in the drawer and came up with some matches and lit the candle. It illuminated Mom's room—the neatly made bed, the dresser, the bookshelf by the window. The bathroom doors were both open, and as I stood up and held the candle a little higher, I could just make out the motionless figure lying in Mrs. Bishop's bed.

The old lady was still sleeping peacefully, just as she had been when I had come down from the attic into the empty house. I must be back in the real house. Weird. The worlds had switched again, somehow, while I was sitting on the stairs after the crash. Except—if this was the real house, where was Mom?

I took a step toward Mrs. Bishop. I could see her white hair gleaming against her pillow in the candlelight. I stood there for a moment, just staring at her. I felt like the whole house was holding its breath with me.

I let my breath out. The hand holding the candle was shaking. I couldn't go any closer to her.

I wanted this to be over. I was so tired. I just wanted to go back to sleep. Why shouldn't I? When I woke up, it would be morning, and Mom would be there, and maybe Dad and Mary and Lily, and everything would be back to normal.

I turned away from the old woman sleeping in the bed, back into Mom's room, and then walked slowly across the hall, holding the candle up high to guide my way. I walked carefully into my room, the candlelight flickering over the rich carpet and the silky green bed curtains. They were closed.

I stopped. I knew I had left them open.

I took another step. The rain pelting down incessantly outside made me feel like I was inside a drum. The window was wide open, and I could smell that sweet, fresh smell of rain in summer. The bed curtains stirred. From the wind? It had to be the wind that was making them billow and shift.

I took another step. My heart was thudding in my chest. I reached out a hand and slowly pulled the curtain back, feeling the fine silk of the real bed curtains, not the coarser silk of the dollhouse bed curtains.

There was somebody in my bed. I could just see the huddled shape under the blankets.

I swear my heart stopped at that moment. I know my breath did.

A girl in a pretty white nightgown was sleeping in my bed, her red hair fanned out against the pillow.

Fizz.

Fizz, in my bed, in a deep sleep. In the real house, not the dollhouse. And Mrs. Bishop across the hall, asleep in her bed, also in the real house.

I shook my head, trying to clear it. Was this the real house? Or was this somewhere else entirely, that was neither dollhouse nor real house? Some kind of . . . in-between place? Where Fizz and Mrs. Bishop could both be asleep and dreaming?

And then my dream flashed back to me again. In the dream, it was me, not Fizz, who was sleeping in the bed. It was me. Sleeping for years and years while the world went on around me. All alone in my little green world, waiting to wake up. Lonely. With a train whistle in the distance, getting closer.

Was it really me who had been sleeping for all that time in my dream? Or was it Fizz?

Part Five

THE DREAMER

Chapter Forty-Six

THE WITCH

I stood, candle in hand, staring down at the sleeping Fizz. Whose dream was it? Mine or hers?

A loud, screeching buzzer shattered the silence, echoing through the empty house.

Mrs. Bishop's bell.

I jumped and let out a shriek. I just managed not to drop the candle. My scream seemed to blend in with the echoes of the bell, and the sound died away like a train whistle charging into the distance.

I steadied myself by grabbing the post of the bed, waiting for the adrenaline rush to pass.

Fizz hadn't stirred.

Hmmm. I reached out my hand to her white arm and gave it a quick pinch.

"Fizz! Wake up!"

She still didn't move. Her breath came evenly, her chest rising and falling peacefully.

I pinched again, harder. "Fizz!"

She didn't react.

In sleep her expression was soft, with a little smile at the corner of her lips. Whatever she was dreaming about, it wasn't the train crash.

Mrs. Bishop's bell cut through the house again, high-pitched, insistent.

I turned away from sleeping Fizz and made my way reluctantly out of the room and back across the hall, gripping the candlestick tight. Each step was an effort.

The light from my candle preceded me into her room. My hand was shaking again now, and the light skittered and danced over the thick blue carpet and the rich velvet bed curtains. And then I turned and saw her.

She lay propped up among the pillows, watching me. Something green flickered on her hand.

The emerald ring—which I had last seen twinkling on Harriet's hand at the party when she took the champagne glass from her husband.

I stepped forward and held the candle closer to Mrs. Bishop's face so I could see her more clearly.

Tonight she really did look like a mean old witch, with her long nose, her sharp chin and her jutting eyebrows. I'd never noticed what color her eyes were before, but now I could see a flash of green in the flickering light from the candle.

278

I knew those eyes.

I tried to speak, but my voice was no more than a croak. I swallowed and tried again.

"Fizz?" I whispered.

Her eyes gleamed.

"Took you long enough," she said. "You're not actually a very intelligent child, are you?"

I swallowed again.

"How—how—?" I seemed to have lost the ability to form words.

"Oh for heaven's sake, stop gaping. You look like a fish," she snapped, and then a smile twitched across her mouth. She threw back her head and laughed.

It all came together. Fizz. Fiona. Fiona Bishop. Mrs. Bishop.

This old lady with her white hair and sharp features looked nothing like the Fizz who was sleeping in my bed with her red hair and smooth skin. Only the eyes were similar, but when she laughed, it was like the two people merged and I could see that she really was Fizz—or some version of Fizz.

"I—I don't understand," I said feebly.

"No, that's obvious," said Mrs. Bishop. "You take a very long time to catch on to things, don't you?"

That was pure Fizz. Acting superior because she knew something I didn't.

I stared at Mrs. Bishop for a moment, trying to see how she and Fizz could possibly be the same person. Fizz did have a sharpish nose and a sharpish chin, but her face was so young and full that they didn't stand out the way they did on

Mrs. Bishop. And the lines and wrinkles on Mrs. Bishop's face seemed to emphasize her features, while Fizz's face was unlined and clear of all the wear and tear the years had put on Mrs. Bishop.

Her hands were an old woman's hands, stiff with arthritis—

"The ring," I said slowly. "Harriet's ring."

She glanced at it. "So you did notice something," she said. "She left it behind in her jewelry box when they went to the city. I put it on that awful night, and I've been wearing it ever since." She raised her hand and turned the ring slowly so the candlelight glinted in the dark-green shadows within.

"So it's all true," I said finally, pulling my eyes away from the hypnotic radiance of the emerald and looking at her face again. "Everything that happened? Everything I saw?"

She looked up at me. The smirk was gone now and she just looked sad.

"Yes," she said. "It all happened. Long ago."

"The train crash?" I whispered, remembering the train cars flying into the air and Fizz sobbing in Betsy's arms.

She nodded. "They all died," she said. "Bubble. My mother. My father. Fizz."

"Fizz?" I asked. "But Fizz didn't die in the crash. You're Fizz."

"No," she said softly. "I used to be, but I'm not anymore. I'm Fiona. Everything that was Fizz was destroyed that night. She's been dead for sixty-eight years."

Chapter Forty-Seven

LOCKED AWAY

I tried to make sense of what she was saying. Everything I thought I knew was flying around like a bunch of juggler's balls about to cut loose and tumble into the audience. I tried to grab at something.

"She's not dead," I said stupidly. "She's sleeping in my bed."

"She might as well be dead," said Mrs. Bishop slowly, as if each word hurt her to say. "That girl, the girl that was me, died out there on that hillside when the train crashed. I was only Fiona after that, and that was the end of Fizz. I shut her away in the dollhouse. Then I closed up this house and the horrors of that awful night and left it all behind."

She fell silent. I thought of this house locked up all that time, the curtains shut tight against the light, the lovely furniture draped in sheets. And the dollhouse in the attic, identical curtains pulled across the windows, little sheets over the little chairs and sofas and beds.

And Fizz, sleeping in the dollhouse bed, all that time, dreaming as the world turned and time passed without her.

Mrs. Bishop seemed to have forgotten me. Her eyes looked far beyond what I could see. I felt like she and I were marooned in a small island of candlelight while the darkness lapped around us like waves against the shore.

"How long?" I asked finally. "How long was it all closed away?"

She gave a big sigh. "Sixty-seven years. I went away to boarding school in September 1929, after the train crash, and I didn't come back until last year. Sixty-seven years. It was closed up all that time. Mr. Brock—Fred—my father's lawyer and best friend, looked after it at first, along with Betsy, our housekeeper."

Her eyes were sad, and it seemed that she was dialing back the years in her mind. "I wanted to get rid of the house. Just sell it. But because of the way my grandfather's will was written, I couldn't. He tied everything up in a special trust, and then my father tied up the dollhouse with it in his will. My grandfather wanted the house to stay in the family. But there was no family. Only me."

Her voice faded in and out, as if she was talking to herself, not to me. I had to strain to hear her.

"I tried to forget about it. I did my best. I had my life in England. But the whole time there was a darkness niggling away at me, deep inside. I always knew that Blackwood House was here, all locked up, with everything inside just the way it had been left. Not just the furniture. Not just the dollhouse. My parents. My sister. My childhood self. All here, as if they were frozen in time on that terrible night. No. I could bury it, but I could never completely forget it."

She looked over at me then, as if she had just remembered I was there.

"I had to keep it. The only way I could get rid of it was to die and leave it to somebody else in my will. The house was well cared for over the years. When Fred Brock retired, his son took over the law firm, and when Betsy got too old to come in and clean, her daughter took her place. And a long time after that, it fell to Fred's grandson and Mary, Betsy's granddaughter. Three generations. They, all of them, kept my trust all those years and didn't speak of it to anyone.

"All the locals remembered was that the family was killed in a train crash. When I came back, people around here thought I was an eccentric old lady from England who had bought the house. And that was fine with me. I didn't want it all brought up again and talked about. I didn't want anyone to know who I really was."

"But why did you come back?" I asked. "If you hated it so much? Why didn't you just stay in England?"

She looked at me directly then, and again I felt the power of those intense green eyes.

"As the years went by, that dark little corner of my mind where I had locked everything up began to take up more space. Memories of my life before the train crash began to surface at the oddest times—things I'd done with Bubble, conversations with my father, arguments with my mother. I tried to shut them down and close them away again, but they kept coming back. Then when I was about seventy-eight, I had some health problems, and I could see my own death coming closer and closer, and the darkness began to take over. It grew bigger and bigger until it was all I could do to focus on anything else.

"I thought I was going mad. I could see my family when I closed my eyes at night before I went to sleep. I could hear their voices in my sleep. And then I started to have a recurring dream that I was young again, lying in my bed with the green curtains, sleeping while the world turned without me.

"For the first time since I left this house when I was twelve, I wanted to come back. I needed to come back. I needed to come back to this house to die where my parents and my sister had died. The house was calling me back. Death was calling me back."

The candle flame flickered in a sudden draft from the window. I shivered. I could almost hear the house calling to her, whispering like the wind outside in the trees, sending its ghostly message across the miles and miles of land and ocean to where she lived in England.

"I ran away from it all my life," said Mrs. Bishop quietly. "And finally there was nowhere to run but back. But a very strange thing happened, Alice. As I felt Death pulling me back here, there was something else. A tiny spark of hope. Because I knew everything was still here—the house, the furniture, the books. And the dollhouse. And the dolls. Even though they were wrapped in a death shroud for all that time, they were here. I started to believe, against all reason, that they were waiting for me to come back and wake them up. That I might be able to get back through the dollhouse and be with them again, the way it was before the crash."

Her voice trembled a little, and if possible, her eyes grew even more intense, boring into mine.

"I don't believe in magic. I don't believe in ghosts. I don't believe in God. But I believed that somehow if I came back here, I could taste it again. Taste my childhood. Through the dollhouse.

"I knew it was a mad idea. All my life in England was built on being an objective journalist. I had no room in my life for wild flights of the imagination.

"But as I drew closer to my death, I began to see the world differently. I had nothing to lose anymore. So I came home. Hoping beyond hope to somehow find my family again."

Her wild green eyes were fastened on mine, her face flushed. She looked like a madwoman.

And I was trapped with her in this place, somewhere in between the dollhouse and the real house, and I didn't know how to get out.

Chapter Forty-Eight

BROKEN GLASS

She must have seen something of what I was feeling in the expression on my face because she gave a witch-like little cackle of laughter and began to mock me, just the way Fizz would have done.

"You're scared of me now, aren't you, Alice? You think I'm insane. But it's not me you should be afraid of. It's this house. It's what's in this house, all around us."

I shivered again as she said that and glanced back over my shoulder. I could almost hear the darkness whispering to me. I was aware of the open door behind me leading into the hall and the cavern of the stairs curving down into the deep darkness of the rest of the house.

"What happened?" I asked. My mouth was so dry that I

could barely give voice to the words. I swallowed. "When you came back? What happened?"

She laughed again, but this time there was a bitterness in her laughter that I had never seen in Fizz.

"Nothing happened. As soon as I walked in the door, I knew I'd made a mistake. The house was filled with shadows but no ghosts. Everything was sad here. Sadder than sad. I had the house and furniture restored to what it had been, except the kitchen—I had a new kitchen put in, with doors to the terrace. But everything else was the same as when I was a child.

"But the house was empty. There was nothing for me here. I would climb the stairs to the attic every day and play with the dollhouse, all by myself, when Mary was gone. I'd move the dolls around. I'd dress them in the clothes that were identical to the clothes we wore. I'd sit there for hours.

"But nothing came alive. The only thing that came back was the pain. It grew until it was as sharp inside me as it was the day that train crashed. It hurt to breathe. It hurt to walk. It hurt every minute of every day. And finally, I couldn't stand it anymore and—"

She broke off. The words had been pouring out of her and she seemed out of breath. She took a moment to calm herself down, and then began to speak again, so softly that I had to lean in closer to be able to hear her.

"I stood at the top of the stairs. Those stairs have always been treacherous. I felt like I was living inside a bag of broken glass, and every time I moved, shards of glass would pierce my skin. And I stood there, looking down the stairs and then I let everything go and I fell.

"I thought it would hurt for just a few more moments, till I reached the bottom of the stairs, and then it would stop."

I felt that feeling of suspension again as she spoke, like the world was holding its breath.

"I fell slowly at first, but then I bounced off the wall where the stairs turn, and I picked up speed. My leg twisted under me and then I was at the bottom, lying there looking up at the chandelier. Still alive. Still in agony. Only now it was my head and my leg that were hurting as much as my spirit had been hurting before.

"I used every swear word I had ever heard. I even made up some. All I had done was make everything worse. I was lying in helpless pain on the floor, and Mary wouldn't be in until nine the next morning. Not only was I not dead, but now I wouldn't even be able to climb the stairs to the attic and look at the dollhouse.

"And then I started to laugh." She grinned, and for just a moment, she was Fizz again. "It was just so funny! I had made a complete mess of it. But laughing made my head hurt, so I stopped.

"I suppose I was unconscious for a while. I had that dream again. I dreamed I was Fizz, sleeping in my bed with the green curtains in the summer heat. Sleeping for days and weeks and months and years. Dimly aware of sounds outside and life going on, but still asleep. Delicious, deep, wonderful sleep."

She smiled. "The best of sleeps. A happy sleep, knowing that when I woke up everything was going to be fun. A summer holiday sleep. And as I lay there in that beautiful dream, I heard the far-off sound of a train whistle. And then I knew that someone was going to come soon and wake me up and pull me into the daytime world."

She stopped talking. She looked sleepy now, as if talking about that wonderful sleep was putting her back there.

I reached out and gave her arm a little shake.

"Then what happened?" I said.

Her eyes snapped out of their sleepiness and she frowned.

"What do you think happened?" she said crossly. "I woke up in the hospital with a concussion and a broken leg."

Chapter Forty-Nine
THE CONNECTION

The wind stirred the curtains and that fresh after-the-rain smell wafted in again. The house was so quiet. I imagined Mrs. Bishop lying twisted at the bottom of the stairs, all alone, with this dense darkness all around her, knowing that it would be hours before anyone came to help her. In and out of consciousness—dreaming.

"That dream you had," I said slowly. "That was my dream too. The same dream."

"It's Fizz's dream," said Mrs. Bishop. "Not yours, not mine. That was what she was dreaming all those years while she lay locked away in the dollhouse."

"Like Sleeping Beauty," I said. "Sleeping for a hundred years."

"Sixty-eight years," corrected Mrs. Bishop. "But yes, like

Sleeping Beauty. And like Sleeping Beauty, she needed someone to wake her up. Not me. Somebody else."

There was a brief silence.

"Me. You mean me, don't you?" I said. "I was the one to wake her up."

Mrs. Bishop nodded.

"That night you came here, that was the sixty-eighth anniversary of the train crash that killed my family. I was lying in bed trying not to think about it, but I couldn't help myself. Every year on June 21 it's the same—I try not to remember, but it all comes back to me anyway. And then the train came, and then the sound of a crash, and for a moment I was right back there on the hillside watching the train cars fly up into the air. I could smell the smoke; I could hear the people screaming, just as if it had happened all over again.

"But I saw it too! That first night, I mean. When I woke up after the accident, I remembered a much worse accident than what really happened. I saw all that."

"You saw it because Fizz saw it. Because I . . . saw it. Somehow we were connected in that moment and we've been connected ever since."

I thought about this for a moment. It seemed bizarre.

Mrs. Bishop went on. "I know the minute we became connected. Right at that moment, reliving the crash, I saw something new, something I'd never seen in all the times I've been haunted by those awful memories. A young girl with blood running down her face. You."

"Me?" I squeaked.

"Well, I didn't know it was you, not until I saw you the next morning. Then I recognized you at once. But by then I knew you were the one to wake Fizz up."

"How . . . how did you know?"

"Because when you went to sleep that night and dreamed you saw Fizz sleeping beside you, I saw her too. I was dreaming what you were dreaming. And it's been like that ever since. Every time you have the dream about going into the dollhouse, I'm with you. I've seen them all. Bubble, Mother, Father, Sailor—" She broke off, smiling. "Good old Sailor."

"But how—" I began. "How did you get inside my dreams? That's what I don't understand. And I wasn't the first person to wake Fizz up. Lily woke her up before I even got here."

"She did?"

Finally, something Mrs. Bishop didn't know about.

"Yes, the night Lily slept in that bed, after you got back from the hospital. Fizz woke up and called her Bubble. She said it wasn't time yet."

Mrs. Bishop frowned. "Hmmm. I guess Lily wasn't the right person." Then her face cleared. "That must be because I had no connection with Lily. After the train crash, you and I were connected, and we had the same dreams. It wouldn't work with Lily because she wasn't in the train crash. You were."

She spoke as if it all made perfect sense. But it was still impossible, all of it.

Except that it had happened.

"Oh, and I heard the two of you sneaking up the stairs to play with the dollhouse," she said. "Not much happens in this house that I don't know about. I hear every little squeak of the stairs or the floorboards. Nothing wrong with my hearing." She laughed. It was Fizz's laugh, loud and infectious.

Except I didn't feel like laughing.

"And, of course, I arranged for you to find the keys in my dressing table that day," she went on. "I wanted you to go up there, Alice, I wanted you to pull out all the dolls and play with them and wake everything up. Then you'd be all the more likely to dream of them at night. And you thought you were being so careful, you and Lily, hiding around the house." She laughed again.

"I still don't understand," I said. "I still don't understand how you and I can be dreaming the same thing. About the dollhouse. About Fizz. Why are we so connected?"

"You know, I've been thinking about that too, Alice. I didn't figure it out until tonight, when we dreamed about the train crash and what happened on that awful night."

A picture of the upturned train cars, the smoke and Fizz struggling to break free of the conductor flashed into my head.

"What about it?" I asked, my voice shaking just a bit.

"You had another dream tonight, didn't you?"

And there it was.

The image I had been trying to push away ever since I saw it. The image of the motionless girl with the blood in her hair on the train with my mother crying beside her.

Chapter Fifty

DEATH

I couldn't say it.

"You mean—you mean—" My voice came out as half croak, half whisper.

Mrs. Bishop looked at me calmly.

"You know what I mean. Fizz kept telling you. The train crash. Your train crash." She spoke slowly, each word hammering against my skull. "Your train crashed sixty-eight years to the day of the crash that killed my family. On a night near the summer solstice when the moon was full and a tree fell across the train tracks, just like what happened in the crash in 1929, which was also on a night near the summer solstice when the moon was full. When your train crashed, you must have been hurt more badly than anyone realized. That's why you've been able to go into the dollhouse world. And that's why you were the one who could wake Fizz up and help her."

"No," I whispered feebly.

"Fizz has been trying to tell you all along, but you wouldn't believe her," said Mrs. Bishop, her green eyes gleaming.

I shook my head.

"I don't know why you're still fighting this, Alice," said Mrs. Bishop in a very reasonable, patient voice. "It's all around us. Can't you feel it?"

Panic took over. "What?" I yelled, jumping to my feet. "Feel what? Tell me! Stop playing with me like you're a cat and I'm a mouse. You're so much like Fizz it makes me sick! You're mean and cruel and—" I floundered. "And nasty!"

She laughed, and her laugh was pure Fizz. "You're so funny, Alice. She's told you again and again. You're in my dollhouse because you're dead. Or as good as."

The word seemed to echo in the silence of the house, and the fear that had been simmering ever since I came to Blackwood House boiled over and swooshed through me like the scalding steam from a kettle. I couldn't breathe or move. A darkness began to close around Mrs. Bishop and me.

But it wasn't an empty darkness. There was a presence here, filling the house, filling the sky, filling the world. A massive presence that was slowly wrapping itself around us, pulling us into its dark heart.

It wasn't cruel. It wasn't kind. It was bigger than cruel or kind. Nothing could stop it.

I realized this wasn't the first time I had felt it. Every time I came back from the dollhouse world, that darkness was there. And in the sudden, profound silence after the train crash, as I lay on the ground breathing in the metallic smell of the train with the grass tickling my nose, I felt that huge, relentless presence enfolding all the people who were dying. Taking them away.

And now I felt it here. Spreading up the curving staircase. Creeping along the thick carpets. Sidling around the corners into this room with Mrs. Bishop and me.

"No," I whispered. "No." I took a deep, shuddering breath.

Mrs. Bishop was watching me closely with an air of grim satisfaction.

"No!" I said more loudly. I grabbed her hand and turned it over, feeling for her pulse the way my mother had taught me. The thump, thump, thump of her blood beat a steady rhythm through my fingers.

She let me do it, watching me with that annoying, superior half-smile I found so infuriating in Fizz.

"You're not dead!" I said, letting go of her wrist and holding my own for a moment. A reassuring thump, thump, thump vibrated through my fingers. "And neither am I. And neither is Fizz."

"Very good," she said, with patient condescension, as if she was a teacher encouraging a hopeless student. "You're right. We're not completely dead. Not yet. But Death is here. It's all around us. It's waiting. You feel it just as I do."

I shivered as she said that and I knew it was true. I glanced quickly over my shoulder.

Darkness. Darkness was all around us. Only the flickering flame of the candle seemed to hold it at bay.

I kept finding it hard to breathe. Like whatever was there in the house with us was stealing my breath. Snatching it away.

"It's no use fighting it," said Mrs. Bishop, watching me struggling with my breath. Her green eyes glowed in the candle-light like two bright, hard emeralds.

I focused on drawing each breath more deeply into my lungs. I didn't know if it was the fear or that thing all around us that was making it so hard for me to breathe, but I wasn't going to stop breathing. Not yet.

Mrs. Bishop spoke up again. Her voice was soft, insistent, almost kind.

"It's better to face it, Alice. You can't run forever. I learned that. I locked it up in this house years ago and I've been running from it ever since. But it's no good. It brought me back here and now it's going to take me. And you. And Fizz."

Chapter Fifty-One

CANDLES

I closed my eyes. I felt like I couldn't move. Fear engulfed me. I was going to die.

And in that moment, beyond hope, I heard my granny's voice whispering to me.

"Cast off the works of darkness and put on the armor of light."

We weren't a religious family. We hardly ever went to church. But my granny, who died when I was five, was a great believer. I had a lot of nightmares when I little, and I was afraid of the dark, and my grandmother used to sit with me sometimes and say this Bible verse to me. "Let us cast off the works of darkness and put on the armor of light." And I would drift off to sleep, imagining myself clothed in shining silver armor made of tiny beams of light. When she died, she left me this verse in a little silver frame, and my mother hung it above my bed.

Cast off the darkness. Put on the armor of light. The armor of light.

"No!" I cried, and this time my voice came out loud and clear. I snatched the candle from Mrs. Bishop's bedside table and took it over to the mantelpiece.

Four silver candlesticks stood there. With trembling hands I took one down, lit it from my candle, then placed it back on the mantelpiece. Then I took a second one down and did the same. I could feel the darkness rustling around me, and I still found it hard to breathe properly, but by the time I had the fourth candle lit, my hands weren't shaking quite so much.

Light flooded the room—a warm glow that brought out the blue and yellow colors in the bed, the curtains and the rug.

Mrs. Bishop looked at me and shook her head, smiling slightly.

"It's no use," she said.

I ignored her and walked out into the dark hallway. The blackness beyond my candle flame seemed to eddy and flow like waves coming up the deep well of the staircase. I crossed into my room.

The thin light from my candle flickered over Fizz, still sleeping in my bed. I went directly to the mantelpiece, where two tall candles in brass holders framed the mirror. I placed them one by one on the floor and lit them from my candle. My hands were shaking and some hot wax fell to the carpet.

I returned them to the mantel, then spun around and was out of my room and into Bubble's. I lit the candles on her mantelpiece. Then into my mother's room, finding another one on her dresser and lighting that. Then back to the hall to light a candle on the desk there. I was sharply aware of Mrs. Bishop lying silently in her bed beyond her doorway.

I headed down the stairs, candle in one hand and banister in the other. As I descended into the hall, I could feel the heavy darkness pressing all around me. Although I moved within the steady center of a circle of light, the darkness closed in behind. My breath was coming in little shallow gasps. I reached the bottom and turned into the living room. I knew there were rows of silver candlesticks on the mantelpieces, the same ones that had been lit for Harriet's party.

I walked carefully between the couches and chairs while the darkness seemed to pull at me, tangling in my hair, sending tingles up and down the back of my neck. I ignored it the best I could, but a chill was spreading through me.

I reached up and lit the first candle. Then the second. Then the third.

The lovely room materialized around me—soft, silky, welcoming.

I made my way to the other mantelpiece and lit the candles there. Turning, I could see the entire room now, dappled with light and shadow. But I could still feel that brooding presence that was hovering just beyond the candlelight. Watching me. Waiting.

I went from room to room, lighting every candle I found. In the study. The hallway. The dining room. And then I went down the stairs to the kitchen.

The modern kitchen. Everything was clean, scrubbed and empty. I found some tea lights in a drawer and set six of them on the table on a plate, then lit them.

As I stood in that silent kitchen, watching the glow spread from the tea lights, I felt a flicker of fear. What if I couldn't get back to the other world? Where my mother was bustling about up and down the stairs with trays for Mrs. Bishop. Where Lily sat drawing at the kitchen table. Where my father was running his hand along the silky white couch and strolling through the rooms, gazing up at the architectural details in wonder. Where Mary was talking on and on and serving up her horrible jellied salad.

I wanted to be back there. I would have given anything to be back there and forget all about Fizz and the dollhouse and Mrs. Bishop and the train crash. I gritted my teeth. I was going to get back. Somehow.

I went back upstairs, through the dining room, bright with candlelight, and into the hall, where the crystal drops on the chandelier high above me reflected tiny sparks of the light from the candle I had lit below.

I went up the staircase slowly, placing my feet firmly on each step.

The whole house was shimmering with light. But the big, impersonal presence had been with me every step of the way, and it still lurked just beyond the golden, wavering light of my candles.

I walked slowly through the doorway into Mrs. Bishop's room. She lay back against her pillows, as I had left her. She looked very tired.

I sat down in the chair beside her bed and placed the candle back on the bedside table. We sat in silence for a while. I could feel her sadness spreading out from her bed and into me.

"What do you want?" I said finally.

She didn't say anything, but her mouth tightened and then a tear fell slowly down her cheek.

"I want them back," she whispered. "I want them all back. I want everything that we had back the way it was. I want my mother alive. And my father. And Bubble. I want to be in this house with them the way it was." Now the tears were spilling down her face.

I put out my hand to her and she grasped it, holding tight.

"After you woke Fizz up, I was back with my family. They were all alive. I want that again." She pulled her hand away and fumbled in her pajama sleeve for a handkerchief.

"But you weren't happy," I said. "None of you were happy. Except maybe Bubble."

She laughed through her tears, wiping her eyes. "Bubble was always happy. Like Lily. Oh, she'd have her tantrums, now and then, whenever things got too frustrating for her. But most of the time, she was just—happy."

"But the rest of you weren't," I insisted. "Fizz was miserable.

Your mother and father were about to get a divorce, as far as I could tell, like mine."

"You're right. We weren't happy. But we were alive."

The darkness seemed to press more closely around us.

I watched her struggling to gain control of her tears.

"Do you think you'll be with them all again if you die?" I asked slowly. "In the dollhouse?"

She laughed bitterly and shook her head. "I told you. I don't believe in any of that. Heaven. God."

"You believe in Death," I said slowly, feeling it murmur around me as I said its name.

"Because I've experienced it," she said. "That night, when the train crashed. And after, when Fizz died inside me. I know Death, so I believe in it."

I began to shiver again.

"It's coming for me," she said simply. "I know it. I can feel it. And so can you because it's coming for you too."

"No," I said loudly. "It's not! It may be your time to die but it's not mine. I have my mother and my father waiting for me, not Death. I have things to do in my life. I have to live my life. It's not my time!"

"Do you think it was Bubble's time?" she asked, angry again. "Do you think it was my mother's time? And my father's time? And Fizz? We all had things to do in our lives, too, but it still came. And it's coming again. I can't stop it and you can't stop it."

A pain sharper than anything I had ever felt in my life knifed through my head and I bent over, my hands to my head, trying to breathe. It seemed to blot everything out so that there was no Mrs. Bishop, no candlelight, no bedroom. Just darkness and this piercing agony.

Chapter Fifty-Two
SLEEPING BEAUTY

I had never experienced anything like it. I felt like my head was going to burst open. I closed my eyes, rocking back and forth, breathing hard, saying, "No, no, no, no," over and over again.

There was nothing else in the world, only the unbearable hammering in my head. It went on and on.

I needed my mother. I needed to go to the hospital. I stumbled to my feet and out of the room, still holding my head, through the bathroom into Mom's room.

The candle burned steadily on the dresser. The bed was neatly made.

No Mom.

Of course. This was the dollhouse. No, not the dollhouse.

The place in between the dollhouse and the real house. Mom wasn't here. Only Mrs. Bishop and Fizz. And me.

I had to get back to the real house. The real world. To my mother. And my father. And Dr. West, who maybe could help me stop this awful pain.

Unless it was too late. Unless that image of me so still in the train was true and I was dead.

But being dead wasn't supposed to hurt like this. Was it?

I staggered across the hall to my bedroom, clutching the doorframe for a moment for balance, then focused on the bed. One step. Two steps. If I lay down and closed my eyes, maybe I would wake up in the real house. And Mom would be there.

The bed loomed up before me, a pale green bubble. And someone was in it.

Fizz. Sleeping. The blinding, overwhelming pain had made me forget about her.

I sank down to the rug and held my head tight between my two hands, as if by holding it I could stop my head from exploding, which is what it felt like was going to happen any minute.

And then I could feel the darkness circling around me, closing in on me from the corners of the room. If I took just one more breath, would it sweep me up and take me away and make this agony stop?

I took another breath. But it didn't stop. I was past caring about anything except this huge, raging headache that was eating me alive. I lost all sense of time or place.

And then gradually, in the depths of that void, I became aware of someone else's voice there with me.

"No, no, no, no—"

I opened my eyes. Through the curtain of pain, I saw Fizz sitting up in the bed, clutching her head just like I was, crying.

"Fizz?" I gasped. "Fizz?"

And then the battering in my head stopped. Just like that. I felt breathless, and somehow lighter, as if a huge weight had suddenly been lifted away from me.

But Fizz kept crying, and rocking back and forth in agony, like she would never stop. It was as if the unbearable pressure in my head had left me and gone to her.

I didn't know how, or why. In the sweet relief that came with the absence of pain, I began to understand something. Maybe what Mrs. Bishop said was right. She and I were connected, from the moment my train crashed and I hit my head. Fizz—Mrs. Bishop—and I were in this together.

I stood up and went to the bed and reached out my hand to touch her shoulder. She was shuddering with sobs.

"Fizz?" I said again, softly. "Can I help you?"

Then she opened her eyes. They were such a beautiful green. But they were blank. She didn't see me. It was as if she were still asleep. She was in that dark place, all by herself, consumed by the anguish of losing her family.

She curled herself into a ball and lay there, crying. I sat down on the bed beside her and smoothed her hair back from her forehead, the way my mother did when I was sick.

She gave no indication that she knew I was there, or could feel my hand, but I kept smoothing her hair back and murmuring, "It's okay, it's okay."

Only it wasn't. It would never be okay for Fizz. I had felt an echo of what she felt, ripping through my head. Mine was a physical pain, but what Fizz felt was even bigger. No wonder Mrs. Bishop had locked it all up in the dollhouse and gone away.

Fizz finally stopped crying, but every now and then a little sob worked its way out between breaths.

The house was quiet. I felt like I'd been wrung out like a dishrag. I was aware of those candles all burning steadily, from the basement up through the ground floor and the second floor. Like the whole house was a candle, lighting up the darkness that was all around us. The armor of light.

A whisper of a breeze feathered in through the window, bringing that sweet after-rain smell of wet leaves and grass.

There was no sound from Mrs. Bishop's room.

And then suddenly, there was a small noise from my closet.

A click—followed by a squeak—followed by a slow creak.

Immediately I was alert, adrenaline rushing through me, bracing myself for whatever was coming.

A muffled, spooky whisper. "Ahhh . . . lisss."

And then louder and more ghost-like: "Ahhh . . . lisss."

I watched as a white hand reached out of the darkness of the closet, followed by a shadowy form that seemed to bend and flicker in the candlelight and then resolve itself into a form.

Lily.

Lily, emerging from the secret passage to Bubble's room, with a big smile on her face.

"Hi, Alice! Did I scare you?"

I let go of the breath I didn't know I'd been holding.

"Yes! Yes, you did! But oh, Lily, I'm so glad to see you!"

She laughed, and then walked slowly across the floor toward me. "I came to see you, but your mother said to let you sleep. I got tired of waiting. I came by the secret passage."

Was I back in the real world? But no, Fizz was still there, sleeping in my bed. What was Lily doing here? Was I in the dollhouse again, dreaming?

She came right up to me and peered into my face. "Do you feel better?"

"A little, I guess," I replied.

She put her warm hand into mine and gave it a squeeze. Then her eyes slid over to Fizz, who had started crying softly again.

"What's wrong with Fizz?" asked Lily. She didn't seem at all surprised to see her in my bed.

I didn't know how to begin to tell her.

"Is she having a bad dream?" asked Lily, her forehead knotted in concern.

"Yes," I replied. "She is."

Lily watched her for a moment.

Fizz's crying was soft but incessant. It would grow quieter one moment and then pick up strength the next. It was the crying of someone who could never be comforted.

"Wake her up," said Lily. "That's what Mom does when I have a bad dream. Wake her up. Then she'll stop dreaming. I think so."

I leaned over Fizz and shook her shoulder gently.

"Fizz!" I said. "Fizz, wake up!"

She kept crying, her eyes closed, completely unaware of me.

I tried again, speaking more loudly. "FIZZ! Wake UP!"

Nothing.

"It's no good," I said to Lily. "She's been sleeping for years. She won't wake up."

"A hundred years?" asked Lily. "Like Sleeping Beauty?"

"Yes. That's exactly what she's like."

"She was awake before," said Lily. "You said she was awake in your dream. In the dollhouse."

"That was a different dream."

"She needs a prince," said Lily. "That's who woke up Sleeping Beauty. I think so."

"We haven't got a prince," I said.

Lily looked at Fizz for a moment. Her hopeless crying was enough to break your heart.

"I can try," said Lily, and she leaned over and kissed Fizz softly on her cheek. "Wake up, Fizz," she said gently, looking into her face. "Don't cry anymore."

Fizz's eyes fluttered. Her sobs caught in her throat, and she opened her eyes and looked into Lily's.

"Bubble?" she said.

Lily smiled her radiant, contagious smile. "Hi, Fizz," she said. "You were crying and wouldn't wake up. I woke you up. Just like Prince Charming. I think so."

Fizz sat up, wiping her cheeks. She looked at Lily, taking her in, and then looked at me. The tears welled up again.

"Alice," she said. "Alice, they're gone."

Chapter Fifty-Three
DOUBLE TROUBLE

That searing pain flashed briefly through my head again and I saw it reflected in her eyes. Then it was gone.

"They're all dead," she said dully. "Bubble, Mother, Dad. They've all left me."

"No," I said. "They're not all dead."

"But the train—" said Fizz. "They all died."

"No, Fizz," I said again. "There was one survivor."

"Who?" said Fizz.

"I'll show you," I replied, and reached out my hand to her. Lily took her other hand and we walked slowly out of the room.

The hall was hushed and soft in the candlelight. Mrs. Bishop's room was dark. We crossed the hall and went in.

"Who—?" began Fizz, and then stopped when she saw Mrs. Bishop.

Mrs. Bishop struggled to sit up. I dropped Fizz's hand and went to help, propping up the pillows behind her again.

Fizz just stood there, staring at her. It was like she was looking into a mirror that showed her what she would look like in sixty-eight years. Lily stood gaping at them.

The eyes were almost identical, but Mrs. Bishop's face was Fizz's carved more distinctly and weathered by the years. Her nose seemed longer, her chin sharper. And where Fizz's cheek was smooth and fair, Mrs. Bishop's was wrinkled and dark. But even though there were lines around Mrs. Bishop's mouth and none around Fizz's, they were the same shape.

Fizz reached out her hand and gently touched Mrs. Bishop's cheek.

"You're really old," said Fizz, a sense of wonder in her voice.

"And you're really rude," countered Mrs. Bishop.

They stared at each other for a moment, then they both threw back their heads and laughed.

Lily slipped her hand into mine.

"They're the same person," she whispered, her eyes big. "Mrs. Bishop is Fizz grown up!"

"Yes," I whispered back.

"Are you really me?" asked Fizz. "I don't understand."

"I came back to find you," said Mrs. Bishop. "I left you here in the dollhouse after the train crash. I should have taken you with me. I would have had more fun."

"Why didn't you take me?" asked Fizz.

Mrs. Bishop looked over at me for a moment. In her eyes I could see everything she had told me. She looked back at Fizz.

"Because it hurt too much," she whispered. "It just hurt too much."

"Yes," said Fizz, "I know," and tears began to spill down her cheeks. Mrs. Bishop opened up her arms and folded her into a hug.

"I'm sorry," said Mrs. Bishop.

For a moment all I could hear was the moaning of the wind outside and Fizz crying softly.

Lily squeezed my hand again.

"Will they be happy now?" she asked. "Now that they're together again?"

Mrs. Bishop's eyes met mine over Fizz's head.

"I don't know," I said uncertainly. "I don't know what's going to happen next."

"I do," said Mrs. Bishop, and then I realized that the wind wasn't just moaning outside, it was beginning to howl. The curtains billowed in at the windows and then a violent gust of wind blew them up in the air and the candles flickered. I could feel the darkness I had tried to keep at bay pressing in on us from all sides.

Lily slipped her hand into mine.

"Alice?" she said uncertainly.

Mrs. Bishop's voice rang out above the growing tumult of the wind.

"It's over, Alice. It was always going to come to this, no matter how many candles you lit. You were hurt too badly in that train accident, even though nobody could tell. And it's all for the best. Now we can all rest."

Fizz pulled away from Mrs. Bishop and turned to face us.

"We're all going to sleep now, Alice," she said, smiling. "A deep, happy sleep. You'll see."

Seeing the two of them together, both with the identical all-knowing smirks on their faces, was more than I could bear.

"You two may want to die," I said, "but Lily and I do not."

"Oh, Lily isn't really here," said Fizz. "She's just part of your dream."

"I am not!" said Lily. "I'm just as real as you, you stupid doll! I think so!"

Mrs. Bishop laughed. "You couldn't possibly understand, Lily. This is beyond you."

"I understand that you're mean," said Lily. "And so is Fizz. You're both mean. Come on, Alice, let's get out of here."

"And where, exactly, do you think you can go, Lily?" asked Mrs. Bishop sweetly.

The wind had picked up even more and the house seemed to be trembling around us. The candle flames faltered and then came back again, sending strange shadows across the room.

"Home," said Lily. "Back to the real house. We'll wake up and everything will be okay. I think so."

Fizz laughed. "Maybe you can do that, Lily, but Alice can't. She's already fading."

Lily turned to me and her face fell.

"Alice?" she said in a small voice. "Are you feeling okay? You look funny."

I grabbed the candle from the bedside table and took it over to the dresser with the three mirrors. My face looked back at me, multiplied by three, quivering in the uneven light. All three of me were very pale, and there was something wrong with my hair at the back, where it was sticking up. I put up my hand to feel.

It came away wet and red.

"You're bleeding, Alice," said Lily beside me. "We gotta get you home so Dr. West can fix you. I think so."

Chapter Fifty-Four

THE ILLUMINATED DOLLHOUSE

I turned back to the bed, where Fizz and Mrs. Bishop were sitting side by side, watching me. They weren't laughing anymore.

"I'm sorry, Alice," said Fizz. "I told you. You wouldn't believe me."

"I'm not dead yet," I said. "Come on, Lily." I pulled her into the hallway, where the candle flames were dancing madly.

The wind was screeching now, tearing around the house like so many howling banshees trying to get in.

"Where can we go, Alice?" cried Lily, gripping my hand with two of hers.

"To the dollhouse," I said. The magic dollhouse. I couldn't think of anywhere else to go. The dollhouse had been the key right from the beginning. Maybe now, somehow, it could help us get back.

As we passed from the hall into my room, a rush of wind scooted after us and blew out all the candles. The house plunged into darkness.

I stopped.

"We have to go up in the dark, Lily," I said.

"No, we don't," she replied, letting go of my hands and fumbling with something.

A couple of seconds later a faint, narrow beam of light trickled out from something she held in her hand.

"It's a penlight," she said triumphantly. "I think so. Dr. West gave it to me for my birthday. I always carry it in my pocket."

The door of the dollhouse room stood open, as I had left it, and a strange, bright glow was coming from the room beyond. A yellow, flickering light.

Lily and I stopped at the threshold and peered in.

The dollhouse was alight with candles, like a huge birthday cake. Both sides stood open, and inside, all the candles I had lit in the bigger house were burning brightly. Tiny perfect candles, lighting up the house.

"Oh!" gasped Lily, clasping her hands. "It's so beautiful!"

It was. The house was at its very best, with the rich fabrics of curtains and couches gleaming in the soft candlelight, the paintings illuminated, the chandelier sparkling in the downstairs hall. We circled around it, almost breathless with the magic of this dazzling, impossibly beautiful miniature world.

There were no dolls. It was empty, as it had been when I came up here after my nap.

"Alice," said Lily softly, slipping her hand into mine. "I have never seen such a wondrous sight in all my life. I think so."

I had to agree.

Just then I became aware of two things almost at the same time. The first was the wind, which had continued to growl and moan around the house ever since we left Mrs. Bishop and Fizz. A gust tore through the open window and all the candle flames in the dollhouse flickered, then grew larger. The second thing I became aware of was the smell of something burning.

I looked more closely at the nearest candles, which were on the mantelpiece in Fizz's bedroom. The flames were blowing this way and that and the bed curtains were smoking. As I gazed at them, a flame flicked up and suddenly the bed was on fire.

Lily grabbed my arm and screamed. All at once, everywhere in the dollhouse, the candle flames were being fanned by the wind and all those lovely, sumptuous fabrics were catching fire. The rugs in the living room, the couches, the chairs, the bed curtains in Bubble's room.

The fire was spreading incredibly fast, fed by the wind that whistled in through the window. I ran over and pulled it shut, but it was too late. The dollhouse walls were burning now, and I could feel the crackling heat scorching my face.

"Lily!" I yelled. "We have to get out of here!"

We raced out the door, and I shut it behind me, hoping to stop the spread of the fire. Then we stumbled down the stairs, through my room and into the hall.

The house was very dark. The roaring of the wind filled our ears, and underneath that, the ominous crackle of flames in the dollhouse room upstairs.

I thought of Mrs. Bishop, lying helplessly in bed, with Fizz beside her. Moving through the hallway was like moving through a pot of black paint, with the narrow light from Lily's flashlight barely breaking through the dense darkness. I held her hand and led her into Mrs. Bishop's room.

"Mrs. Bishop," I began. "We have to get you out of here—" And then I stopped. The penlight's wavering beam passed over the empty bed.

Mrs. Bishop and Fizz were gone.

No sooner did I see that the bed was empty, than Lily's flashlight blinked out. She dropped my hand.

"Lily?" I said, reaching for her.

There was no answer.

I was alone.

Chapter Fifty-Five

THE STAIRS

The darkness was complete. No moonlight coming in through the windows. No starlight. Just deep darkness all around me. The wind picked up, screeching around the outside of the house, sweeping in the windows.

I felt my way out of the room into the hallway. The wind began to howl and sing, and I could hear curtains flapping and things falling off shelves and breaking.

And all the while the darkness thickened around me like a big, dark blanket. I could barely breathe. The darkness had an intense, quiet energy that was big enough to swallow the whole house. The whole world.

It was coming for me. Like Mrs. Bishop had said. Had it already taken her and Fizz away? How could I possibly stop it? Death was all around me, silent, relentless. Completely impersonal.

I was going to die.

I fell to my knees in the hall, covering my head with my hands, trying to hide from Death.

And as I crouched there, wind and darkness all around me, something completely unexpected happened. Images of my mother came into my mind. Laughing as she told me stories of her cooking disasters while I put the macaroni and cheese together for Mrs. Bishop. Shouting at Dad over the muffins when he said he had to work for six more months before he could quit. Crying on the train all afternoon as we traveled away from the city toward Blackwood House. Bursting into my room after I first saw the ghost in my bed, her hair sticking up. Smoothing my forehead as I lay in bed with my everlasting headache.

And then came images of my dad. Standing on the doorstep in his wrinkled suit, his eyes lighting up when he saw me. Pleading with my mother to give him another chance, that he really meant it this time. Hugging me tight, smelling of soap and aftershave.

What would they do without me? What would I do without them?

"No," I whispered to that insidious, all-powerful darkness. "Not yet."

I scrambled to my feet. A sound like a freight train bearing down on the house filled my ears.

I'd seen a movie about a hurricane once. This was definitely starting to feel like a hurricane. A hurricane that was barreling through Blackwood House.

I had to get out.

With one hand groping along the wall to my right, I took careful steps toward the stairs. If I could just get down the stairs and outside, maybe I would be okay.

Suddenly there was no more floor under my left foot—just air. I struggled not to lose my balance, but at that moment a tremendous blast of wind came up behind me and pushed me down the stairs.

I felt that sickening rush of adrenaline as I fell into space, and then a horrible jolt as I hit the wall, then went tumbling down. I rolled over and over, banging my head again and again.

The pain in my head came back in a rush, and this time, if possible, it was even worse than before. It seemed to burst out of my head and expand to fill all the rooms in the house. The roaring of the wind and the screaming of the pain in my head seemed to join together until I felt like I was at the center of a galloping storm.

Then I hit the bottom of the stairs and thumped my head one more time. The darkness I had been working so hard to keep at bay closed around me and bore me away.

Part Six

THE UNDISCOVERED COUNTRY

Chapter Fifty-Six

TOUCH AND GO

"Ahhh . . . lisss"

Somebody was calling me softly in a spooky voice.

"Ahhh . . . lisss"

My head hurt. A dull pounding. I opened my eyes, but had to shut them again right away because the room was too bright.

"Alice!" said the voice with delight. "You're awake!"

I squinted my eyes open just a little and saw Lily standing beside my bed, grinning at me.

Except it wasn't my bed. This bed had metal railings on the side, and there was a bright light in the ceiling, bearing down on me.

"Ellie!" called Lily in a loud voice that made me wince. "Mr. Greene! She's awake!"

I turned and saw that the wall on my right was a window, and there were three people standing on the other side, but then they rushed into the room, and my mom was there, and my dad, and they were hugging me and crying and laughing.

"Ouch!" I said as Lily gave me another heartfelt hug. "My head hurts."

"Be careful, Lily," said Mom.

Dr. West was there, too, and he gave me a huge smile.

"Welcome back, Alice," he said. "You gave us all a good scare."

He took my pulse, checked some screens at the back of my bed, and looked into my eyes with a little flashlight. It looked familiar. Didn't Lily have a light like that?

"Head hurt?" he said.

"Yes."

"It will for a while. We'll give you some more painkillers soon. You've been through the wars." He reached out and touched something on my head, and for the first time I realized there was a big bandage wrapped around my head. I put up my hand to feel it.

"What . . . what happened?"

Mom's face appeared beside Dr. West's. "You've had surgery, Alice. It turned out that there was a little bleed in your brain, caused when you hit your head in the train, but it was so small it didn't show up on the CAT scan. When Lily went to wake you up, she couldn't rouse you, so she came and got me. You were unconscious. We got you to the hospital in an ambulance, they found the bleed and went in and stopped it."

"Am . . . am I going to die?" I asked, my voice trembling.

Mom put her hand over her mouth and shook her head, tears in her eyes. She couldn't answer me.

Dr. West jumped in. "No, Alice, you are not going to die. You're going to be fine. You just need a few days in hospital and then some quiet time, and you'll be going swimming again with Lily in a couple of weeks."

A huge sense of relief flooded through me. Mrs. Bishop was wrong. It wasn't my time.

"But what about Mrs. Bishop?" I asked. "Is she okay? Did she die?"

Mom frowned. "She's fine. Mary's with her. Why do you ask?"

"Oh. I don't know," I replied. "I was worried about her."

"Don't worry about anything," put in Dad, coming closer and planting a kiss on my forehead. "You're going to be fine; Mrs. Bishop is already fine. And I'm going to stay around for an extra week or two till you feel better."

I looked from him to Mom. "Are you and Mom fine too?" I asked.

"Lily, let's leave Alice alone with her parents for a while," said Dr. West. "How about some ice cream from the cafeteria?"

"Okay," said Lily, with a little bounce. "I'll see you later, Alice."

After they left, Mom and Dad sat down, one on each side of my bed, each of them holding one of my hands.

"We were so worried," said Mom. She sniffed and then pulled a Kleenex out of her pocket and wiped her eyes.

"We thought we were going to lose you," said Dad.

"Really? Could I have died from this? Mom?" My voice rose into a squeak.

"Stephen, for goodness' sake," snapped Mom. "You're scaring her."

"No, I need to know," I said. "Could I have died?"

"You're fine now," said Mom. "We caught it in time. But if Lily hadn't gone in and tried to wake you up when she did . . . well, it would have been touch and go." Then she started to cry again, and Dad went around the side of the bed and wrapped her in his arms.

After a while she stopped crying and turned back to me. "I felt terrible we hadn't realized earlier that there was something wrong, but your symptoms were those of someone who had a mild concussion, and we just had no way of knowing."

My head was aching worse now, after all the excitement. I closed my eyes for a minute.

"We should let you sleep," said my mother.

"No . . . wait!" I said, opening my eyes again and reaching out to clutch at her arm. I needed to ask her one more thing. "You and Dad . . . are you going to be okay? Are you going to . . . get a divorce?"

They exchanged looks. Then Dad spoke.

"Alice, I have to go back to LA for a while to work over the next few months, but I'm leaving the company at Christmas, and I'm going to find work that keeps me close to you, no matter what happens."

"You mean . . . you might still get a divorce?"

"Alice," said Mom, "we just don't know. Right now all you have to worry about is going back to sleep and getting better."

She bent over and kissed me. Then Dad did the same, and then they left.

I closed my eyes. I felt I could just slip away, into the darkness again.

I opened my eyes quickly. Into the darkness. I didn't want to go there. What if there was another bleed, if they still hadn't caught everything? What if I went to sleep and never woke up?

The thin hospital blanket was pale green, and it felt soft under my hand. Someone had turned the overhead light off and the room had lost its glare. I had no idea what time it was, or what day it was. My head hurt, and I was so tired.

My eyes closed again. Mrs. Bishop had been wrong. It wasn't her time yet. And it wasn't my time either. That dream I had of Mom in the train, crying over my dead body, it was just that: a dream. Something I was afraid of, something I had imagined happening, but something that hadn't really happened.

Or had it really happened and I changed it somehow? By lighting the candles against the dark? By burning down the dollhouse? Had I really burned it down? I forgot to ask Mom about the fire. Was that all part of the dream?

And what about Fizz? Where was she now if the dollhouse was gone? Was she still in Mrs. Bishop's bed? Haunting her instead of me? Or were she and Mrs. Bishop one person now, the way they were supposed to be?

Poor Fizz, sleeping and sleeping all those years while the world went on without her. Sleeping . . .

I opened my eyes again with a jerk. I couldn't go to sleep. It was too dangerous. I didn't know when my time would come. It could be five minutes from now or it could be seventy years.

I couldn't possibly stay awake that long.

Chapter Fifty-Seven
A GUARDIAN ANGEL

I listened to the muted sounds of the hospital. People walking by in the hall, talking, their voices rising and falling as they drew nearer my room and then passed on by. A kind of humming noise—electricity? Air conditioning? I listened, all my senses alert, wondering if I could feel that gathering darkness I had felt in the dollhouse. The darkness that was Death.

Then I heard footsteps coming along the hall, approaching my room. Stopping at my door.

I opened my eyes. I didn't even know I'd closed them again.

"Alice?" said a small voice. "Are you still awake?"

"Yes." My voice was a dry croak again. "Come in, Lily."

"I brought you some ice cream," she said, coming into the room and showing me a bowl of chocolate ice cream and a spoon. "Dr. West says you can have it."

I looked beyond her, and Dr. West was standing in the doorway, grinning and nodding his head. For a moment he reminded me so much of that daydream I had of a different dad, living on a hillside, welcoming Mom and me home. A very comfortable, predictable dad.

"Go ahead, it will do you good," he said, then turned and walked away down the hall.

After I finished the ice cream, I lay back against my pillows. Now I was really tired. My eyes closed. The darkness started to move in. I jerked them open with a gasp.

"Alice?" said Lily, looking alarmed. "What's wrong, Alice? Does your head hurt again? Should I get Dr. West?"

"No, it's not that."

"What is it then?"

I searched her face. "Do you remember anything, Lily? Anything about being in the dollhouse with me? Talking to Fizz and Mrs. Bishop? The wind? The fire?"

Lily frowned. "There was a fire. Did your mom tell you about that? I don't remember any of the other stuff."

"What fire?" I struggled to sit up.

"The dollhouse. After you came to the hospital. My mom and me were staying with Mrs. Bishop. Mom smelled smoke coming from the attic. The dollhouse was on fire! The fire engines came and everything. It was so exciting, Alice! I think so. But the dollhouse burned away and it's all gone now.

Mrs. Bishop was sad. We had a good talk after. She told me it was her dollhouse from when she was a little girl. I asked her why she kept it a secret and she said, 'Some things are better locked away, Lily; you'll find that out yourself someday,' but I don't think so. I think it's better to keep things like the dollhouse unlocked, so anyone can play with them. What do you think, Alice?"

I lay back against the pillows. "I think you're right. People shouldn't lock things away." I sighed. I was so tired. I closed my eyes.

We were quiet for a while. I felt myself drifting off and opened my eyes. Lily was sitting beside me, gazing out the window.

"Lily?"

"Yup?"

"Lily, have you ever been afraid to go to sleep?"

"Afraid?"

"Yes, afraid. Because of what might happen while you're sleeping?"

She frowned. "Like a bad dream?"

"Yes. Like a bad dream."

"I used to be. But my mom said I had a guardian angel that watches me while I sleep and keeps me safe no matter what. So now I don't worry."

"Do you think everyone has a guardian angel, Lily?"

"Sure. They must. That's how it works. I think so."

I smiled. "Lily, I think maybe you're my guardian angel. Mom says you saved my life."

Lily leaned in closer to me, a little frown creasing her forehead. "I was so scared, Alice. Your mom told me it was time to wake you up. I shook your arm and shouted really loud, but you kept sleeping. Then I thought maybe you were like Sleeping Beauty and needed someone to kiss you, so I kissed you. But you still didn't wake up. So I went and got your mom. I think so."

"That was the right thing to do, Lily," I said sleepily. Maybe that's why I dreamed that Lily had kissed Fizz. But it was me she kissed. Everything was mixed up.

"You were so sad," she continued. "Crying. In your sleep. When I couldn't wake you up. I felt so sorry for you. You were crying and crying." She reached out and took my hand. "Are you still sad, Alice?"

I gave her hand a squeeze. "No, Lily. I'm happy now. I just wish I wasn't so scared to go to sleep."

"You can go to sleep now, Alice," she said. "I'll stay right here with you." She smiled at me, one of those joyful, beaming Lily-smiles, and gave my hand a little pat. "You won't have nightmares. You're safe now. I think so."

I smiled back and let my eyes close. The darkness came in, but now it was a friendly darkness, and I could feel the warmth of Lily's hand in mine. I let everything go—and fell instantly and deliciously to sleep.

Chapter Fifty-Eight

QUESTIONS

Lily came to visit me nearly every day over the week I was in the hospital. Her mother would drop her off then pick her up a couple of hours later. Mom and Dad came too, and I saw Dr. West every day. But it was Lily I looked forward to seeing the most. I felt calm when she was there, and her happiness seemed to spread to me. Whenever I was drifting off to sleep, I'd imagine that she was there still, watching over me. My guardian angel.

I had a lot of time to think in the hospital. I didn't feel like watching TV or reading, because my head still ached, so I lay there quietly a lot of the time, thinking about what had happened.

Was it all a dream? A hallucination? Something caused by the injury in my brain? Mom explained what a bleed was:

a tiny blood vessel burst and leaked blood into my brain. So my brain wasn't quite working properly. Is that why events and people in my life were transformed into the people in my dream?

I became Fizz. Lily became Bubble. Dr. West was Adrian—but that was a bit of a stretch, because Adrian was vain and good-looking, and Dr. West was ordinary-looking and kind. And Mom wasn't anything like Harriet, and Dad wasn't anything like Bob—except that he was away a lot at work. The train accident that killed everyone—well, it was a much worse version of my train accident. And Mrs. Bishop was just Mrs. Bishop. A cantankerous old lady.

I went on thinking like that, trying to draw the parallels, trying to work it out.

Everything that had happened in the dollhouse did have a dream-like quality to it, where things were turned around and unexpected and sometimes really scary. But it also felt completely real.

There was one way to find out. Or maybe two ways. One would have to wait till I got home. But I could do the other from the hospital.

The next time Mary came in to pick up Lily and say hello, I told her I needed to speak to her alone, so she sent Lily down to the cafeteria for ice cream.

"What is it, Alice?" said Mary once we were alone, looking a little puzzled.

I took the plunge.

"Mary, you need to help me. I . . . I found out some things, and you need to tell me if they're true. It's very important, because I don't know if I dreamed it all. When I was sick."

"I'll help you if I can, Alice," she said. "What kind of things?"

"Well, is it true that Mrs. Bishop lived in Blackwood House when she was a little girl?"

Mary's mouth fell open. I waited.

She seemed to recover herself. Then she nodded. "Well, yes. It is true. It's not something she wants known, so I keep it to myself."

I swallowed. "And is it true that her whole family was killed in a train accident? A long, long time ago? Say, in the 1920s?"

Mary nodded again, her eyes filling with tears. "I don't know how you've discovered these things, Alice, but it's true. It was terrible. She lost all of them, and she was only your age. Just a girl."

"And is it true that after that Blackwood House was locked up and no one ever lived in it again till she came back last summer?"

"Alice, how do you know all this?"

"It's true, then?"

"Yes, it's true, but how did you find out about it? Did Mrs. Bishop tell you?"

I thought back to the candlelit room with Mrs. Bishop propped up against her pillows, telling me how she came back to Blackwood House.

"Yes. But I wondered if I dreamed it."

Mary sighed. "No. It's true. I've kept her secret, and my mother and my grandmother before me have all kept her secret. People around here thought the house was sold long ago. All kinds of rumors have sprung up over the years, but we never told. It's important to Mrs. Bishop that nobody know her business. I'm surprised she told you."

I said nothing. My head was reeling again. If that part of the story was true, then what about the rest? Was I just dreaming that I went into the dollhouse whenever I fell asleep? Or was I really there? Would I ever know?

But now at least I knew that the train crash was real. It happened, all that long time ago. Fizz lost everyone.

I thought of the only time I saw her whole family together, the night of the party, with Bubble looking so beautiful in her grown-up dress, laughing when her father broke open the bottle of champagne, and Harriet sparkling on the couch, and Bob teasing the girls and making them go through the ritual of how they got their nicknames. And Fizz rolling her eyes, but enjoying it nonetheless. All of them so alive, so vibrantly alive. And then all of them gone. In a moment. When the train crashed.

Poor Fizz. Poor Mrs. Bishop.

Beside me, Mary stirred. "Well, I can see you're tired," she said. "You need to get your rest. I'll go find Lily and take her home." She stood up to leave.

"One more thing, Mary." I put out my hand to stop her. "Lily said there was a fire—and the dollhouse burned down?"

"You know about the dollhouse too?"

I nodded.

"For goodness' sake! Is nothing secret?"

"But why did it burn down?"

"The fire chief said they couldn't figure it out. A complete mystery. Spontaneous combustion maybe, I don't know, but it's an awful shame. Such a beautiful dollhouse, but of course nobody could play with it except Her Nibs, and she hasn't been up to look at it since she broke her leg. I'm surprised she's not more upset about it, but she seems resigned. Funny, nothing else in the attic was affected. Just the dollhouse. By the time the firemen got there, the fire was out. Nothing but a pile of ashes, with the rug burned away underneath, but that's all."

"Weird," I said.

"Yes, very weird. Now, I must get Lily. I don't know how you know all my secrets, Missy, but you better keep them to yourself. Mrs. Bishop wouldn't want the whole world knowing her business."

"I won't tell anyone," I promised.

"That's a good girl," she said, giving my hand a squeeze, and she left.

I lay back on my pillows and closed my eyes.

* * *

The day they let me go home, Dad came to collect me, saying Mom had something she was busy with. I was a little miffed that she hadn't come herself, but Dad was cheerful, driving me home in Mrs. Bishop's car.

When we pulled up in the driveway, the first thing I saw was a paper banner across the front door that read "Welcome Home Alice" in uneven painted letters, and Lily burst through the door with a bunch of balloons, hopping up and down in excitement. Mom and Mary appeared behind her and then led me downstairs to the kitchen, where I discovered what Mom had been busy with: a "lunch." It was just as lavish as the lunch Mary had made for us the night we arrived.

The kitchen was festooned with streamers, and there was a big chocolate cake with sloppy pink rosebuds and another "Welcome Home Alice" message straggled across it in pink icing.

"Your mom let me ice the cake," said Lily.

There were tuna sandwiches, potato chips, ginger ale, carrot sticks and radishes cut to look like rosebuds. "My specialty!" said Mary. And she had brought her other specialty, a jellied salad, this time red with weird green slivers of something in it and multicolored mini-marshmallows.

We took our plates out to the terrace and sat at the table under the umbrella to eat. It wasn't as hot today, and a light breeze stirred the trees. Lily and Mary kept up a steady chatter, with Mom and Dad and me joining in when we could.

Just when we were finishing our second pieces of cake, a train whistle blew down the valley.

"That's the twelve-thirty passenger," said Mary, and forked a large piece of cake into her mouth.

I put my fork down on my plate. I suddenly felt a little sick. Mom noticed.

"I think you've had enough excitement for today, Alice," she said, and pushed back her chair. "Come on, let's get you settled in bed for a nap."

I didn't protest. I said goodbye to Dad and followed Mom up the basement stairs to the dining room, and then around the corner and up the steep curving staircase.

I got up to the bend in the stairs and then a wave of vertigo hit me. For a moment, the world began to spin around me. I clutched at Mom's arm.

"You okay, honey?" she said, putting her arm around me.

"I'm a bit dizzy," I whispered.

"That's to be expected," she said. "Take a deep breath."

I did. The dizziness faded.

"When I was sick, that last day, I dreamed I fell down these stairs."

"Well, you didn't. You were in your bed the whole time."

Mom helped me up the rest of the stairs. I glanced over to Mrs. Bishop's door, which was shut.

"Mrs. Bishop is having a nap, but she wants to see you later, after your rest, to welcome you home."

I let Mom tuck me into bed, leaving the bed curtains open so I could see out the window. She bent over and kissed my forehead.

"Sleep well. You'll feel so much better when you wake up."

And she left.

Chapter Fifty-Nine
CHOCOLATE CAKE

When I woke up the light had changed. I felt groggy, uncertain of how long I had slept. One hour? Two? I had been out like a light, with no awareness whatsoever of being asleep or time passing.

I swung my legs out over the side of the bed and dropped to the floor on the window side so I could look out.

The shadows were lengthening on the lawn. The air smelled sweet and fresh. Warm, but not hot. I must have slept for three or four hours. I was used to long naps in the hospital, so it was no surprise.

I heard a train whistle, and I braced myself. I was going to have to get used to it, since about six trains passed every day. The whistle shrieked as the train sped down the valley, and then I could hear the train rumbling and it whooshed past.

Then the trees stirred in the wind like a lady settling her full skirts, and the train thundered into the distance.

It was a beautiful spot, with the lawn stretching out to the hill, the pretty flowerbeds, the pale blue lake in the distance, and the summerhouse just visible off to the right. A peaceful spot. If it wasn't for the trains.

I shivered. A cool breeze fluttered the curtains. I turned away from the window and went to the closet to find a sweater.

As I stood there, still sleepy, I noticed that someone had hung up the midnight blue cocktail dress I had worn to the party. The spangles shimmered in the dim, shadowy closet. The dress Fiona had given to me to wear. In the dollhouse.

"Alice?" Mom called from my room. "Are you up?"

I dropped my hand and walked out of the closet to meet her. "Yes."

"Feeling better?"

"Yes." And I was.

"Mrs. Bishop wants you to come and have a cup of tea with her in her room. I've brought her some of your cake. Better brush your hair and wash your face first."

As I walked across the carpet to fetch my hairbrush from the closet, I felt something hard under my bare right foot. Hard and a little lumpy.

I looked down. Something had spilled on the carpet. But it was stuck. Gum?

I crouched down to inspect it.

It was a little puddle of dried candle wax. Big enough that I would have noticed it before if it had been there. And then it came back to me, as clear as if it was happening all over again.

I came running in here from the hallway, trying to light all the candles in the house, trying to beat back the encroaching darkness. I placed the candlesticks from the mantelpiece on the floor to light them from the candle in my hand, my hands were shaking, and some hot wax fell to the carpet.

Just here.

Not a dream then.

Thoughtfully, I continued to the closet and found my hairbrush.

After tidying myself up, I knocked gently on Mrs. Bishop's door. She called out for me to come in.

Mom had set up a tea tray on a little folding table beside the bed.

"You can pour the tea, Alice," said Mom, smiling. "I'll leave you two alone so you can have a nice visit."

I approached Mrs. Bishop warily. She was sitting upright in bed, wearing yellow pajamas with little blue flowers. Her hair was neatly brushed, held in place by a blue headband. She matched the room.

"Hello, Mrs. Bishop," I said.

"Hello, Alice," she replied politely. "How are you feeling?"

"Much better, thank you."

"Well, your mother says you can pour the tea, so why don't you get on with it," she said, with the familiar edge to her voice.

I did so. Playing tea parties was always one of my favorite games when I was little, so I knew how to do it.

"Milk?" I asked.

"Yes."

I poured the milk into the pretty blue-and-white china teacup. Then I filled it up with steaming tea.

"Sugar?" I asked.

"Yes," she replied.

There were silver sugar tongs, so I picked up a lump of sugar.

"One lump or two?"

"Four," said Mrs. Bishop firmly.

I nearly dropped the tongs. Then I did as she asked. Each sugar lump plopped into the tea like a stone, sending up a little wave. Four plops.

I handed her the tea, and she stirred it with one of the silver spoons Mom had provided, then took a ladylike sip.

"Perfect," she said.

There were two dainty pieces of cake set out on separate plates with silver dessert forks. I put one plate beside her teacup, then helped myself to tea and cake.

I drank my tea slowly, watching her. Neither of us spoke.

It seemed like a battle—who was going to hold out the longest?

I finally gave in. I knew she could last much longer than I could.

"I thought you'd be dead by now," I said. "You and Fizz."

Mrs. Bishop was right in the middle of a sip, and she sputtered and nearly choked on it. She recovered and put down her teacup. She fixed me with a stare from her startling green eyes.

"There was a change of plan," she said. Then she threw back her head and laughed. At that moment, she was both of them: Fizz and Mrs. Bishop, melded into one.

When she stopped laughing, she looked down at the small piece of chocolate cake on her plate.

"That's not nearly enough," she said. "Alice, we need more cake."

THE END

ACKNOWLEDGMENTS

My inspiration for *The Dollhouse: A Ghost Story* came from two people and one glorious house.

The very first glimmer of the story appeared one day years ago when my father told me about an impressive but scary staircase he had climbed in the Georgian house of a friend. Being the kind of person who falls in love with houses, I wanted to see it, and soon I was head over heels with a wonderful house that had been lovingly restored. The owner was Ruth Redelmeier, who had been at university with my mother, whom I had recently lost. I took great comfort in hearing stories about my mother from Ruth, who was very generous with her time and attention. We became friends, and soon I was visiting her regularly. She had a dollhouse in her bedroom, and she introduced me to the tiny treasures she had collected. Slowly the idea for my book began to grow. Ruth let me wander around her house whenever I visited, with one exception: she didn't want me to go into the attic by myself, because the stairs were so steep. One day I enlisted the help of a friend, Robert Cramer, who also has an enthusiasm for old houses, and we climbed up to the attic. The large room was shadowy and quiet; wide floorboards cut from pine trees nearly two hundred years ago stretched the full width of the house between two gracefully arched windows. The empty space seemed to hold the unseen history of the house. Over time, this house and this attic began to live inside me, whispering secrets, and slowly became inhabited with Alice, Fizz and Mrs. Bishop.

My other inspiration was Sarah Legakis, a young woman at my father's church. I noticed her right away in the choir: she was very pretty and had a joyful, open expression. She seemed to radiate goodwill. I was drawn to her, and over time, I gradually got to know her better. I liked her a lot: she was engaging, affectionate and enthusiastic. I learned that she had developmental differences, and would always have a child's outlook on life. I couldn't stop thinking about her, and I knew I wanted a character like her in one of my books. Sarah was the bright spark that led to the creation of Lily and Bubble.

So I would like to thank my two muses: Ruth and Sarah.

Ruth, your friendship and kindness to me over the last few years has been a great source of happiness. I admire your patience, independence and practical outlook. You have helped me through many a difficult time, and I have fond memories of chatting over cups of tea, playing with your dollhouse, and prowling through your house with characters and scenes from my book dancing through my head. Thank you for everything.

Thank you Sarah for being yourself so completely and for all the bounce and joy you bring to everyone you meet.

I'd also like to thank Anne Finlay, Sarah's mother, for being so open and welcoming to me when I approached her about creating a character inspired by Sarah. Anne gave me the benefit of her considerable experience and insight, and her input and feedback were essential as I developed the characters of Lily and Bubble. And thank you to Kate Legakis, who helped me understand what it was like to live with a sister with developmental differences.

There's a golden retriever in Western Bay named Bear, who was the inspiration for Buttercakes/Sailor. Either Tracey Crummey or her brother Wade walk Bear by my house every day, and one day he walked right into the story.

A very big thank you to my agent, Hilary McMahon of Westwood Creative, for all her hard work on this book and the faith she has in my work.

My heartfelt thanks and appreciation go to my excellent editor, Sam Swenson, who has seen me through four novels now and always brings her clear insights and high standards to my work. Sam challenges me and asks all the questions that need to be asked. She gives my books a good shake and they are so much stronger afterwards! Thanks also to everyone at Tundra, especially Sam Devotta, Margot Blankier and Tara Walker. Special thanks to Chloe Bristol for creating such an imaginative and striking cover, and to Emma Dolan for her inspired design. And thank you to ArtsNL,* who gave me a much-needed grant that helped me buy some time to work on the book.

As with all my books, I have depended on the kindness and hospitality of my friends, especially those in Ontario who open up their homes to me and welcome me into their lives:

Laurie Coulter, Erich Volk, Pat Green and Margaret Gardonio. Your steadfast encouragement, good dinners, sympathy and laughter is an ongoing source of strength for me. In St. John's, Barb Neis, Peter Armitage, Beni Malone and Marian Frances White offer a similar bed-and-breakfast form of support. Kitty Whalen, Tom Whalen and Rick Clarke are my stellar neighbors who bring me groceries when I'm in isolation, splits for my woodstove and dessert all too often. My good friends Christopher Thorpe, Marie Alexander, Wanda Nowakowska, and Michael Worek have all cheered me on over the years as I wrote *The Dollhouse*. Jo Caragh and George Miranda have been warmly supportive. Frieda Wishinsky and her husband Bill generously offered me their house in Toronto for several weeks while they were away, and I spent much of that time working on this book. Thank you Robert Cramer for exploring the attic with me and being such a good friend, and thank you Robin Cleland for your continuing insight and support for my work.

A special thank you to Vanessa Shields, my enthusiastic and loving writing sister, who is quite simply always there for me. Working with Vanessa at hand on FaceTime during the pandemic has added so much to my writing life and has eased some of the challenges of solitude. Thank you, Vanessa, for the inspirational writing retreats, the daily accountability, and especially, The Complaints Department!

My first reader is always my dad, Graham Cotter, and his respect for my work, his suggestions and his ongoing encouragement are essential to me. My daughter, Zoe Cleland, is another early reader who gives me insight, ideas and appreciation. Her childhood experiences and her unique perspective have informed all of my writing for children.

A quiet thank you to my mother, whose spirit is never very far away, and who would recognize Mrs. Bishop's sense of humor, her hairbands and her nose. And finally thank you to all the other spirits who come and go, haunting houses and haunting me, whispering their stories to me again and again, until I write them down.

* I acknowledge the support of ArtsNL, which last year invested $3.2 million to foster and promote the creation and enjoyment of the arts for the benefit of all Newfoundlanders and Labradorians.

NEWFOUNDLAND AND LABRADOR ARTS COUNCIL